Hold Your Horses

LOUISE TURNER & WANDA JENNINGS

BOOK SEVEN OF THE MAGNOLIA MANOR SERIES

Printed in the United States of America
First Printed October 2022
Cover Art by Victoria L. Hawkins

Published by:

Southern Willow Publishing, LLC
1114 Highway 96,
Suite C-1, #340
Kathleen, Georgia 31047

ISBN: 978-1-956544-23-7

Working in all types of weather, through hardships, floods, famines, and even pandemics, farmers provide our nation and the entire world with food and life sustaining materials. Their efforts all too often go unnoticed and underappreciated. It is to these unsung heroes of our nation that we dedicate this book.

[Chapter One]

"I saw the Ferris wheel going up on my way into town this morning," Wilbur said. He drained his coffee mug and handed it to Mona behind the counter who refilled it. The coffee at the Starlight Café was the best in town.

"The fair is so romantic!" Mavis squealed next to him. "I can't wait to ride the Ferris wheel and look over all of Junction!"

"Don't even ask, Mavis. I'm not riding the Ferris wheel with you," Wilbur shook his head. He wasn't afraid of much, but heights topped the short list of things he feared.

"Ew! Why would I want to go on a romantic ride with you, Wilbur?" Mavis rolled her eyes.

"I didn't mean it like that," he replied hastily. "I just meant that you have a way of dragging me into things I don't want to do. I can't stand those deathtraps, and I'm putting my foot down this year. There's no telling how dangerous those contraptions are."

"Wilbur's right," Mona nodded. "Harry was just telling me about an accident over yonder in Texas a few weeks ago. So sad," she lamented. Harry merely grunted in agreement behind the counter as he flipped a stack of pancakes onto a plate for Mavis.

Wilbur gave Mavis a knowing look, but it didn't faze her. She had been looking forward to the once annual county fair coming back to town. It hadn't been back to Junction in nearly ten years, and she was beside herself with excitement.

"Thank you," she smiled as Harry handed her the heaping plate. "These sure look good."

"Alright," Wilbur said with a sigh. "I better get a move on. I've got to haul that load of firewood over to Johnson's farm and then pick up Opal's chicken wire from the hardware store and get it set up for her. She's got more chickens than she knows what to do with these days."

"How is she doing?" Mona asked as Wilbur paid his tab.

"She's alright," Wilbur said. "She's doing much better than she has been. Her mind isn't as sharp as it once was, but it doesn't stop her any. She's always on the go. Mavis can tell you; she near about runs circles around us still. She and Ms. Maude."

"Oh, Ms. Maude was in here the other day," Mona chuckled. "She near about rioted when I told her we'd run out of apple pie slices. She said she'd just have to go back to the Pig and get her a whole pie and how it was cheaper to do that anyway. Then she mumbled something about young'uns not knowing how to respect their elders. Harry and me were laughing too hard to hear her finish."

Wilbur and Mavis both blushed. There was no telling what Maude was liable to say. She was always a hot-head, and the older she got, the less of a filter she had. While Maude and Opal weren't blood related to either of them, Wilbur and Mavis both looked after them as best they could. Those two women had been in their lives forever and helped raise them. They were the only sense of family either of them had left.

"I'm sorry about that, Mona," Mavis winced.

"Don't be!" Mona shushed her. "That woman is a town legend!"

Wilbur shook his head with a smile and tipped his hat to Harry who was frying up the next customer's order. "See you tomorrow, Mona. See you later, Mavis. Be at Opal's around five for supper. You know Ms. Maude has to eat on a tight schedule." He waved to a few more friends on the way out.

"Why does she have to get on a strict schedule?" Mona asked. "Is she sick?"

"No," Mavis giggled. "Just ornery."

Mona and Mavis laughed and made small talk while Mavis finished her breakfast. She and Wilbur had a standing supper invitation at either Opal or Maude's house every Thursday evening, and they knew better than to miss it. Neither Opal or Maude cooked much anymore, so Mavis and Wilbur took turns bringing food over. Tonight was Mavis' turn and she had planned on going over to the Piggly Wiggly and buying a few boxes of the fried chicken from the deli, along with some sides and a cake from their bakery.

Mavis paid her tab and scooted outside to her car. On the short drive to the grocery store, she made a mental list of things to buy. She knew there was no point in writing an actual list on a piece of paper because she never went by it anyway. Mavis was more of the follow your heart type of shopper. And today her heart told her the two for one sale on hummingbird cakes was the right choice.

She bought two boxes of chicken and accompanying sides before remembering that Opal was a vegetarian. She always seemed to forget that tidbit. Even in her old age and scatterbrained mind, Opal took her dietary habits very seriously, just as she always had. She had shocked Mavis one time when Mavis was a little girl when she told her one night that she could never eat any kind of chicken because she raised them at her house. Mavis always loved to go over to Opal's backyard and play with her chickens and quail, but she also didn't have a problem eating any kind of bird for supper. Opal said there was a fine line between pet and food, but Mavis was just as happy to cross that line any time she laid her eyes on fried chicken, or beef, or pork. Mavis loved all animals, but she loved being a foodie even more.

After perusing the produce section for salad items, Mavis skipped over to the frozen section and loaded her buggy up with ice cream. She was a firm believer that one could never have too many cartons of ice cream in the freezer. Ice cream stayed good forever, not that it lasted too long at Magnolia Manor. There used to be the cutest little ice cream shop in downtown Rhinestone, but it had closed when Mavis was a teenager. So mass produced frozen cartons would have to do. She kept the homemade vanilla stocked for Wilbur and the chocolate ice cream for Ms. Maude who always made it a point to take one or two cartons home with her whenever she visited the Manor. The birthday cake and mint chocolate chip were for Mavis alone. She kept those hidden in the deep freeze in the laundry room under lock and key. The best memories were of the times she and Big Daddy Jameson shared a pint of mint chocolate chip ice cream before bed, long after Big Mama Ruby had dozed off in her recliner after cleaning the kitchen after supper.

Mavis couldn't believe that it would soon be sixteen years that her grandfather had passed away. Her grandmother, the matriarch of the family, Ruby Montgomery, had been gone for a little over three years now. Some days it felt like ages, others just like yesterday. So much had changed in the years since their passings, but a few traditions and relationships had survived, just like that old, weathered magnolia tree in the front yard that gave Magnolia Manor its moniker.

Mavis was getting teary-eyed in front of the sorbets again. She often thought about her beloved grandparents who had raised her from the time she was a baby. Without them, there was no telling what would have happened to her. Her mother, Melanie, has been unable to take care of herself, let alone raise a baby, so her parents had stepped in and tried to help them both. Unfortunately, Melanie died young. It was very tragic for Ruby and Jameson, but they leaned on the Lord and on young Mavis who was only a toddler. Together they gave Mavis the best life anyone could ever imagine. When Wilbur joined their family when she was six, her life got even better. Not only was Wilbur still her closest friend, but he was also the brother she had always needed. All these years later, they looked after Maude and Opal, lifelong best friends and the surviving members of the Stone Sisters, a nickname given to Maude, Opal, and Ruby in their childhood. Those three women were never without one another, and even after three years, it still pained Mavis to see Maude and Opal go on adventures without Ruby. She couldn't imagine how they felt without their best friend, but they honored Ruby's memory everywhere they went.

The year after Ruby passed, Mavis traveled off and on in the same spirit. A few times Wilbur had accompanied her, and she always felt like Ruby was smiling down on her seeing her check off items on her own bucket list.

"Mavis? Is that you?" a voice croaked behind her.

She whipped around and saw Nadine Waters, another lifelong familiar face, in a wheelchair behind her. Her niece, Maureen, was on her cell phone and waved at Mavis as she continued her conversation. Nadine lived across the street from Maude and had been friends with Ruby and Opal nearly all their lives. One would think that that would automatically mean that Nadine was friends with Maude, too, but one would be wrong. The two women were more like frenemies who seemed to find joy in constantly annoying each other. There had hardly been a time in either of their long lives where one hadn't been thinking of the next best way to prank or irritate the other.

"Good morning, Ms. Waters," Mavis smiled. "How are you?"

"Fine, fine," Nadine said. She eyes the tubs of ice cream in Mavis' buggy and zeroed in on the chocolate. "Are those for Maude?" she asked.

"Yes ma'am," Mavis nodded. "She sure loves her chocolate ice cream alright!"

Nadine nodded and mumbled that it would sure be a shame if Mavis got her sugar-free and fat-free chocolate instead on account of Maude's diabetes.

"But Ms. Waters, she doesn't have diabetes," Mavis frowned. At least, she didn't think Maude had diabetes.

"Sure would be a shame," Nadine repeated. She shrugged her shoulders as Maureen whispered, "Sorry, I'm on hold with one of her doctors." Maureen and Nadine walked on and left Mavis staring after them as they headed towards the checkout line.

Nadine had always been the most put together person Rhinestone had to offer. She dressed in fancy clothes and drove the latest sports car up and down the country roads. She had never married or had any children after inheriting and selling the business her father, an oil tycoon, had built. Last year she had been diagnosed with lung cancer, long after giving up smoking in the seventies. The treatments had taken a lot out of her, but she insisted on living her life to the fullest. Mavis knew that she had returned home last month from a Caribbean cruise with some of her fellow church ladies, but she looked extra tired and somewhat sad today.

It was hard watching the people she loved age, but that was another consequence of life. No one lived forever, though Opal had often boasted of drinking from the fabled Fountain of Youth, which Maude would inevitably sigh and say, "that was the Trevi Fountain in Rome, you old bat! You near about drowned in it, too!"

Mavis shook the memories out of her brain and tried to focus on the task at hand. According to her watch, it was nearly noon and she had a list of things to accomplish at the Manor before she could head over to Opal's and help her and Wilbur with the chicken coop. Chores like laundry were mundane, but it must be done. She much preferred to dust the living room while her work out tapes blared in the background. She liked to work up a sweet while she cleaned. Then she'd have to vacuum and out the dishes away from the dishwasher before showering. It was a full afternoon and she needed something sweet to boost her energy. She followed her nose back to the bakery and chose a few boxes of freshly baked cookies to fuel her later workout. By the time she made it to the check-out line, Nadine had already been rung out. She made a mental note to ask Maude about her later this afternoon.

When she got to the Manor, Mavis unloaded the groceries and changed into her gym clothes. The neon pink spandex made her look and feel good while she cleaned. The particular workout tape she had chosen was 80's hair band themed, which made her power through her to-do list in record time. She tossed the last of her dirty laundry into the washing machine and went upstairs to her room. After she showered and got the stuff for dinner out of the fridge, it was time to head to

Opal's house. Wilbur had been there since lunchtime and would probably be worn out. Maude and Opal usually worked him to the bone with projects. Mavis grabbed him a water bottle and a snack bag of cookies and shoved them in her purse before walking back outside to her car.

She could hear Maude shrieking before she saw them. As soon as she turned off her car in Opal's driveway, she heard Maude raising cane in the backyard in between the squawks of twenty or so chickens. She hurried to the backyard and saw Maude standing in front of what looked like a freshly built lemonade stand. Wilbur saw Mavis walking up and waved. "Welcome to the funny farm," he chuckled.

"What's going on here?" Mavis asked.

"I'll tell you what's going on," Maude huffed. "Opal's got it in her head that she's going to set up a booth at the fair! Can you believe that!" Maude threw up her hands and walked towards the chicken coop where Opal was sitting down by the gate with her arms full of chickens.

"What kind of booth?" Mavis asked Wilbur.

"A fortune telling booth, or something like that," Wilbur smiled. "Wants to call herself Madame Opalina."

"I love that!" Mavis exclaimed.

"I figured you would," Wilbur chuckled. "Ms. Maude doesn't reckon it's a good idea, but I helped Opal build this booth this afternoon. We've still got to paint it, but I don't see any harm in it. We'll all be there to help her run it though. Everyone here in Rhinestone appreciates Opal's antics, but the fair tends to bring out all kinds of folks over in Junction."

Mavis nodded and helped Wilbur open the cans of paint at his feet. "Let me get the food in the house and then we'll paint really quick before supper," Mavis suggested.

"I'll paint a few coats if you take those two inside and get ready to eat. I can probably do it quicker if they aren't around," Wilbur laughed.

Mavis understood exactly what he meant. She called over to the two older ladies in the chicken coop and motioned for them to follow her to the house. They did so begrudgingly, all the while arguing about the fair and some old crystal ball that Maude said was probably made of Pyrex.

"Please hurry," Mavis whispered to Wilbur. He merely smiled as he watched the three women carry the shopping bags into the house.

[Chapter Two]

"I don't see why y'all have to go along with her foolishness!" Maude sputtered. She inhaled another bite of mashed potatoes and sighed. "I'm afraid we're getting too old for this."

"Ms. Maude! Are you sick?" Mavis gasped. Even Wilbur looked a little taken aback by Maude's phrasing. She had never been one to speak about her age or act it.

"I'm just saying," Maude whispered. "Opal's been through a lot. Some days she forgets things, and y'all know she ain't as sharp as she used to be. That second stroke two years ago almost killed her."

Mavis and Wilbur exchanged quick glances and looked over at Opal who seemed to be in a trance. Her eyes were closed and she was humming a tune that neither of them could quite place. Opal had indeed been through a lot over the past few years, but she always sprang back in time. Maude had never let her miss a single doctor or therapy appointment.

"We'll be there, too," Wilbur smiled softly. "It'll be good for both of you to get out of the house and be out and about. It's been a while since y'all have had an adventure. It's been a while since any of us have had an adventure," he chuckled.

"We've had enough adventures to last a lifetime," Maude said. "You really think we need one more?"

"Wilbur's right," Mavis nodded. "Don't get used to hearing that, Wilbur," she added with a sideways glance. "We'll all be there. And just think about all the food and animals and people we'll see. I can't wait for Saturday!"

"I see plenty of animals and people here on my street. But I do like the fair food," Maude said slowly. "Ok, I guess it can't hurt. As long as Opal plays by the rules."

"When has that ever happened?" Mavis whispered sarcastically to Wilbur under her breath.

"What was that Mavis?" Maude asked. "Who said anything about clapping? You might want to get your ears checked out."

"Yes ma'am," Mavis nodded.

"Opal, snap out of it. Finish your salad. Mavis brought a cake over on the stove and I aim to eat it in peace," Maude snapped.

Opal shook her head and took a deep breath and picked at her plate piled high with leafy vegetables. "I'm not deaf, you know," she sassed back.

"No one said you were dead," Maude huffed.

Opal winked at Mavis and Wilbur before dutifully eating the rest of her meal. She gathered up the plates when everyone was finished and placed them in the sink. Mavis cut the hummingbird cake and gave everyone a giant slice. It was absolutely delicious and melted in their mouths. It was easy to see why that particular kind of cake was a crowd favorite. Mavis reckoned she could eat it every day and never get tired of it. It was made with different fruits, so it was healthy. Crushed pineapple, bananas, and pecans made for the perfect combination.

"I knew I should have worn my stretchy pants," Maude said as she loosened the button of her jeans. Her eyes had grown to the size of saucers at the sight of the cake slice.

"What are you doing?" Mavis gasped. "You've got to keep your clothes on, Ms. Maude!"

"Don't get naked," Opal shook her head.

"You're one to talk about getting naked. You've been a worldwide streaker your whole life," Maude told her. "And besides, I'm not getting naked. I'm just giving everything a little room to breathe."

Mavis looked over at Wilbur who was putting the rest of the leftovers in Opal's refrigerator. He shook his head without a word. Nothing these women did or said surprised him anymore.

"Ms. Maude, we got you a plate here to take home. And a big ol' piece of this cake, too," Mavis told her.

"I'll help you carry it over to your house whenever you're ready to go home, Ms. Maude. But there's no rush. We can stay here and visit as long as you like," Wilbur smiled.

"Get naked at your own house," Opal mumbled. She shook her head and frowned at Maude.

"I ain't getting naked!" Maude shrieked again. "I swear, the older y'all get, the worse you get.

Opal, I'll pick you up in the morning. Wilbur, you gotta take that thing with you and get it set up. We've got to go shopping for all the mess she needs for that voodoo contraption before we get to the fair."

"Voodoo contraption?" Mavis asked.

"That fortune telling mess is close enough to witchcraft," Maude said. "I don't need anyone guessing my future."

"It's not a guess," Opal yawned.

Maude shook her head vehemently. "Only the good Lord knows my future. Though if you see anything about winning lottery numbers, let me know."

"You still play the lottery, Ms. Maude?" Mavis laughed.

"Of course, I do! Why wouldn't I?" Maude looked aghast.

"Well, I," Mavis began. "Oh, never mind." She knew that Maude had more money than she knew what to do with but getting into that with her was pointless.

Wilbur smirked at Mavis and changed the subject. "What exactly are y'all needing to shop for?" he asked.

"Opal needs a uniform," Maude said.

"Costume," Opal sighed. "Uniforms are for soldiers and firemen."

"Excuse me," Maude said dramatically. "Opal needs a costume. And she can't find her blasted crystal ball that she says is important. I swear I saw it last week on the table," she frowned.

"What table?" Opal asked.

"I don't know. A table's a table," Maude shrugged.

"Wait a minute!" Opal gasped. She shuffled towards her guest bathroom, and they heard a cascade of noise.

"Opal? What in the world are you doing?" Maude shouted from her place at the table. She had already worked her way through most of her cake.

Wilbur and Mavis both hurried down the hallway and found Opal on a stepstool tossing bottles out of the cabinet. "Here it is!" she shrieked happily.

"Here what is?" Mavis asked as she peeked around Wilbur's head in the doorway.

"My ball!" Opal smiled.

"What's going on?" Maude shouted from the kitchen.

"She found her ball," Mavis called back.

"Her ball?" Maude shouted. "Opal ain't got no balls." She shook her head and continued to shove pieces of cake into her mouth.

Opal climbed down from the stool. She cradled a large crystal ball that was wrapped in a purple and gold shawl. She pushed past Wilbur and Mavis and took the find back to the kitchen to show Maude.

"That's the one," Maude nodded. "There's probably a dozen or more of those out in the shed back there.

"Not like this one," Opal shook her head.

"What's so special about that one?" Mavis asked. She had left Wilbur in the bathroom to clean up the mess that Opal had left over the floor.

"This came from the Swiss Alps," Opal breathed. She had an air of mystery in her voice and a twinkle in her eye.

"The Swiss Alps?" Maude rolled her eyes. "More like the Salvation Army."

Opal shot her a look and continued her story. "I ordered it from QVC. It's the real deal."

Wilbur rejoined the women who had moved to the living room. "What time do I need to have the booth setup tomorrow?" he asked.

Opal looked down at her wrist that was bare. "Around noon," she nodded.

"The fair opens to the public at five," Mavis said. "Opening night is going to be so magical."

"It'll be ready by then for sure," Wilbur assured them. "Madame Opalina will be the belle of the ball."

"Why do y'all keep talking about balls?" Maude asked.

"A ball is a dance," Mavis explained gently.

"We ain't dancing," Maude shook her head. "Last time I danced was at a wedding down at the senior center and I near about got married myself. You gotta be careful when you shake your hips like that."

Mavis and Wilbur looked very confused, but Opal nodded along to Maude's story. "It ain't like it used to be," she agreed.

"What are they talking about now?" Mavis whispered to Wilbur.

"Beat's me," he whispered back.

"Why do you want her to beat you?" Maude asked Wilbur. "I swear, this generation is loster than goat out the back barn door!"

"A goat out of a barn door?" Mavis asked.

"Loster?" Wilbur asked at the same time.

Maude and Opal merely shook their heads at Mavis and Wilbur's lack of understanding.

"I don't like lobster," Opal said.

"You want lobster? Wilbur, we just ate," Maude said knowingly. "Did you not get enough? Mavis, go in the kitchen and fix Wilbur some more supper. He was too busy talking and not enough eating earlier."

"I'm fine," Wilbur said. "Anyway, we'll all be ready for the fair tomorrow when it opens. It runs for seven days, right?"

Mavis nodded enthusiastically and could barely contain her excitement. "Yes! Sunday through Saturday. The first and last day aren't full days though. More like half days. On the last day, they do an adoption event for some of the animals," she squealed.

"I don't think that's right," Wilbur interjected.

"What do you mean?" Maude asked.

"You can adopt the animals!" Mavis reiterated. "They put them up for adoption and everything. You bid for them and then take them home."

"It's an action," Wilbur nodded. "But it's for meat, Mavis."

"No, that doesn't sound right. They auctioned off whole cows and pigs. They'd be the cutest little pets!" Mavis affirmed.

"Mavis, they auction them off for people to buy for meat. You can purchase a quarter, half, or a whole cow or hog. You pick it up from the butcher a few days later," Wilbur explained.

"That's where I always got my beef and pork," Maude nodded. "Freshest meat around. Gives those kids pocket money, too. That's what they mean when they say shop local."

Mavis gasped and put her hands to her mouth. "That's terrible!"

"You love beef and pork," Wilbur pointed out.

"But not from animals I pet all week!" Mavis squealed. "I don't want to know the names of the hamburgers or ribs I eat!"

"Circle of life," Maude shrugged. "What goes around comes around."

"Sure is," Opal agreed. "And it comes around time and again."

Mavis shook her head and tried to recenter herself. "I heard that they're going to have live music this year," Mavis said.

"I like jive music," Opal said. "Good for the soul."

"It ain't done it," Maude said. "Music isn't medicinal. You gotta go see a doctor for moles. That's what happened to Nadine. She went to the doctor last year and came back with cancer. I couldn't believe it!"

"Oh! I saw Ms. Waters earlier today. I was going to ask you how she was doing," Mavis said to Maude.

"How should I know? You said you just saw her today. You tell me!" Maude shrugged.

"Well, I just meant that she looked tired and like maybe she wasn't feeling her best," Mavis frowned.

"Cancer at her age can't be fun," Maude said seriously.

"At our age," Opal nodded.

"We ain't got the cancer," Maude corrected. "Nadine has the cancer, but she's supposed to be doing better now. She's going back to the doctor this week for new cans, but we know how that is. One minute you can be fine and the next you're not."

Mavis and Wilbur nodded solemnly. Ruby had passed away from metastatic colon cancer at the end of the summer back in 2018. They all knew more about cancer than they ever wanted to. It seemed to consume her all at once. If truth be told, Ruby had probably been suffering for quite some time, but like all good southern women, she kept things to herself for too long. By the time she voiced any concerns and saw a doctor, it was nearly too late. It was a hard time for everyone. Opal had had a stroke and nearly died, and not long after, Ruby was diagnosed with cancer. She held on for months before it finally overtook her. Even though it had been three years, her death still loomed over all who loved her. Maude was the only one out of the three women who hadn't suffered any major health setbacks, which was surprising seeing as how she was also the only one who smoked diligently and ate whatever she wanted to. Sometimes life was funny like that.

"I think it's about time I turned in," Maude yawned loudly. She belched and buttoned her pants that were still undone. 'Walk me home, Wilbur. You never know what's outside in these here parts."

Wilbur nodded and retrieved Maude's plate from the fridge. "I'll be right back," he said to

Mavis. He held onto Maude's arm and helped her down the porch steps and walked her the short distance to her house. He could see the lights on across the street at Nadine's house and hoped she was doing well.

"Hold your horses, Wilbur!" Maude demanded. "It's dark out here."

"Yes ma'am," Wilbur smiled. He shone the flashlight on the ground for Maude to see the ground in front of her. "Need me to help you inside?"

"I can make it," Maude said. "You go load up that contraption and we'll see you at the fairgrounds tomorrow around lunchtime. You're gonna bring some lunch, right?"

"Yes ma'am," Wilbur nodded. They had never discussed him bringing lunch, but he would add it to his list of things to do. He watched as she climbed the three steps to her porch and heard her lock the front door behind her. Once she was safely inside, he hurried back across the yard to Opal's house. Opal was in the kitchen rinsing off the dishes to put in the dishwasher. Mavis packed up the rest of the cake and slid into her shopping bag. "You all set, Mavis?" he asked.

She nodded and gave Opal a hug. "We'll see you tomorrow," Mavis smiled.

"I'm going to load up the booth in my truck and we'll be at the fairgrounds tomorrow to set it up. Ms. Maude says I'm going to bring lunch for us all to eat before the fair opens to the public," Wilbur explained.

Opal nodded and walked them to the front door. She hugged them both and closed the door behind them. "Ms. Maude told you to bring lunch?" Mavis asked.

"You know how it goes," Wilbur chuckled. "I'll pick you up around ten tomorrow morning and we can go through a drive-thru on the way to Junction."

"Sounds like a plan," Mavis agreed. "Do you need any help loading that booth into your truck?"

Wilbur shook his head and said, "I can manage. See you in the morning."

He loaded the booth and tied it down so it wouldn't fall out. Most of the paint had dried, but it would probably need another coat once he got it set up at the fairgrounds tomorrow. He turned onto the highway and headed to his serene log cabin in the woods. The next seven days of the fair were setting out to be an adventure alright.

[Chapter Three]

True to his word, Wilbur dutifully picked up Mavis on time the next morning. She hurried down the porch steps of Magnolia Manor and climbed into Wilbur's truck. None of the fast-food chains were serving lunch yet, so they drove straight to the fairgrounds to set up the booth in the allotted spot. Wilbur wasn't sure how Opal had done it, but she had somehow gotten the last available booth space the fairgrounds had to offer. Then again, who was going to say no to Opal Tyler?

"There's a lot of interesting looking folks here," Mavis pointed out once they parked. Opal had not told them where they were supposed to set up the booth at, so Wilbur and Mavis walked through the gates and looked for someone to speak to about the setup process. "There's Hector Morales over by the ticket booth," Mavis pointed. Hector was one of the men in charge of the fairgrounds and an old friend of Wilbur's from high school.

Wilbur hurried behind her to where a group of men were standing. "Hey Hec," he called out.

"Hey Wilbur. Morning Mavis!" Hector smiled. "What are y'all doing here so early?"

"Opal Tyler put in last minute to set up a booth and we aren't sure where it's supposed to go. We were hoping you could point us in the right direction," Wilbur said.

Hector scratched his chin and pulled out his phone. "Let me see," he said. "Booth setups are from ten to noon today. Let me look up her name and see. Ok, here it is. Opal Tyler's got spot number twelve under the big red tent over there." He pointed behind him towards two large tents, one blue and one red, about two hundred yards away that were setup to house almost fifty different booths and vendor tables each. "I'll hold the gate open for y'all to drive right up to it. Need any help unloading?"

Wilbur shook his head and thanked him for being so helpful. He and Mavis walked back towards the truck and drove through the gate Hector held open for them. They could see a bunch of people already setting up their own booths and tables. There were booths of homemade soaps, canned jellies and jams, jewelry, artwork, and blankets. Every which way they looked they saw something different for sale.

"Why didn't Opal bring her Color Me Crazy line up here to sell?" Mavis wondered out loud.

"She doesn't need to," Wilbur laughed. "She's already famous internationally for it. Lord knows it'd cause a stampede in here if she brought all that stuff down here. Ever since she sold her salon, the public has been begging her to open another one."

Mavis nodded. Wilbur was right about that. The Comb Over was the premiere salon in Rhinestone for decades. Opal had sold it years ago and it closed not long after. The new owner just didn't have what it took to be an entrepreneur. Thankfully, Opal had already launched her product line internationally and it had taken off immediately. If you wanted any of her products, you had to order it online. The fancy salons in bigger cities carried the line in their stores and shops, but there wasn't anywhere local to purchase them.

"What time do you think they'll roll up in here?" Mavis asked.

Wilbur looked down at his watch and shrugged. "Probably a few minutes before the gates open," he laughed. Maude was not known to be punctual unless the outing revolved around food. There was no telling what adventures Maude and Opal were currently getting into while shopping this morning. Those two were double trouble when they were together.

They got the booth setup in record time. Wilbur slathered on another coat of paint while Mavis painted a sign for the top of the booth with Opal's name and services listed. It was almost noon when they both finished.

"Want to walk around and see if there's any food here?" Wilbur asked. "You know Ms. Maude will riot if I don't have lunch ready like she instructed."

Mavis agreed and smelled the air. "Let's take a right out of here towards the food trucks. I smell pizza," she mused.

Wilbur knew that Mavis' nose was usually spot on. He followed her down the pathway and saw various food trucks set up in rows. There was indeed a pizza truck that looked to be up and running. There was a short line at the window of carnival workers who were sweating out in the hot sun. Mavis and Wilbur joined the line and ordered a whole pizza for the four of them to share. The food truck didn't have any plates, but the woman behind the counter shoved a handful of napkins at Wilbur and called for the next person in line to step forward.

They walked back towards the red tent and saw Maude pulling a wagon behind her. The wagon was loaded down with boxes and shopping bags. Opal, dressed in a floor length cloak, walked behind the wagon to make sure that nothing from the mountain of clutter fell. She held the coveted crystal ball in her hands.

"There y'all are!" Maude huffed. "It's about time! Come help me. This mess is heavy!"

Wilbur handed Mavis the pizza box and jogged towards Maude and took over pulling the wagon. He pulled up in front of the booth and started to unload the bags and boxes.

"This looks good," Opal smiled. She reached out to touch the booth, but Maude slapped her hand. "Don't touch it! The paint looks wet!"

Opal stuck her tongue out at Maude and turned towards Wilbur. "Thank you," she smiled.

"No problem," Wilbur said. "Mavis drew you the sign so everyone would know what you were set up for."

"Thank you," Opal beamed at Mavis.

"Yea, yea, it all looks good," Maude said. "What's for lunch?"

"We've got pizza for lunch," Wilbur assured her. "Let's go over to those picnic tables under the trees for some shade."

"Weighed?" Opal asked. She looked around but didn't see a scale. "I don't they weigh us."

Wilbur and Mavis smiled at Opal as Maude zoomed past them towards the tables and sat down. Wilbur helped Opal over to the tables while Mavis followed behind with the pizza and napkins.

"What kind did you get?" Maude asked.

"They only had cheese," Mavis said. She set the box down on the table and handed each person a napkin and bottle of water.

"I guess that will be fine. Where's the plates?" Maude asked.

"They didn't have any," Mavis explained. She opened the box and inhaled the aroma of melted cheese. The pizza smelled heavenly, and she was anxious to dig in.

"We'll just have to make do," Maude frowned. She reached for the biggest slice and started eating it. Wilbur handed Opal a slice on a napkin and then gave one to Mavis before grabbing one for himself. They polished off the entire pizza in minutes. Wilbur threw away the trash and they all walked back towards the tent that was full of people bustling around.

"It's crowded in here," Maude sniffed. "How long we gotta be at this thing?"

"Hadn't even started getting crowded yet," Wilbur smiled. "Just wait until gate opens to the public."

"You mean more people are going to show up here?" Maude asked.

"Hope so," Opal nodded.

"The fair is from noon until ten most every day. Today it doesn't open until five though," Mavis explained.

"What?" Maude gasped. "There ain't no way I'm sitting out here every day all damn day. No way!"

"Yes, we are!" Opal countered.

"Not for seven days!" Maude shook her head.

"We'll all take turns," Wilbur said gently.

Maude grumbled and pulled out a piece of candy from her purse. "Let's unpack these boxes then," she sighed. "Might as well get this fool contraption set up. We bought enough for it."

"Where all did y'all go this morning?" Mavis asked.

"Everywhere," Maude frowned. "Now that Opal don't drive and I'm her chauffeur, I swear she picks places just to annoy me."

Wilbur swore he saw Opal smirk at Maude's words. They began to unpack the boxes and bags in the wagon. There was a bag full of snacks that Wilbur knew was Maude's, and another sack full of plastic gold coins. One box of smelly wigs was barely held together with tape that probably came from the eighties. They pulled out baskets and bottles of various sizes and four different robes of various colors.

"These are beautiful," Mavis said.

"One for each of us," Opal nodded. She handed the dark blue one to Wilbur, the golden one to Mavis, and kept the purple one for herself.

"Oh, I like yours, Wilbur!" Mavis gushed.

"I look like Lawrence of Arabia," Wilbur laughed as he fastened his robe.

"Where's mine?" Maude asked. She blew out her cigarette and looked around expectantly.

"Right here," Opal said proudly. She held out the remaining robe towards Maude who frowned.

"I ain't wearing that," Maude frowned.

"Why not?" Mavis asked. "It's um, beautiful in its own way. Right, Wilbur?"

"Right," Wilbur nodded. He bit his lip to keep from laughing.

Maude took the robe from Opal and held it up to her. It was shockingly pink and had bright orange polka dots all over it. "I look like a damned flamingo!" she howled.

"But a very pretty one," Mavis added encouragingly.

Maude shot her a look before slipping the pink robe over her head. "I'll wear it for now, but I'm not leaving this booth in this getup," she hissed.

"Someone has to advertise," Opal frowned. "And try on this one." Opal handed Maude a raven-haired wig that looked like it hadn't been brushed since the Middle Ages.

"What?" Maude snapped.

"The brightest has to advertise," Opal shrugged. She handed Maude a bright purple sign that read: Ask Me About Madame Opalina's Fortune Telling Booth. "Pin it to your back."

"Pin it to my back!" Maude thundered. She stomped her foot and refused to take the sign or wig from Opal.

"Fine," Opal smiled wryly. She took the sign and slapped Maude on the back with gusto to secure the sign to Maude's back. "It's just tape," she shrugged. "Or Mavis can sew it."

Wilbur and Mavis were bent over in laughter at the spectacle in front of them. Other people from surrounding booths paused their work to look over at the two old women squabbling. Maude pulled the sign from her back and looked from Wilbur to Mavis and back over to Opal. "I swear, Opal, this is the limit. You've done some stuff before, but this really is too much. This is the craziest thing you've ever tried."

"But Ms. Maude," Mavis began.

"I wouldn't say that," Wilbur said. Opal had many crazy ideas in her eighty plus years.

"No, don't try to defend her this time. This really is too much!" Maude lamented.

"It's not that bad, Ms. Maude," Wilbur said, clearing his throat to keep from laughing.

"I am not a walking billboard!" Maude shouted. "And I dang sure ain't a circus flamingo billboard!"

"You'll stand out, that's for sure," Wilbur chuckled under his breath.

"It's bound to bring business," Mavis added.

"This is not a business! This is one of her hairbrained concoctions!" Maude fumed. "You did this on purpose," she hissed at Opal.

"It's for charity," Opal reminded her. She pulled the wig onto Maude's neck and ignored her screeching and howls.

"To be fair, her hairbrained ideas are usually successful," Mavis added with a weak smile.

"If you think it's such a good idea, then you wear it," Maude told Mavis. "I give enough to charity already. Hell, I'll pay you money to shut this mess down right now." She ripped the wig off of her head and threw it onto the booth's counter.

"Why don't we just set all this aside for right now. We can figure out if we need to advertise after folks start coming in tonight," Wilbur said, taking the sign from Opal and putting it underneath the shelf in the booth.

Maude crossed her arms and huffed. "I still look like a flamingo."

"Flamingoes don't talk," Opal smirked.

"I swear, one of these days, Opal Tyler," Maude mumbled under her breath.

"I can't tell you how many times I've heard her say that over the years," Mavis whispered to Wilbur. He nodded and said she was right about that. Maude often threatened Opal's life, but no one ever took it seriously. Especially Opal, who took it more like a challenge. She knew that Maude was always along for the ride, now and forever.

"We'll know she's really mad if she ever stops saying it," Wilbur laughed.

"It is a pretty big feat that they haven't killed each other yet," Mavis added.

"She does have big feet," Opal nodded seriously. She adjusted a bleach blonde wig in the style of a pixie cut onto her head and beamed at the mirror she had pulled from her purse.

Mavis gasped and Wilbur collapsed into giggles at Opal's frequent misheard conversations.

"Clown shoes," Opal continued. She pointed to Maude's sandals that Maude wore with long tube socks that came to her knees underneath the robe.

"What do we have left to do for this mess?" Maude asked.

Wilbur looked at his watch and shrugged. "I reckon we're done here until they let people in the gate, right Ms. Opal?"

Opal nodded and looked around at the busyness around them. Before anyone could say anything, she shuffled over to their neighbors on the right and started looking at their seashell sculptures. She and the older man behind the counter engaged in a very animated conversation about God knows what. The whole scene was much funnier with Opal in her purple robe and pixie cut wig.

"Good lord! What is she doing now?" Maude asked.

"Being Opal," Wilbur smiled.

"We should probably try to keep an eye on her," Mavis said.

"You mean them," Wilbur laughed as Maude hurried over to the neighboring booth to pester Opal.

"These are pretty," Maude said. She had picked up a couple of the sculptures herself and began to admire them.

"Watch this one," Opal whispered loudly to her new friend. She gestured at Maude and added, "Sticky fingers."

Maude glared at Opal and quickly put down the sculptures she had been admiring. She wiped her fingers on her robe and hissed, "My hands are just fine!"

"I've bailed her out of jail before in Memphis. She almost didn't escape New York either," Opal shrugged.

"Every one of those was your fault!" Maude huffed.

Wilbur and Mavis looked at each other. It was difficult to tell sometimes when Opal was kidding and being serious. The man kept an eye on Maude as she perused the selections just to be safe. The fair brought out all kinds of people.

"Alright, we've got a few hours until the public comes in. Shall we look around to see what the fair has to offer?" Wilbur suggested.

They all agreed that that would be a good idea. Opal climbed into the wagon and ordered Maude to pull her like a sled dog. Wilbur merely shook his head.

[Chapter Four]

Opal didn't last long in the wagon. Maude only dumped her out once before Wilbur picked up the older woman from the ground and decided it was probably best that they all walk. Opal had left her walker at home, so Wilbur made sure to keep her steady with his arm.

Before long, the wagon was filled to the gills with crafts items they had purchased that were made all over the southeastern United States. Boxes and bags full of candles, diffusers, pillows of various sizes, eco-friendly cleaning supplies, various candies and chocolates, soup mixes, and meat and vegetable marinades. Mavis found a booth that sold powdered shakes and put in to buy a year's worth of supply, even though Opal turned up her nose at the list of ingredients. Opal bought Maude a crafting kit in an attempt to keep her entertained during her first shift as Madame Opalina's assistant later that afternoon. The kit included materials and a small print booklet of instructions for the crafter to make her own pair of earrings. It didn't matter that the craft kit was for children, Maude seemed to be excited about it.

After they shopped, Mavis insisted on seeing some of the animals. Wilbur had to drag Mavis away from the petting zoo when it was time to return to the tent. "But Wilbur! They're all so cute! The little piglets and the big grumpy cow begged me to keep feeding them!" she wailed.

"You heard them talking to you?" Opal asked.

"No," Mavis frowned. "They said it with their eyes."

"Don't look them in the eyes," Maude warned. "That bull would sooner gore you because he knows you'll eat him once the fair is done."

"Don't say that!" Mavis wailed. "It's a petting zoo!"

"I'm just saying," Maude shrugged, as they pulled their newfound treasures back into the tent behind Opal's booth. She set to work on opening the craft kit before anyone could stop her.

The gates opened to the throngs of people at exactly five o'clock. It looked like people from all over the tri-state area had come to see what the fair had to offer. While Wilbur helped Opal get into her costume, Mavis and Maude got ready to attract passersby.

"How do people pay for this thing?" Maude asked.

"Cash only," Mavis replied. Opal had decided to donate all of the cash raised from her booth to her favorite local charity. Mavis set the empty fishbowl on the counter and saw a group of people coming near. "Oh! Here they come. What should we do? Where's Madame Opalina?"

"Welcome to Madame Opalina's where we're going to tell you what's going to happen to you," Maude told the first visitor to the booth.

"Ms. Maude, you can't say it like that. You have to be inviting," Mavis coached her.

Maude rolled her eyes, but turned back to the woman and said, "Welcome. Come on up." It wasn't necessarily the warmest invitation, but it was an improvement.

Opal appeared out of nowhere and reached for the woman's hand. She quietly studied the lines on the palm before looking up at the woman and nodding. "Everything is going to work out. He's on his way home as we speak," she said breathily.

"Really?" the lady asked. "Bentley's coming home?"

"Yes," Opal held her hand and nodded.

"Oh, thank you," she hugged Opal around the neck and scampered off. She shoved a fistful of bills into the clear fishbowl on the counter.

Maude looked at Opal. "What in the world was that about?"

Opal shrugged. "The inner eye always knows."

"Ms. Opal, that was amazing!" Mavis gushed.

Opal nodded and smiled in return.

"And everything is really going to be okay for her?" Mavis continued.

"Yes," Opal said. "Her dog is waiting on her porch for her like he always is."

"I wish I knew how to do that," Mavis said.

"Let me try to teach you," Opal said patiently. She took Mavis' hands and began to study them. "Hmm," she murmured. She brow furrowed and she frowned heavily. "He's coming back. It won't end well, at least for him. But he is coming back. And soon."

Mavis stared at her. "Who's he?"

"Yes," Opal murmured.

"Oooh, my goodness. Can you believe it, Wilbur? Ms Opal just told me he's coming back," Mavis said to Wilbur who had just returned from throwing away some of their trash in the receptacles by the tent's exit.

"He who?" Wilbur asked.

"I don't know," Mavis squealed.

Wilbur shrugged his shoulders with a smile. "Well, good for him then, I guess."

"Now do Ms. Maude!" Mavis said.

Maude grunted as Opal reached for her hands. "This is crazy!"

Opal had barely looked at her hands before saying, "Stay away from the brisket."

"For the last time, I am not turning into a vegetarian!" Maude fumed.

"Trust me, you need to stay away from the brisket," Opal warned her again.

"This is nuts! Just because you don't eat meat doesn't mean that the rest of us can't. I swear, Opal, not all of us have to have a crazy diet like you do!" Maude huffed. "I like brisket and it likes me!" Maude turned and walked over to the corner where she stood and fumed for a few minutes.

Mavis was too excited to worry about Maude's doubt. "Now it's Wilbur's turn!" She reached for Wilbur's hand and pulled him over to Opal.

Wilbur offered Opal his hands and waited with a grin on his face.

Opal beamed at him. "The sweetest lady is going to come into your life!"

Wilbur laughed. "I don't know about all that. Sounds like you might be trying to get me into trouble."

"She's going to love you!" Opal said again.

"Okie dokie, well, that's good I guess," Wilbur laughed, but he did pull his hands away quickly before Opal could offer up any more predictions. He didn't always hold such notions, but Opal was a wildcard. He wouldn't be that surprised if her predictions, and warnings, really did happen.

A group of teenage girls walked up to the booth and started asking questions. Mavis smiled at them and told them all about Opal. They were eager to meet her and have their futures read. Especially the redhead in the front of the group who had tears rolling down her cheeks. "My boyfriend just broke up with me," she whispered. "Maybe Madame Opalina can help me fix this."

Mavis nodded and looked around, but Opal was nowhere in sight. "Wilbur, where did she go?"

Wilbur looked over his shoulder and shrugged. "I don't know. She was just right here," he said. "I'll go find her. You two manage here."

Mavis looked at Maude and grabbed her by the arm. Before Maude could argue, Mavis had tugged a wig from the nearby box onto her head and tied a sash around her neck. "You have to be Madame Opalina. Wilbur went to find Opal, but we have a group ready for us!"

"I don't know anything about this future mess. You be Opal," Maude grumbled.

"I can't!" Mavis squealed. "The teenage girls already saw me. I promised them some pretty big things."

"I don't even like teenage girls," Maude frowned. "Not even when I was one. Plus, they're too whiny these days."

"Be that as it may," Mavis began. "You're going to have to handle it. Come on!"

"Alright," Maude hissed. Her jet-black wig hung a little to the side, but that was the least of their worries. She plopped down on the chair behind the booth and bellowed, "Well, come on over. What do we have here?"

The red-headed girl's friend pushed her to the front counter and stood around to watch the spectacle. "My boyfriend just broke up with me. I don't know what I'll do!" the girl cried.

Maude gave the teenager a side-eye look and frowned. She looked far too young to be dating. There was no way she had even driven herself to the fair. Where in the world were her parents? "How long were y'all dating?" Maude asked.

"Two weeks! He said he loved me!" the girl lamented.

"You've got to be kidding me," Maude hissed to Mavis. Mavis cleared her throat loudly and shook her head. Maude sighed and rolled her eyes but decided to finish strong. "You're what? Fourteen?" she asked the girl.

"Fourteen and a half!" the girl shrieked.

Maude took a deep breath. "Let me see your hands."

The girl held out her hands for Maude to examine. Her manicured nails were an immaculate shade of violet that matched her thick eyeshadow that had smudged due to her crying.

Maude adjusted her wig quickly. "Right, well, from the looks of it, your heart vein and your life vein intersect at Jupiter. That's the biggest planet, you know." She looked at Mavis who nodded for confirmation. "Which is good because Mars crosses the path in mid December. Or could be January. That means that this is only a temporary setback. Let him go because he doesn't deserve you. Your true love is coming to meet you on the horizon where Venus intersects Pluto," Maude continued.

"But Pluto isn't a planet," a girl near the back of the group interjected.

"Yes, it is!" Maude snapped. "What are they teaching y'all these days?"

"It's really not," the girl laughed disdainfully.

"Well, in my day it was!" Maude huffed. "Anyway, when that happens, you'll meet the one of your dreams."

"Really?" the girl asked her.

"Absolutely," Maude said.

"When will that be?" the red-haired girl asked. "Tomorrow? Are you sure it's not Andy? I thought we had a connection!"

"Hell, if I know!" Maude snapped.

"But he already unfollowed me on Instagram!" the girl frowned.

Maude was too tired to be dealing with the heartbreaks of this younger generation. Back in her day, this kind of thing didn't happen. Social media had ruined the lives of kids nowadays. Between Facechat or Snapdragon or whatever the channels were called, kids nowadays needed to tighten up

41

and stop being so dramatic. Mavis could see that Maude was about to lose her cool, so she stepped in and took over.

"You need to date yourself," she told the girl. "He doesn't see how great you are. Let him go," she smiled.

The girl didn't seem convinced, which made Mavis evaluate her tactics. "Um, ask his best friend to the movies?" she suggested.

"Oooh! Diabolical," the girl's friend laughed. "I like it."

The group of teenage girls walked off. Apparently, they didn't seem to think that Maude or Mavis' advice was worth any monetary donation. "See? They don't even know the value of a dollar," Maude hissed. She pulled off the wig that had made her head sweat. The robe was comfortable, but it was suffocating in the sweltering heat. The humidity levels were record high this October and she needed a glass of something to cool her off.

"I'm going to get some of that freshly squeezed lemonade," she said to Mavis. "You can handle business while I'm gone."

"Oh, ok," Mavis frowned. Wilbur was still not back from looking for Opal. Maude had not been concerned at Opal's disappearance. She reminded Mavis that Opal had a history of walking off. Mavis would never forget the time that Opal had disappeared into one of her back rooms and tried on some of her lingerie. Or the time that she dove in headfirst in the giant fish tank. Or the time she swam in the church's baptismal. It was always something with Opal Tyler. "Can you bring me back some lemonade?" Mavis called out.

"Sure, sure," Maude replied. She disappeared outside and left Mavis standing next to the booth. Maybe Maude would drum up some business while she was out, but that seemed doubtful. Minutes ticked away and no one seemed to want to stop in, so Mavis adjusted her robe and chose a stunning blonde wig from the box behind the booth. That wig was sure to attract any man who walked by.

A few minutes later, a handsome man in tight blue jeans sauntered right on up to the booth. "Good evening," he smiled. "How much for a pretty lady like you to tell me my future?" he drawled.

Mavis blushed and said, "ten dollars."

"That seems a little high for my price range," the man said. "How about you tell me some things and we'll go from there?"

Mavis nodded and gestured for the man to hold out his hands. "Let me see," she whispered in a Jamaican accent. She wasn't sure where that accent had come from, but the stranger seemed to enjoy it. "I see a lot of money in your future. Big sums of money."

"That's what I'm talking about!" the man said. "I've placed some big wagers on the bull riding tomorrow night. Anything else?"

Mavis bit her lip and continued, "And stay away from the brisket," she parroted.

"Brisket?" he frowned. "I run a brisket truck over yonder." He snatched his hand back and stood at the mouth of the tent about ten feet away.

43

"What are you trying to do, run off all my business?"

Mavis was taken aback. "No, of course not."

"Is this the kind of advice that you've been giving out to the suckers that come in here?" he demanded. "Are you trying to sabotage me?"

"No, I," Mavis stammered. "It's just that," she hesitated before remembering that she was the master of her fate, and no one could ever take that away from her. Not even an irate customer. "That's what the inner eye has foreseen," she declared.

"My hind foot! I better not find out you've been trying to steal my business," he threatened her.

"What's going on here?" Wilbur demanded. He had nearly run himself out of breath over to the booth.

"We're done here!" the man spit. He turned on his heel and stormed out of the tent leaving Mavis to explain what had happened to Wilbur.

"Where's Opal?" Mavis asked.

"Oh God," he winced. "Hold on!" He scanned the crowd and saw Opal sitting in a wooden rocking chair. He hustled over to her and stopped the chair from turning over backwards right in the nick of time. He took her by the hand and brought her back over to her booth where Mavis was still sitting.

"How's business?" Opal asked.

"Lousy," Mavis frowned. "Neither I nor Ms. Maude have the inner eye that you have."

"Yes, I know," Opal nodded. "Where's Maude?"

"I don't know," Mavis sighed.

"Will you please tell me what in the world that was all about?" Wilbur huffed.

"Here's your lemonade," Maude said, holding two giant cups of refreshment. She had appeared out of thin air. "What in the world was that guy stomping off for? And Opal, where did you run off to earlier?"

"Had to see a man about a horse," Opal said.

"What?" Wilbur, Mavis, and Maude all asked.

"You don't have room for a horse!" Maude said.

"Well, technically she does," Wilbur reasoned.

"Mavis had a horse a few years back and I can, too," Opal said.

Wilbur turned to Mavis who shook her head and begged him not to even go there. She changed the subject quickly before either Opal or Maude told the story of the Mavis' lingerie and costume trunk they had accidentally discovered one time. She would never forget the sights she saw that afternoon and quickly donated the entire trunk of leather bustier tops to the local charity shop. Slim Pickens Thrift Store had readily accepted the donation with a smile.

"Anyway! Ms. Maude ran off a group of teenage girls and then left me all alone to deal with that angry man who makes brisket. I was just repeating what you had said earlier," she explained to Opal who merely nodded.

"I see," Opal said. "I was afraid that would happen. I'm back now." She settled into the chair behind the booth, and like magic, a line formed in front of her.

Some women really did have all the luck, Mavis thought.

[Chapter Five]

Day one of the fair was exhausting. Mavis wasn't sure that she would be able to keep up day in and day out for the next week. Even Wilbur was tired, and he was used to being out in the heat and working hard. Not that Mavis wasn't accustomed to hard work, but she wasn't used to dealing with the public for so many hours.

No one had expected Opal's booth to be that popular, besides Opal herself. As soon as Opal returned to the booth after her disappearance, the line of customers wrapped around the outside of the tent. Everyone wanted to see Madame Opalina in action, and Opal knew how to entertain a crowd. It was after midnight before Wilbur and Mavis got home last night. They had followed Maude back to her house to make sure that she and Opal made it home safely. Neither of them were keen on Maude driving so late at night, but Maude insisted that she would be fine. After they watched the two older women go into their respective houses, Wilbur turned towards Mavis and said, "No ifs, ands, or buts about it. One of us has to drive them from here on out to Junction."

Mavis agreed wholeheartedly. Maude had run every red light between Junction and Rhinestone and never dipped below ten over the speed limit. Mavis agreed that she would call them both in the morning and tell them that she would be by to pick them up in her new Chevrolet Suburban with plenty of time to spare before the fair opened. Wilbur had a few projects he needed to attend to before driving over to the fairgrounds, so the responsibility had fallen on Mavis. She truly didn't mind, as long as Opal and Maude stayed where they were supposed to and didn't run off again and leave her to manage the booth.

After the commotion died down last night, Wilbur whispered to Mavis that he had overheard Opal telling the man with the booth next to them about the mechanical bull. "I think she intended to give it a go, but I managed to intervene before she said more. You don't think they'd let her ride it, do you?" he asked.

Mavis shook her head quickly. "Surely not! Well, then again, I'm not so sure," she frowned.

They really wouldn't put it past Opal to at least try to ride the mechanical bull. They would have to keep a better eye on her at all times.

Mavis slept solidly all night long. When she awoke the next morning, she rolled over and saw the sun peeking in through the curtains. It was still pretty early, but she had a list of things she needed to get finished with before she headed to Junction. First, she needed to call Maude.

"Good morning! I hope I didn't wake you," Mavis smiled when Maude answered the phone.

"I rarely sleep," Maude croaked. "What time is it? Are we late?"

"No, no," Mavis assured her. "I'm going to pick you two up at eleven and we can head over to the fairgrounds. How does that sound?"

"I'll drive us," Maude replied. "We can manage ourselves."

Mavis had been expecting that reaction, but she was ready with a plan. "I understand, but I'd really like to show you both my new car. It's so big and roomy. I was even thinking you'd like to sit in the front seat," she smiled. She knew Maude couldn't say no to that.

"No thanks," Maude said. "Me and Opal want to get some things today. She's got her mind set on a new set of rocking chairs and I found me a hammock, and I don't think it'll all fit in your car."

Maude's car was significantly smaller than Mavis' new vehicle, so Mavis had to bring out the big guns. "Oh, Ms. Maude, you won't believe this, but my new car can fit all the rocking chairs you two can think of. And all the snacks. Speaking of which, I'm on my way to the Pig in a few minutes once I finish getting dressed. I'll swing by your house afterwards and you can just ride with me since I'll already be out and about."

Maude thought about what Mavis had said and finally agreed. Mavis had always been a little bossy and it wouldn't hurt for her to drive this once. "Ok," she relented. "Pick me up some peanut oil if they have it. I'm almost out."

"Yes ma'am," Mavis said. She hung up the phone to get ready for the day. If she hurried, she could squeeze in a quick breakfast at the diner on her way to the Piggly Wiggly. She pulled her luscious dark hair into a bun and put on her favorite sundress that accentuated her curves. She completed her outfit with a beautiful sun hat and her favorite pair of light blue sunglasses. There was no need for makeup today because she would surely sweat it off anyway.

Her new Suburban was such a smooth ride. It was the most comfortable vehicle she had ever been in, and she was more than happy with her purchase. The dealership didn't have the color she had been looking for, but she found a body shop a few towns over that was more than willing to configure her custom paint request. No one else had a hot pink Suburban in the area. It was definitely hard to miss!

She pulled into an open spot at the Starlight Cafe and waved at Harry behind the counter. He nodded and continued to flip the stacks of pancakes in front of him. Mona smiled and gestured for Mavis to take a seat at the counter near the register.

"Good morning!" Mavis grinned. "Lord Mona, what's got you so happy this morning?"

Mona's face had broken into a huge grin, and she leaned over to Mavis. "I've got big news!" Harry grunted behind her and she corrected herself. "We've got big news!"

"What is it?" Mavis asked.

"We're selling the cafe," Mona whispered.

"What?" Mavis gasped. The Starlight Cafe had been in Rhinestone since she was a kid. Mona and Harry's parents had started it and it was a landmark for the town.

"Don't worry," Mona said. "It'll still be the same cafe. That was part of the deal. See those two ladies there?" She pointed out two older women who were sitting by the window in the back. "Loretta and Mae," Mona whispered. "They're sisters who have been looking for a restaurant to buy and they've been courting us for weeks. I've been dying to tell you, but we weren't sure how it would all work out. We've never ever considered anyone else running this old place, but Harry and I agreed that it's time."

"Oh, Mona, that's great. If you're happy, I'm happy!" Mavis said. "When does it all happen?"

"We sign the papers tomorrow morning. I almost can't believe it," Mona said. "It was like they were sent from heaven or something."

"What do you mean?" Mavis asked.

"I'm tired, Mavis," Mona said. "I know Harry is, too. We never get a day off and we're both run ragged. Loretta and Mae, well, their daddy died back in May and left them a boatload of money. They're from over near Talladega and said every summer they'd come visit their grandparents who lived between here and Junction and stay the summer. They've always loved this old town. They stopped in about six weeks ago and told us all about it. Said they'd love nothing more than to have a diner just like this. I jokingly said they could have this one, and well, the rest is history."

"That's amazing," Mavis said. She looked over again at the two women who looked to be in their fifties.

"It really is," Mona agreed. "They've got plans to hire employees and fix it up like it used to when my parents first opened it over thirty years ago. We'll finally be out of debt and live a little, you know? I don't know the last time I went on a vacation or even slept in late. I'm getting old, Mavis."

"We're getting old," Mavis corrected. "Life's too short not to follow your dreams. When are you going to tell the folks around here?"

"Harry wants to make sure it happens first," Mona explained. "I think we are both still a little shell shocked, to tell you the truth. Not just anyone will pack up and move to Rhinestone these days, but those two are plum excited about it. They bought McInnis' old farmhouse down by the river last week and everything. Their husbands came with them, both retired from the military, and said they're excited, too."

"It's all happening so fast!" Mavis said. "I just can't believe it."

"Me either," Mona agreed. "That means I'll have more time for yard sales and whatever else you think we can get ourselves into. I feel like I can finally start living my life. You know, ever since you got me to give up cigarettes last year, I've been feeling pretty good about myself. Might even go on a few dates now that I have time for a social life!"

"Yes!" Mavis cheered. She was so proud of Mona for the way she had cut out cigarettes over the past year. It hadn't been easy, but with Mavis' coaching, she was able to finally beat her addiction. She had even lost some weight and started dressing in things other than her diner uniform. It was like she was a brand-new woman.

"Ever since mama and daddy died, Harry and I have been through so much. It hasn't ever been easy, but it's been worth it," Mona continued. "Right, Harry?"

Harry nodded and Mavis swore she saw a smile on the corner of his lips. "To celebrate, how about you both meet me and Wilbur at the fair on Tuesday for lunch? Madame Opalina can even read your palms and everything!" Mavis smiled.

Mona looked at Harry who nodded. "That sounds like fun. I think Tuesday is when the FFA kids are showing their animals, too. It'll be like old times for Harry," Mona said.

"Perfect. Mind if I let Wilbur know?" Mavis said. "Or do you want to tell him?"

"You can tell him," Mona said. "Oh, Mavis, I can hardly stand it. Tomorrow my whole life is going to change."

Mavis reached over and gave her friend a big hug. Harry and Mona deserved for good things to come their way. They worked so hard day in and day out. Mavis hoped that it all worked out for the best. Mona took down her order of blueberry pancakes and extra bacon and handed the order to Harry. She moved on to take care of other customers, but never lost the smile on her face.

Once Harry finished cooking her breakfast, Mavis gulfed it down in record time. After she paid her bill, she hurried outside to her car and drove straight to the Pig. She loaded up on bottles of water and assorted snacks for the four of them. She almost forgot Maude's cooking oil but hurried back and grabbed two jugs just to be on the safe side. She checked out and loaded everything up in the trunk. She would be cutting it close, but she should arrive in Maude's driveway around eleven as promised.

Maude and Opal were both waiting for her on Maude's porch. "We didn't think you were going to make it," Opal said.

Mavis looked down at her watch and then back at the two women. It was only five minutes past eleven, but she knew better than to argue. She helped them into the car and then backed out of the driveway.

"This is nice," Opal said. "Smells new."

"Smells like manure?" Maude asked. "I don't think so. More like leather."

"Who's Heather?" Opal asked. "I had a client at the salon named Heather. Had the prettiest red hair I ever did see. That was back in eighty-nine, or maybe ninety. She's probably grown up by now."

Maude rolled her eyes and snapped, "Of course she's grown! That was thirty odd years ago!"

"Time flies," Opal nodded.

Maude let out the most exasperated sigh and turned around in her seat. "We've been through this a million times! You can't fly, Opal!"

"I can, too!" Opal sassed back.

Mavis turned on the radio to drown out their arguing and prayed silently that Wilbur would hurry up to relieve her. She loved Maude and Opal very much, but they could get exhausting quickly with their bickering and general oddness. By the time that they arrived at the fairgrounds, they had settled in nicely. Opal had fallen asleep, and Maude had found the bag of snacks Mavis had hidden under her seat. Those were the particular snacks that Mavis had not wanted to share with anyone, but Maude's nose was more direct than a bloodhound. At least it kept her quiet and occupied.

They had just enough time to walk to Opal's booth and help her freshen up when the gates opened. Sunday afternoon was a big day for the fair. It was still the weekend and fair food after church ranked high on most everybody's list.

The line stayed long for most of the afternoon. Mavis was thrilled to see Wilbur walk over at half past three. She was famished and Maude was past the stages of hangry, but Mavis had been afraid to leave the two women alone or worse, send Maude after some lunch. Wilbur had barely waved hello before Mavis jumped up and told him she'd be back soon with lunch. As soon as she walked off, Maude whispered, "She near about starves us every time."

"I would have brought y'all lunch," Wilbur said. "I figured y'all had already eaten by now."

"Me, too," Maude grumbled.

Wilbur noticed a bag of trash full of candy and snack wrappers near Maude's feet, so he wasn't too worried about them. He was glad that the booth was popular. Opal had raked in a lot of donations already, and it was only day two! There was no telling how much she could raise by the end of the fair. Word had spread far and wide about Madame Opalina. and Opal was locked in! Wilbur watched her dazzle the crowd and watched as her fishbowl continually filled up. He had remembered to bring a portable safe with him today and made a mental note to collect the cash every thirty or so minutes to lock in the safe that he left in the truck.

Mavis came back thirty minutes later with nachos, cheese sticks, two turkey legs, a bucket of popcorn, a giant ear of roasted corn, and a brisket sandwich. She set the food down on the fold up table behind the booth and pulled napkins out of her purse. "I had a hard time choosing," she blushed.

Maude grabbed the brisket sandwich and inhaled it in three bites. Wilbur handed her a napkin as she licked the sauce off of her fingers. "How was it?" he asked her.

"Not half bad," Maude said. "Not the best, but not the worst thing I've ever eaten." She rubbed her stomach and looked at what was left of the pile of food. Mavis had already claimed the two turkey legs and had set aside the nachos for Opal, so Maude nibbled on the corn. Wilbur watched her out of the corner of his eye as she set the corn down after a few minutes.

"What's wrong?" he asked her. She looked a little green and held onto her stomach. Before he could ask again, she excused herself to the port-a-potties near the tent's exit, knocking over the wagon full of water bottles and snacks in the process.

"Ms. Maude?" Mavis shouted, but Maude ignored her in her beeline for the restroom.

"What did she eat?" Opal asked over her shoulder.

"A sandwich," Mavis answered. "A brisket sandwich."

"I told her to stay away from the brisket," Opal sighed, before turning back to the waiting customer in front of her.

[Chapter Six]

By the time Maude came back to the booth, Wilbur had already been out to his truck two different times to store the cash donations. He and Opal would have to go to the bank to deposit the cash in the morning because it was quite the loaded sum.

Maude sank down in the chair Wilbur offered her and sipped some water from her bottle. Wilbur was pretty sure it was water, but he didn't want to ask and find out. Opal glanced at Maude and shook her head, "one of these days," she spouted. "One of these days you'll listen to me."

Maude didn't have the energy to argue with her. She explained that she felt better, but still wasn't back to normal. Wilbur offered to take her home, but she waved him off. "If I'm going to be miserable, I might as well be at the fair." Wilbur knew she wasn't feeling well because anytime someone in line had food with them, she turned her back to them so she couldn't see or smell what was in the wrappers. He offered to find her some medicine, but she waved him off again and said that she didn't trust any medicine you could buy at the fair.

"I can run over to the store," Wilbur offered.

"No thanks," Maude said. "It's all out of me now. I'll tell you what though, I don't think I can ever eat brisket again. Not when it comes out like that."

Wilbur grimaced at the thought. If that was the case, then the brisket would surely have made others sick as well, but there wasn't any way of proving that. It was a strange coincidence how things had worked out. But after the hundreds of predictions Opal had made in the past two days, one or two were bound to come true.

"Do you think Opal cursed her?" Mavis whispered to Wilbur.

Wilbur shook his head. "If Opal had the power to curse people, she would have cursed Maude a long time ago," he laughed.

"Oh, Wilbur! I almost forgot to tell you!" Mavis suddenly shrieked. She launched into the story about how she had seen Mona earlier that morning and brought him up to speed. He was just as dumbfounded as she had been.

"I can't believe it," he said in awe.

"That's exactly what I said!" Mavis nodded. "We'll have a lot to talk about Tuesday at lunch."

"We always do," Wilbur chuckled.

Mavis laughed and picked at the popcorn that was almost gone in the bucket. There was something special about fair food. Even though it was low in nutrition and full of grease and who knew what else, it was so tasty. The county would have to wait at least another year for the fair and its many food trucks and booths to return.

"I'm going to get a funnel cake. Does anyone want one?" Mavis asked.

Wilbur nodded and asked Opal if she wanted one. She closed her eyes and slowly shook her head. "Let me guess! That one is poisoned, too?" Maude asked.

"No," Opal said. "I just don't want that much sugar. It's safe for you though."

Maude eyed her warily before nodding to Mavis. "Ok, three regular funnel cakes," Mavis smiled. "I'll be right back."

"Hopefully, she'll bring us some more napkins," Wilbur said aloud. Funnel cakes were downright messy when eaten properly.

"Use your robe cloaky thing," Maude said. "Practically the same thing."

Mavis returned with three big funnel cakes and napkins. She handed them out and sat down to eat. Even though Maude had a stack of napkins in front of her, she seemed to prefer to wipe the powdered sugar off on her robe. It would need a thorough washing before it could be worn again. Wilbur looked down at his own robe and saw that it too was sprinkled with powdered sugar. It wouldn't be a bad idea to take all of the costumes home for a good cleaning. He brushed off the crumbs and tidied up the back area of the booth a bit. The line was still pretty steady. He noticed that a few customers were repeat customers who had been the day before. He reckoned they must have liked what they had heard and either came back for more or brought some friends.

As the evening wound down, Mavis offered to walk with Maude around the midway to see what all else the fair had to offer. They had already seen most of the booths and pop-up shops, as well as the petting zoo the day before. Maude agreed, which left Wilbur to attend to Opal and her adoring crowd. He sat down next to Opal on a stool and watched as she explored the many futures in front of her. She stayed in full character for each visit, and even though some of her predictions weren't necessarily positive or good, she had a way of framing them so that person on the receiving end wasn't angry or afraid. She either had a true gift or she was the most talented actress this side of the Mississippi!

Maude and Mavis slipped out of the large tent and crossed the length of the fairgrounds towards the midway. The lights from the fair rides lit up the entire night sky. It was hard to believe that only a week or so ago, this place had been a giant empty field. It amazed Mavis how quickly they could get such an area ready for thousands of people. Thankfully, the weather had been cooperative. Even though it was uncharacteristically warm outside for this time of year, the skies had been clear and were predicted to stay clear for the next week or so.

As they got closer to the nearest ride, a large boat like structure where people buckled themselves in and rode off the ground side to side, Maude shivered. "You couldn't pay me a million dollars to get on one of those," Maude pointed. "On none of these."

"Have you ever ridden a carnival ride?" Mavis inquired. She couldn't picture Maude on anything that willingly took her feet off the ground.

Maude nodded and mumbled something about Coney Island and a group of nuns and Nadine, but Mavis couldn't be sure that she heard her correctly. Why would a group of nuns be at a theme park in New York? And why would Maude be traveling with a group of nuns? She wasn't what anyone would call ultra pious when it came to certain things. She knew that Maude, Opal, and Ruby had been to New York City, but she wasn't sure what all they had done on that trip. All Mavis remembered was that they had brought back toys and a lot of postcards from that particular trip. How in the world did Nadine factor into that?

Nadine Waters and Maude had a very complicated relationship. From the time they were children, the two of them had made it their life's mission to irritate and at times downright infuriate the other. While most of the pranks were harmless, there were times where they both got too invested. It wasn't all bad though. In their later years especially, something had softened between them. When Ruby died, Nadine had been so wonderful for the grieving family. Everyone in town loved Ruby Montgomery and took her death hard. Maude and Nadine still randomly pranked each other, but long gone were the days of feral cats in the backseats of new convertibles or fertilized yards of chicken manure. The last thing had been when Nadine had called into the radio station and announced Maude's birthday on the air in September, as well as Maude's phone number for everyone listening to text or call her. It took a week for that hullabaloo to die down, so Maude retaliated by having a barbershop quartet show up on the hour for ten hours straight to sing Nadine a song on her front porch. Nadine's sickness had been hard on Maude. She wouldn't admit it, but the cantankerous old woman enjoyed the spite and back and forth that Nadine brought to her life. Mavis hoped their back and forth lasted forever. Things like that helped keep a mind sharp.

"That coaster almost killed me," Maude continued. "Never again."

Mavis shrugged and continued to point out the various lights and sounds of the midway. Children laughed and teenagers screamed on the thrill rides. There was something for everyone to enjoy. The tall swings rose over their heads and Mavis watched as the people in each swing whipped by. The children's sized roller coaster on the wooden track clunked each time it came by. The spinning bowl shaped ride made her feel nauseated just by watching it. The bumper cars crashed and made zapping noises every time one car hit the other. The carousel went round and round with children and their parents. The Ferris wheel loomed in the near distance high above every other ride. Mavis wasn't keen on many of the rides, but she had her heart set on the big wheel. "Come on, Ms. Maude! Just one go around the wheel," Mavis suggested.

"Never again," Maude snapped.

"But we'll be able to see all over Junction. I bet if we try hard enough, we could see all the way to Rhinestone!" Mavis grinned. She knew that was impossible, but it would be fun to try.

Maude cut her eyes at Mavis and shook her head. Mavis knew there was no way other than to drag the woman on it. "Oh, fine," Mavis frowned.

She looked around but didn't see anyone she knew to ride with her. It was too fancy of a ride to ride alone. Plus, she did get a little afraid once it stopped at the very top.

They continued to look at the different rides that had not been there the week before. Maude made small talk about how amazing it was that the rides could be set up and torn down almost overnight. Hopefully, they had the brightest minds of the ages working on them, but that was rarely the case. Mavis had seen handmade posters stuck to posts near the entrance of the fairgrounds announcing job opportunities for anyone who wanted to work a few hours when the fair ended the following weekend to help clean up the fairgrounds and help tear down the rides. Maybe it was for the best that she didn't have anyone to ride with after all. Who knew how secure those things really were.

As they made their way back to the path that led the way to their tent, Maude's eyes lit up. "You see those over there?" Maude gestured to the rows of carnival games. "Opal can win every single time."

"Really?" Mavis gasped. "No one ever wins those kinds of things."

"I don't know how she does it. Probably magic or something," Maude shrugged. "But she can't lose. It's the damnedest thing."

"Let's try our luck," Mavis offered. To her surprise, Maude agreed. She said that she had watched Opal enough over the years and thought she had a few tricks up her sleeve. It was certainly worth a try.

The first game they came to was a simple basketball hoop. Each woman got one try to sink the ball into the hoop. If they managed, they could win any of the giant stuffed animals that were lined up in front of the hoop. There were bright pink dogs and brilliantly blue cats, and one giant purple whale. Mavis squinted her eyes and held her breath. Her shot bounced off the rim and the man behind the counter caught the ball. It had looked so simple, but she should have known better. These games weren't designed with ease in mind. The man nodded for Maude to go next, but she couldn't even manage to get the ball anywhere close to the rim. Even though Mavis wanted that stuffed whale, she didn't want to expend all her energy just yet. There were a ton of other midway games down the line to try.

Mavis was sure that their defeat would cause Maude to want to go back to the booth, but it seemed to drive her in the opposite direction. She walked over to the next game in the row and saw a small pool full of rubber ducks. The object of the game was to pick two random ducks and match the numbers on the bottom. After four tries, Maude had not managed to find a matching pair. She threw the rubber ducks back into the shallow water and scowled at the carnie.

Mavis chose the next game. There was a line of targets in a small shooting gallery. There were two plastic rifles that could be fired at will at the targets in front of them. All they had to do was knock down all eight targets in sixty seconds. Maude grinned and said, "now this one looks easy!"

Mavis was relieved that they had finally found a game that Maude was sure to win. She had grown up shooting guns, so this game should be second nature for her. Only it wasn't. After three separate tries, Maude was only able to get three of the targets. Whether it was due to user error, or the game actually being rigged, Maude was furious. If they didn't find a game she could win quickly, she was liable to lose her mind.

"What about this one?" Mavis suggested. All they had to do was toss a ring onto the top of a milk jug. They each got five rings and could win a prize for each ring they landed. Maude landed one, and Mavis landed two. That meant a total of three different prizes. While these prize options weren't grandiose like the giant stuffed animals, this booth did offer some interesting ones. Mavis chose two butterfly keychains and Maude chose the dinosaur one. While they weren't the most exciting prize options, Mavis and Maude were both content with finally achieving a win. They eyed a few more games, including one that had small bowls of goldfish as the prizes. Mavis thought about winning her catfish Clive a little friend, but Maude was antsy.

"Let's get back and see if Opal is packed up for the night," Maude said.

Mavis looked at her watch and saw that the fair would be closing in the next few minutes. "I didn't even realize what time it was!" Mavis gasped. They had better go check on Wilbur and Opal and help them wind down.

Maude led the way past the last row of carnival games. Nestled between the two small tents that sheltered throwing games with giant prized teddy bears was a rickety table with a poster board duct taped to the front. A thin man with a protruding gut and very few scraggly black hairs stood behind it with his lips pursed. Mavis had never seen a kissing booth look so rough. She ducked behind the man in front of her and hurried her pace so she wouldn't be seen.

"How about a lil' kiss fo' a fine man," the voice drawled in a choppy Cajun accent to the unsuspecting woman closest to him.

Mavis would know that beak and snarl anywhere.

Earl Thibodeaux Boudreaux was back.

[Chapter Seven]

Mavis could hardly fall asleep that night. Even though she was exhausted from helping out at Madame Opalina's, every time she closed her eyes, the buzzard-like face of Earl Thibodeaux Boudreaux came flying back to the forefront of her mind with all the excitement that preceded a root canal.

She had been so stunned by his sudden appearance that she remained rooted to the spot for what seemed like ages. In reality, it was only a couple of seconds, but time had a way of slowing down whenever Earl was around. Much like watching a slow-motion video of a dumpster fire, Earl was a walking disaster waiting to happen. She had thought she was finally rid of him when Wilbur rescued her from his dilapidated trailer in the middle of the bayous of Louisiana back in 2018, but he had showed up again last year in Rhinestone. During his mini reign of terror, he had aimed his powers of chaos toward Mavis by way of Mona and Magnolia Manor.

Mavis had tossed and turned most of the night reliving the last time he had strolled into town. On that occasion, he had hatched a scheme to undermine Mavis of the responsibility and ownership of the Manor, before turning his so-called charms on Mona. That little adventure saw him carted off to jail for a list of offenses as long as Mavis' arm, thanks to Wilbur and Mona, and a handful of others. She was certain that she had been able to shake him off for good. But here he was again! He was like a cockroach!

She thought that would be the last time she ever saw her former beau, but alas, he had managed to get out of jail once again. She wasn't sure how or why the justice system had seen fit to let him wander the streets as a free man, but she knew with all his natural talent, he was bound to land in trouble once more. She only hoped he kept his adventures far away from her.

Then she remembered Opal's prediction. Opal had warned her that he, although Mavis didn't know who he was at the time, was coming back, and that things wouldn't end well for him. Opal had a way of knowing things that most people didn't. The first part of the prediction had already come true. Surely that meant the powers that be had already set his demise in order. If that was the case, Mavis could sit back and let fate take its course. She wouldn't need to be involved at all. All she needed to do was stay well clear of his shenanigans while he got himself into trouble. Greatly relieved with this new plan of inaction, Mavis rolled over and dozed off for a few more hours of sleep.

The next morning, she woke up with a start realizing that she had slept past her alarm. She didn't have time to eat breakfast or brew a pot of coffee. She quickly threw on some clothes and raced over to Maude and Opal's. Hopefully, they hadn't left yet!

When she pulled into Opal's driveway fifteen minutes later, Maude was already loading a large bag of snacks in her car. "I thought you forgot about us," she hollered over as Mavis stepped out of her SUV.

"Ms. Maude, you know I'd never forget about y'all. We've got plenty of time to get there," Mavis told her.

"Not the way you drive," Maude said.

"Mavis doesn't know how to fly," Opal corrected. "Well, she might."

"No ma'am, I don't know how to fly," Mavis told Opal. "And Ms. Maude, I drive five miles over the speed limit usually."

"Not yesterday you didn't," Maude muttered. "Felt like we were crawling." She still had the keys to her car in her hand.

"Well, I assure you we were not," Mavis sighed. She reached in the backseat of Maude's car and grabbed the overstuffed bag of snacks. "Now let's get you all loaded up and we'll head on over."

They made it to the fairgrounds with plenty of time to spare, although Maude kept encouraging her to drive a bit faster. For a woman who hadn't wanted to be involved in the Madame Opalina adventure, Maude was certainly in a hurry to get back there.

"We're early, Ms. Maude," Mavis kept saying, but it did little to calm Maude's nerves. She was certainly in a hurry this morning. By the time they walked into the large tent, Maude was beside herself.

"Ms. Maude, the fair hasn't even opened up to the public yet. We've got more than enough time to set everything up. Don't worry. We'll be ready to open," Mavis assured her, although the strain of being patient without her morning cup of coffee was starting to show in her voice.

"Set up? What in the world are you talking about?" Maude stared at her.

"Setting up for Madame Opalina," Mavis explained.

"Do you think I was in a hurry because I was worried about this voodoo stuff?" Maude asked. She looked aghast at Mavis' suggestion.

"Well, why else would you need to rush over here?" Mavis was on her last tether.

"Ribs!" Maude said.

"Ribs?" Mavis asked. What was wrong with the old woman's ribs?

"You should have known she thinks with her stomach," Opal said gently.

Mavis shook her head. "Her stomach? Ms. Maude, what exactly are you talking about?"

Maude rolled her eyes and looked out of sorts. "The rib truck at the end of row, way down there past the funnel cakes," Maude sighed impatiently. "He's selling racks for half price to all the workers here until the fair opens. Then they go back up to full price!" Maude thrust a handful of cash at Mavis. "Go on down there and get me a couple racks. Buy some for you and Wilbur, too. But you need to hurry."

Mavis looked from the money to Maude. "But I need to help Opal."

"I'll help her put her wig on. It'll be fine," Maude said, trying to push Mavis out of the tent.

"Don't worry, Ms. Maude. I'll get you some ribs even if I have to pay full price for them," Mavis offered the money back to Maude, but she threw her hands up in frustration.

"We ain't doing this! The reason I have so much money now is because I know when to buy things at half price," Maude countered. She pushed the money back to Mavis. "Go on now. You ain't got but twenty minutes to get there. God, I hope they aren't sold out."

"Are you sure you don't want to go?" Mavis asked. "I didn't see a cooler to put them in. Should I call Wilbur to bring one?"

Opal chuckled as Maude grunted, "I'm too old to want to run all the way over there." She reached in her purse and pulled out some more money. "Here, pick up some rabbit food for Opal. You know, something healthy with no flavor. The greener the better."

"But the cooler?" Mavis repeated.

"I don't need no cooler," Maude shushed her. "They're best eaten fresh. Tell Wilbur to hurry up if he wants some."

Resigned to her fate, Mavis shuffled out of the tent and headed over to the rib truck as directed. She prayed silently for the rib man to have ribs left, or else Maude was liable to hurt him.

"I wonder where Wilbur is?" Opal said.

"He said he'd be running a little late today, but he should be here before it gets too busy," Maude said. She fastened Opal's cloak around her throat and adjusted her wig. Once Opal was satisfied, she put on her own robe and fluffed her wig that Opal insisted she wear. The booth looked fine and didn't need any major attention. Wilbur had stayed late last night and added a few hanging lights and a makeshift tent to store their wagon, snacks, bags, and costume trunk out of the way. Opal sat down in her comfy chair and got ready for her customers. Maude snuck a few cookies from her purse and then settled down and made herself comfortable across the two aluminum chairs behind Opal.

A few minutes later, Opal heard the sawmill-like wheeze of Maude's snores. She turned to see Maude stretched out between two folding chairs, the robe draped loosely around her shoulders, and her wig pushed down to cover her eyes. Opal decided it was best to let sleeping bears lie. She still had a few minutes before the gates opened, so she drank some water and polished her crystal ball. She glanced up with a slight start and gasped. A strange man was standing in front of her booth with a snaggle-tooth grin.

"How you doin' dis fine mornin'?" he said with a smile from ear to ear.

"Good morning. Won't you have a seat?" Opal offered him a chair in front of the counter. She sat down and waited for him to sit down. He eyed her cautiously and looked over at Maude who was snoring behind her.

"You's reckon you see da future, huh?" he questioned her.

Opal smiled kindly but gave nothing away. "The inner eye sees in many directions," she smiled.

"Da inner eye ain't seeing much towards yo' jar over dere," he pointed at the empty jar. Wilbur had taken all the cash out of it before they left last night, but this stranger didn't need to know that.

"We work with the donations we receive," she said calmly.

"We sho do," he nodded firmly. "Now dat dere is a fact if I ever hear one."

"And what is your name?" Opal asked.

The man scrunched up his face and furrowed his brow. "Theodore Bear," he said hesitantly. "My friends call me Teddy," he smiled again.

"And how may I help you?" Opal continued to study the man.

He sat down in the chair and sighed. "Well, you see, I been a bit down on my luck lately. I was wonderin' when things were gonna pick up a bit," he smiled. He leered once more at the empty jar. His eyes darted around at the woman before him and her friend sleeping in the corner.

Opal shook her head. "Your luck will continue along its same path for the foreseeable future," Opal told him. She grimaced at her prediction which indicated that his luck wasn't on a hot streak.

He puffed up his chest. "Dat's not a nice thing to say. Aren't you supposed to look through yo' crystal ball or somethin'?"

"There was no need. Your future is perfectly clear," Opal said. She stared back into the dark eyes of the frustrated stranger who leapt to his feet. His chair clanged to the ground in his haste.

"You not who I thought you was! Now we knows why you ain't got no money in dat jar over dere! Tellin' people stuff like dat. You know dat ain't right!" he howled. He swiped the empty donation jar off the counter and it fell to the ground. Thankfully, the fishbowl didn't break.

Opal sat calmly and stared at him as he had his tantrum. The sudden noise of his chair turning over caused Maude to grunt. "What's happening?" she hissed. She tumbled out of the chair and landed hard on her side. The wig completely obscured her face, so she didn't see the man stomp off. "What in the world?" Maude howled. She ripped the wig off her head and tossed it to the ground. "Who was that?" she asked Opal.

Opal was silent as she watched the man angrily exit the tent. He had to be a worker or a fellow vendor to be inside the fairgrounds this early. He was dressed in ripped up jeans and a tattered flannel shirt, but there was no indication of any company, so maybe he was what the kids called a carnie. Either way, hopefully he wouldn't come back and stir up trouble. Opal had enough to deal with between Maude and her incessant need for pork.

"Who was that?" Maude repeated.

Opal shrugged and looked at her crystal ball. "He's not who he said he was, that's for sure," she nodded.

"What?" Maude asked. "That don't make no sense, Opal." Before Opal could respond, she put her hands on her hip and frowned. "Where's

Mavis? She shoulda been back here by now." She sank back down into her chair and took a few sips from her water bottle. "And where is Wilbur? The gates are about to open."

"I'll call him," Opal said. She was still staring at the tent flap hoping that strange man stayed away.

Wilbur picked up on the third ring and told Opal that he was parking his truck and would be there in a few minutes. Ten minutes later, he entered the tent and wiped the sweat from his brow. "I'm sorry I'm late," Wilbur said. He was out of breath as he sat down next to Maude behind Opal's booth. "Where's Mavis?"

"She better be in line getting my ribs," Maude frowned.

"Your ribs?" he asked.

Maude launched back into her impassioned tale of half-priced ribs. She checked her watch and lamented that it had already been forty minutes and the trailer was either sold out or back to full price by now. Wilbur assured her that Mavis would get things taken care of. At least, he hoped for her sake that she got the ribs. No one wanted to deal with a hungry or agitated Maude.

"Would you like me to go check on things?" Wilbur asked.

"If you leave, who knows who will show up here!" Maude huffed.

Wilbur looked confused. "Is that a no?" he asked Maude.

"I'll go myself," Maude said. "You watch Opal and make sure that man doesn't come back to stir up trouble." She shuffled towards the tent's exit to fetch Mavis.

"What man?" Wilbur asked Opal once there was a break in the line of customers.

Opal sighed inwardly. "He said his name was Teddy Bear, but I don't believe that's his real name. He seems familiar though," she frowned. She knew she had seen this strange man before, but she couldn't for the life of her remember where.

"Who was he?" Wilbur asked again. "What did he look like?"

Opal sat still for a second and said dreamily, "a bird. An overgrown bird."

Wilbur took out this handkerchief and wiped his head. A bird? The first person to pop into his mind was Earl, but Earl was in jail somewhere in Louisiana. He had been extradited back to Baton Rouge, and a slew of other places, to face his many crimes after being arrested in Rhinestone last year.

"What do you mean?" Wilbur asked Opal.

"He looked like a bird," she repeated. "Even squawked like one with his accent."

"What kind of accent?" Wilbur asked.

"I haven't heard a true accent like that in some time," Opal mused.

"Opal, what kind of accent did this man have?" Wilbur asked.

"Cajun," Opal nodded. "Definitely a true Cajun."

Wilbur's stomach fell to his knees.

[Chapter Eight]

Before Wilbur could fully digest the fact that Earl had returned, Mavis and Maude returned with lunch. Maude looked much happier than when she left. She had a bucket full of ribs and a bag full of sauce packets. Neither woman had thought to grab any napkins, but thankfully Wilbur had brought a roll of paper towels from his house the day before.

"Here's your rabbit food," Maude said to Opal. She handed her a salad in a plastic container that had been drenched in ranch. "It got a little shaken up on our trip back."

"I see," Opal said. "Thank you."

"And here you go, Wilbur," Maude said. She handed him a slab of ribs with her bare hand. He didn't have anywhere to set it down, so he held the oozing slab and stared back at her. The red sauce dripped off the meat onto his boots. "Do we have any plates?" he asked.

"I think there's some in the wagon," Mavis said. She rummaged around and found a stack of flimsy paper plates. Wilbur reckoned they were better than nothing, so he set his messy slab on the plate Mavis held out and wiped his hands on the paper towels.

"Why do you need a plate?" Maude asked. She was already onto her second slab. Bits of pork and sauce flew out of her mouth as she spoke. Wilbur handed her a clean paper towel and she grabbed it with her messy fingers. "Thanks! Better eat them while they're hot. Mavis got the last few. Good job, Mavis girl!" She clapped Mavis on the back and left a barbeque handprint on Mavis' dandelion yellow shirt.

It didn't take them long to scarf down the ribs. Cleaning up after the messy lunch took much longer. Maude licked the sauce off her fingers and mumbled under her breath when Mavis handed her some hand wipes from her purse. Wilbur bagged up their trash and discarded bones and took them to the dumpster outside of the tent.

There was no good way to get the sauce stain out of Mavis' shirt, which frustrated her. She sank down on a blanket behind Opal and pulled a book out of her purse. Wilbur offered to walk around with her, but she said there was no way she could possibly be seen in public with such a heinous stain.

"I'll walk around with you," Maude offered Wilbur. "There's a booth somewhere around here with some dessert, I just know it." She grabbed Wilbur's arm and led him away from the booth towards other vendors.

It didn't take her long to find what she was looking for. Three rows over from Opal was a large booth with two tables full of cakes, pies, brownies, and cookies. Maude's eyes grew to the size of saucers. She bought a plate of chocolate chip cookies, a pan of brownies, and a vanilla pound cake. After Wilbur assured her that he didn't need anything, she checked out and let the woman behind the counter bag up her items in a large brown paper sack. Her eyes lit up when the woman told her about a cake walk they were hosting in one of the air-conditioned buildings. She handed Maude a piece of paper with a schedule printed on it and Maude promised she would see her there. Wilbur offered to carry the bags of treats for her, and she happily agreed. He started to head back towards Opal's booth, but Maude wasn't quite ready to return to Madame Opalina's just yet. She put in to visit the other nearby booths and left Wilbur in the dust. He scanned the people around them as he and Maude walked through the vendors. The idea that Earl had returned to the area was unsettling, to say the least. He wasn't sure how in the world he would tell Mavis the news. On the other hand, maybe it wasn't Earl after all. Earl couldn't be the only bird-like man in these parts. And he certainly wasn't the only man to have a distinct Cajun accent. Wilbur decided to go investigate a little bit before he mentioned anything to Mavis. It would probably be best to confirm his suspicions first and foremost.

"Wilbur!" Maude said. "What are you doing? Quit lollygagging."

"Ma'am?" Wilbur turned his head. "Oh, I'm sorry."

"Where in the world are you? Your mind is a million miles away," Maude said.

"Nothing much. I'm just thinking about that man that came by the tent this morning," Wilbur told her.

"He wasn't much to look at," Maude said. "Well, not from what I saw. That damned wig near about blinded me. He made a big old fuss though! Could barely understand him."

"Right," Wilbur nodded. "A big fuss, huh?"

"Wilbur! I may be old, but I'm not dumb. What's going on in that head of yours?" Maude asked. She jerked his arm and steered him towards an empty bench.

"Well, I can't say for sure, but I think I know that man," Wilbur said as he sat down.

"What do you mean?" Maude asked. "Who was it?"

"I think it was Earl," Wilbur said quietly.

"You need to hurl?" Maude gasped. "Hold your horses, let me get a trash can!"

"No ma'am," Wilbur chuckled. He helped Maude sit back down and get settled before he explained. "I think it was Earl. I know you never had the um, pleasure of meeting him, but you must remember the name."

"That buffoon from Louisiana?" Maude sneered. "I did meet him once."

"Where?" Wilbur gasped.

"At Beaver Crossing," Maude said. "He was talking to Reverend Simmons and me and Opal were over there, and he yelled at us!"

Wilbur was shocked. Maude not Opal had ever mentioned meeting Earl before. "Are you sure?" Wilbur asked.

Maude rolled her eyes at Wilbur and shook her head. "I didn't know it was him at the time, but I found out later from Simmons who he was. I didn't want to bother you or Mavis since he was finally gone, but dadgummit! I can't stand that man!"

"There's so much about him," Wilbur shook his head. "This is bad news if it's really him."

"He's the one that near about ruined things for our Mavis," Maude snapped.

Wilbur nodded, but Maude wasn't finished. "The one who embarrassed Ruby and tried to steal the Manor time and again!"

Wilbur continued to nod as Maude got angrier. "Oooh, he makes me so mad! You know what I mean?" she snapped.

"Yes ma'am," Wilbur said.

"Let me at him!" Maude said with ferocity. "I'll show him where he can stick it!" She held up her balled-up fist and shook with anger.

"Now Ms. Maude, let's calm down. I don't know for sure that it's him," Wilbur said.

"I bet it is," Maude grimaced. "He's done messed with us all now!" She leapt with gusto back to her feet and left the bag of desserts on the bench. Wilbur grabbed the bag and scrambled to catch up with her. When Maude was furious, she moved quickly. He wasn't sure where she was headed, so he called after her. "Wait for me!" When he finally caught up with her, he saw that she was headed back towards Opal's booth. "Wait a minute!" Wilbur said. He grabbed her arm gently and pulled her out of sight before Opal or Mavis could see her.

"What in tarnation are you doing?" Maude snapped. "We've got to go handle him!"

"Ms. Maude, we need to be smart about this," Wilbur said breathlessly.

"What do you mean by that?" she hissed.

If Wilbur wasn't careful, Maude might turn her angry energy back on him. "We need to make sure he is back before we worry Mavis," Wilbur explained. "I don't want to upset her. Let's do some digging first."

"What are we digging for?" Opal asked gleefully.

"Dear God, Opal! What is wrong with you?" Maude gasped.

Neither Wilbur nor Maude had heard Opal come up behind them. "Where's Mavis?" Wilbur asked.

"She's at the booth," Opal shrugged. "Are we digging for treasure?"

"No!" Maude said. "Now be quiet before anyone hears you. Y'all are both so loud! Come over here," she directed.

Wilbur and Opal followed her outside the large tent into the bright sunshine. Wilbur told Opal his assumption and watched her eyes widen in surprise. "I should've known," Opal said. "The inner eye knew all along he'd be back."

"Wait a minute!" Maude gasped. "You did tell her he'd be back!"

Opal nodded. "Yes, I did say that," she remembered.

"But it might not be him," Wilbur reminded them. "We need to find out for sure."

"It's him," Opal said. "I'm sure of it."

"We need a plan," Maude agreed.

"You two continue your digging. I'll keep Mavis busy at the booth," Opal said. She walked off just as quickly as she had appeared.

"How does she do that?" Wilbur asked.

"I've known her all my life, Wilbur, and I still don't understand her," Maude said. "But we can't focus on that right now. We need to figure this out!" Once again, Maude was off to the races. Wilbur hurried behind her and dodged people walking in every direction.

"I don't know how we're going to find him," Wilbur said loudly. "It's like finding a needle in a haystack."

"I've found more than a needle in a haystack before," Maude shouted back.

Wilbur wasn't sure what that meant or how that was relevant, but he shrugged it off and finally caught up with her in front of a donut truck. Maude ordered a bag of powdered sugar donuts and turned to ask Wilbur what he would like. He knew better than to say nothing, so he ordered a bag of cinnamon sugar donuts to appease her. After they received their donuts, Maude inhaled her treats quickly and was back on the move.

"Do you know what he was wearing?" Wilbur asked.

"How should I know?" Maude shrugged. She bumped into a large man in front of her who had abruptly stopped. "Ouch!"

Wilbur caught her before she toppled over backwards. "I don't know how we're going to find him in this crowd, Ms. Maude," Wilbur said.

Maude steadied herself and yelled loudly. "Earl? Where you at?"

"Shh! What are you doing?" Wilbur gasped. He clamped his hand over her mouth and promptly howled in pain. "You bit me!"

"Never silence a woman," Maude admonished him. "Especially one who still has all her teeth."

Wilbur rubbed his bitten hand against his jeans and grimaced. "Please stop shouting his name. We don't want him onto us."

Maude nodded and continued to look around. "Let's go this way. Maybe he's working one of the carnival rides," Maude suggested.

Wilbur nodded and followed her towards the midway. They looked over every ride they walked past, but no one stuck out. Wilbur was feeling very dejected when they decided to walk back towards the tent full of vendors. They passed the rows of midway games that Maude scoffed at. "They're all rigged," she told Wilbur loudly. "Don't waste your money!"

Wilbur couldn't blame her for her feelings. Most of those games were indeed rigged. He walked past the games and ignored the calls from the workers to try his luck. They were almost back to the path that led to the vendor tents when he saw him out of the corner of his eye. Dressed in what could only be described as a lion tamer's outfit from an ancient circus, Earl was standing behind a makeshift booth made from a rotten pallet and some old milk jug crates. "Ten dollas fo' a kiss!" he called out to every attractive woman who passed by.

"He'd have to pay me two hundred dollars to kiss him," Maude guffawed.

"That's him!" Wilbur hissed.

"Kim? Who's Kim?" Maude asked.

"Ms. Maude, that is Earl," Wilbur jerked his finger towards Earl who was now in a shouting match with a very muscular man and a blonde woman in a tight black mini skirt. It seemed that Earl had flirted with the wrong woman! "That's him alright. Let's get out of here before he sees us."

Wilbur and Maude hurried out of sight and made their way back to Opal's booth. Her booth was easy to spot. It was easily the most popular one most of the day. Mavis had gotten up from her spot on the ground and was happily collecting the donations from people in line. Opal saw Wilbur and Maude approach and smiled when Wilbur gave her a thumbs up. He hoped she understood what he was trying to communicate.

"Where have you two been?" Mavis asked.

"Exploring," Maude shrugged. "How's it going here?"

"It's been amazing," Mavis gushed. "Reverend Simmons came through about half an hour ago and, well, I don't know exactly what Madame Opalina whispered to him, but he got all excited and jumped up and near about caused a domino effect with the line behind him!"

"What in the world?" Wilbur asked.

"Whatever it was was life-changing! I've never seen him get that excited before," Mavis giggled. "He hopped around and thanked her profusely. Then he went down the line and yelled something about the Lord's blessings showering us all. I don't know," Mavis shrugged.

"Opal! What in the hell did you tell the preacher?" Maude asked.

Opal ignored her and took the hands of the next customer and continued her act.

"That poor man needs some happiness in his life. He's come a long way," Mavis said. "I can remember when he couldn't even look someone in the eye. And he stuttered something fierce. I'm so proud of him!"

"He has come a long way," Maude agreed, although she still didn't care for him. "The last time he had a fit in church was when me and Opal were there, and Opal took a dive in the baptismal."

"What?" Wilbur gasped. Mavis laughed and said that she had heard all about it.

"Yea," Maude nodded. "That was when we saw, oh never mind," she swallowed hard. She had almost said that was when she and Opal saw Earl but thought better of it. "So, just a few more hours here. Here Mavis, I bought you some brownies." She snatched the brown bag from Wilbur and handed the pan of brownies to Mavis.

"Thank you," Mavis smiled. She handed Wilbur the fishbowl that was full of bills and change. He emptied the bowl and stuffed the cash into a large envelope. He set the envelope in the wagon and sat down next to Mavis who was eating some of the brownies. "Want one?" she asked.

"No thanks," Wilbur smiled. "Ms. Maude already force fed me some donuts."

Mavis yawned and stretched her arms high above her head. "I don't know how they do this," she said. "I'm literally exhausted and I'm half their age."

"They go a mile a minute," Wilbur agreed. "I don't know how we can all keep this up for the rest of the time though."

"She's raised a lot of money so far," Mavis said. "I definitely want to be like them both when I grow up."

"Me too," Wilbur smiled. He halfway listened to Mavis shoot the breeze for the rest of the afternoon as he agonized over how to tell her later that her worst nightmare was back in town.

[Chapter Nine]

Mavis was already in her lilac pajamas drinking hot chamomile tea in the kitchen when Wilbur knocked on her front door a few minutes before midnight. "What in the world?" she asked when she opened the door. "Is everything ok? What's wrong?"

"I called you, but you didn't answer. I just wanted to make sure you were ok," Wilbur said. He was out of breath and looked around the entryway as if he was looking for someone.

"I'm fine," she replied. As soon as the fair closed for the evening, she had packed Maude and Opal into her car and dropped them back off at their respective houses. She took a quick shower and got into her warm pajamas and made a hot cup of tea before bed. She was exhausted, but she couldn't seem to clear her mind. She had brewed a kettle of herbal tea on the stove and poured some into Ruby's favorite teacup that she had bought at the antique mall a few years before she died. "I left my cell phone upstairs. What's going on? Are you ok?"

Wilbur hadn't meant to startle her, but he needed to make sure that Earl wasn't anywhere near the Manor. He also needed to let Mavis know that he was back. Once he was satisfied that no one else was in the house, he followed Mavis to the kitchen and watched as she made him a cup of hot tea in another one of Ruby's prized mugs. She could see that something was really bothering him. She added some lemon, his favorite, and set the steaming mug in front of him at the small breakfast table. "What's got you all in a bother?" she asked.

"I'm just going to come right out with it," Wilbur sighed. He didn't want to beat around the bush about it. "Earl's back. He's back in town."

He had expected Mavis to jump and shout and have a full-blown panic attack, or maybe even cry. But to his surprise, she stayed silent and still. For some reason, that made him even more concerned. "Mavis, did you hear what I said?" Wilbur asked.

"I heard you," Mavis nodded. She sipped her tea and breathed deeply, careful not to meet his questioning eyes.

Wilbur was at a loss for words. Mavis wasn't responding at all like he had thought she would. She didn't look shocked to hear the news at all. Did she know something that he didn't, or was she in shock? Wilbur cleared his throat and asked if she was ok.

"Wilbur, I saw him last night," Mavis said quietly.

"What?" Wilbur roared. "You're seeing him again? Mavis!" He rose from the chair and started pacing the floor like a mad man.

"Wilbur," Mavis squeaked.

"I can't believe it!" Wilbur repeated over and over again.

"Wilbur!" Mavis said.

"I thought you had finally gotten over that fool," Wilbur said. "And here you go again! I swear!"

"Wilbur! Listen to me!" Mavis squealed.

"What?" Wilbur snapped. He turned away from the sink to face Mavis. "I cannot believe this."

"Are you going to let me talk or what?" Mavis asked angrily.

"Tell me what? You just said you're seeing him!" Wilbur lamented.

"Will you hush? I'm trying to tell you," Mavis began again, but Wilbur cut her off. "I just can't believe it," he sighed.

"Wilbur! I said I had seen him," Mavis rolled her eyes. "I saw him with my two eyes. And that was it!"

Wilbur looked dumbfounded. "Wait. What?" He scratched his head and walked back to the table.

"All I said was that I saw him last night and now you're losing your mind," Mavis sighed.

Wilbur looked like Mavis had slugged him in the jaw. He didn't know what to say. He scrunched up his forehead and looked back at her. "So," Wilbur said. "Are you dating him again or not?"

"God no!" Mavis yelled. "I'm not stupid, Wilbur."

Wilbur looked gob smacked. He really didn't know what to say in response. He was sure that something fishy was going on. Why else would Earl be back in Junction this close to Rhinestone? Mavis could see the confusion on Wilbur's face.

"Wilbur, that ship sailed a long time ago. Well, I wouldn't call it a ship exactly. Not even a boat. More like a one paddle canoe, or raft. Anyway, it doesn't matter," Mavis said. "The point is never again."

Wilbur shook his head and sighed. "Thank you for that explanation," he rolled his eyes. "But I'm glad to hear that y'all aren't back together. He's bad news, Mavis."

"You ain't wrong about that," Mavis agreed. "How'd you know he was back?"

"It's a long story," he laughed.

"Hold on, this calls for cake," Mavis interrupted. She walked over to the refrigerator and pulled out an uncut cheesecake. She rummaged around and found a jar of preserves and opened it. She cut both her and Wilbur a large slice of cheesecake and added a good dollop of strawberry preserve to the top.

"This looks good! Where'd you get it?" Wilbur asked.

"I made it," Mavis lied. She saw Wilbur's unconvinced look and laughed. "Ok, I bought it from the bake sale at the fair. It's a pretty one!"

"Tastes good, too," Wilbur agreed. He took another bite and savored the taste.

"Ok, now I'm ready," Mavis said. She settled back into her chair and dug into her slice of cheesecake.

"He was at the fair today," Wilbur explained. "Ms. Maude and I saw him. Had his own booth and everything. Well, Opal saw him first. He came by her booth while you were out getting lunch. She said he acted up and woke Maude up from her nap. She did say he gave her a different name. I don't think she knew who he was then, but I knew as soon as she told me. So we went and found him. Wasn't too hard. He was tied up with some strong fella who looked like he wanted to whoop him. It'd serve him right," Wilbur shrugged.

"At his little kissing booth?" Mavis chuckled.

"You saw that?" Wilbur asked. "I don't reckon he's getting much business. I'm thinking he came by to visit Opal to see how she was fairing money wise. Word is she's pretty popular."

"You're probably right," Mavis nodded. She got up and cut herself another slice of cheesecake and topped it with more preserves. "Did he see you?"

"No," Wilbur shook his head. "I don't think he recognized Maude and Opal either. Otherwise, I bet he would have asked about you. You didn't talk to him, did you?"

"Wilbur, I swear!" Mavis snapped. "You must think I'm an idiot or something." She jabbed her fork into the slice of cheesecake and sent bits of the strawberry preserve all over the table.

"Ok, ok," Wilbur said calmly. "It was just a question." He hadn't meant to set off Mavis' temper. Mavis was easy going most of the time, but when she got going, it was hard to calm her down. "I just want to make sure he leaves you and the Manor alone."

"Earl knows better than to come sneaking around here again," Mavis said.

"He's here for a reason," Wilbur said. "I don't think it's a coincidence that he's back."

Mavis nodded. "How is he back?" she asked. "Harlan and them promised he'd be gone for a good long while. It doesn't make any sense."

"I know," Wilbur sighed. "It doesn't make any sense to me either. I'll see what I can find out, but I wouldn't put anything past him. Let's just keep an eye out. Probably best he doesn't see either of us."

"If I know Earl, it won't be long before he gets himself in some kind of trouble," Mavis said. She finished her slice and wrapped up the rest of the cake. "Don't forget that we're having lunch with Mona and Harry tomorrow. I meant to call them today, but I lost track of time. I hope it all went well."

"Reckon we better tell Mona about Earl?" Wilbur asked.

"I think we ought to," Mavis nodded. "I don't want to ruin their good news, but she deserves to know. God, I hope he doesn't wander back to the diner. Harry's liable to whoop him this time!"

"If the diner's really been sold, it won't be their problem anymore," Wilbur reminded her. "Alright, I better go. I'll be here around nine thirty and then we can go get Opal and Maude. What do you say?"

"See you then," Mavis said. "Thanks for telling me about Earl. I was going to tell you, I just needed to process it all first. He gets me all out of sorts. And before you start, no, it's not because I love him. He repulses me. I just can't believe that slimy worm has inched his way back to our homeland."

"It'll be ok," Wilbur said. "We've got the edge on him this time." He rinsed his plate in the sink and grabbed his truck keys from the counter. He reminded Mavis to lock the door behind him and walked down the porch to his truck.

Both he and Mavis felt better after their chat. Even though they didn't get much sleep, they both felt better knowing that they were on the same side regarding Earl and his antics. When Mavis and Wilbur arrived at Opal's the next morning, both women were sitting on the porch waiting for them.

"You think they'll be alright while we get together with Harry and Mona?" Mavis asked.

"They'll be fine," Wilbur nodded. "I think. We'll just have to keep checking on them."

They helped the two older women into the middle seat of Mavis' car. Opal had a large cup of water and a smoothie bowl that she was happily eating, but Maude looked at it with disdain. "She tried to poison me with that thing," she pointed to the smoothie bowl. "I'm gonna let you take me through a drive-thru for some real food."

"Fried food doesn't mean it's real," Opal mumbled.

"It ain't natural to eat that much fruit," Maude countered. "And all you drink is water and tea or more of that blended up fruit or veggie mess. It ain't American. Americans drink coffee and beer and eat fried chicken. Animals eat that mess." She pointed once again to Opal's pink smoothie bowl.

"Fruits and vegetables are natural," Wilbur pointed out. "And we all could be better about our water intake."

Mavis smiled under her breath at Wilbur's response. She knew Maude would have something to say about it.

"No, no. Bodies need protein," Maude continued. "I don't eat any of that rodent food and look at me, I'm as healthy as a horse!"

"A Clydesdale," Opal mumbled.

Mavis and Wilbur laughed loudly, which only aggravated Maude further. She swatted at Opal's arm and stuck out her tongue. "That chicken place once you get off the highway will be fine. I'll get me two chicken biscuits and a big, sweet tea. Last time they gave me unsweet. Can you believe that? Why do they even make that mess?"

"I thought you said tea wasn't American?" Mavis giggled.

"Sweet tea ain't like regular tea," Maude sighed. "It's a special formula and everything. Y'all don't get it."

Mavis dutifully pulled into the fast food's parking lot and saw the line for the drive-through wrapped around the building. She asked Maude if she was sure that she wanted to stop here, and the older woman said she would get out and go inside by herself. She asked if anyone else wanted anything, and they all shook their heads. Wilbur had brought over a hash brown casserole to the Manor, and they had hurriedly eaten breakfast together before driving over to Opal's.

Mavis, Wilbur, and Opal waited in the running car while Maude ran inside. She was in and out of the restaurant in less than ten minutes. She came out with three paper bags full of breakfast sandwiches, hash browns, and enough condiments to outfit a small army. By the time they had parked at the fairgrounds, she had worked her way through one of the food bags.

As soon as they arrived at the large tent and walked down the aisle to Opal's booth, they could tell that something was awry. The chairs were tipped over and the wagon was on its side. The costume trunk had been rifled through, but it didn't look like anything had been taken. "I bet this was Earl's handiwork," Wilbur hissed to Mavis.

They cleaned up as best they could and got everything ready for the opening of the fair. As soon as Opal was dressed in her cloak and wig and ready for her customers, Mavis and Wilbur got ready to meet Mona and Harry. Maude promised that they would be fine and told them both to have a good time with their friends. "My eyes are peeled for that lunatic," she whispered to Wilbur. "I'm ready for him if he gets into my snacks again."

Mavis and Wilbur waved goodbye and walked out of the tent towards the food trucks. They saw Mona and Harry near the hotdog truck waiting for them. From the look on their faces, everything had gone well with the sale of the diner. Mavis elbowed Wilbur and whispered, "let's wait on the Earl news. I don't want to rain on their parade." Wilbur agreed and congratulated Harry and Mona enthusiastically.

They ordered their hotdogs and French fries and sodas and sat down at an empty picnic table to hear all about it. Mona nor Harry had any idea what to do with all of the newfound free time. After they ate their greasy food, Mavis suggested that they walk around the various animal barns. She wanted to stay as far away from the midway, and Earl, as possible. She wasn't quite ready to tell Mona about Earl's return yet. She was in too good of a mood to ruin. They came to the horse barn first and saw all of the beautiful colts, racing stallions, and show mares.

In the sheep barn they got to pet the lambs and watch the bigger ewes get sheered. Wilbur had to tear Mavis away from newborn piglets in the pig barn and the baby chicks under the lights in the chicken coops. She had already researched on her phone how long it would take Wilbur to build a small pigpen in Jameson's old barn.

"Let's go see the dairy cows," Harry suggested. He had a softness for the cows and was almost giddy at the thought of stepping back into the old show barn. It had been decades since he had been back to this place. He owed everything he had to the old gray barn with the circular show ring. The barn hadn't changed a bit. He still remembered it like it was just yesterday.

[Chapter Ten]

Harry had ended up being the youngest FFA scholarship winner in Rhinestone's history. It was unconventional, at least for those who had known the erudite teenager, but history had been made at the county fair that year.

Harry knew everything there was to know on the SAT. He was, what many would call, a genius. However, there were very few accolades for brains at Rhinestone High. Those awards and community scholarships were given to seniors and to those students whose families could probably already afford to pay for college. Unfortunately, that didn't include Harry's family. Though the diner was a nice avenue to keep the family afloat, it didn't provide the kind of opportunities that Harry needed for his future. He knew he would have to find another way, besides his intelligence, to make it out of Rhinestone.

His twin sister, on the other hand, was perfectly content with just getting by grade wise. Mona wasn't interested in grammar or the Pythagorean theorem. She didn't care about history class or any electives. All Mona cared about was her latest boyfriend and dreamed of one day taking over the Starlight Cafe from her parents with her husband and their yard full of kids.

Their parents encouraged their kids to try out different sports and clubs, but neither Harry nor Mona cared about school sanctioned extracurricular activities. Until one particular extracurricular activity offered a bit more than Harry had previously thought. One day, after hearing his friend talk about how much money he had made selling his show cow, Harry's ears perked up. He didn't necessarily have any interest in raising or training a cow, but he had an interest in making money. Once he learned that these competitions offered scholarships, he was completely sold. His parents were thrilled, but they had one condition. They wanted him to encourage Mona to join FFA, Future Farmers of America, with him. Harry knew that was an impossible task. Mona didn't like dirt or animals or people for that matter. He was pretty sure that Mona was afraid of cows anyway.

Over the next few weeks, Harry tried his best to convince Mona to join the class. Like he knew she would, she refused time and again. Finally, his parents agreed that showing cows or pigs or anything else resembling food was not up Mona's alley. They allowed Harry to sign up his sophomore year of high school and bought him a cow to work with. Harry took to showing like a duck to water. It was yet another thing he was good at. In the evenings, Mona would sometimes come out to the small barn and watch Harry and Lola, his Brahman cow, practice. She had to admit that the velvety brown cow was cute, but she could never see herself prancing through the mud and the muck with a slab of beef for any amount of money.

Harry began to collect a lot of money from his wins at shows. During his junior year of high school, he was set to become the most winning shower this county had ever seen. When the annual fair came around, Harry and Lola stole the show. The final weekend of the fair was the final round of shows for this competition, and if he won, he would be set for his first year of college in Junction. Even though he had accumulated enough money to attend the local community college for a few semesters, his eyes were set on the ultimate prize. The ultimate prize was a full ride scholarship to one of the top agricultural schools in the state, plus an all expenses paid round trip to the national competition three states over.

Nothing could go wrong for him, until one day it did.

Harry woke the morning of the final round with a raging fever and heavy cough. Every time he swallowed, it felt like razor blades were cutting his throat. His mother promptly sent him upstairs to bed and wouldn't hear another word about any competition or commitment. His health came first. His father agreed with his mother and hurried off to the diner before Harry could protest further. If only he could clone himself! Then he could be in two different places at once. He had always loved being a twin, but for the first time, he wished he had an identical twin brother instead of a fraternal twin sister.

Mona skipped by his room on the way outside when it struck him. He called for her to come back to his room and she begrudgingly followed him.

"Your ears are red," she said. She placed her hand on his forehead and swore. "Damn, Harry, you're hotter than a two-dollar pistol. Stay away from me. I can't be getting sick." She wiped her palms on her jeans and grimaced.

"I don't have time to be sick either," he frowned. He reminded her about the final round later this afternoon and what the ultimate prize was.

Mona frowned with him and agreed that it sure was a shame that he would have to miss it. She said he was sure to win, but there was always next year.

"I have an idea," Harry whispered. He beckoned Mona to lean in closer and whispered his idea to her so their mother wouldn't overhear.

"You've got to be kidding me!" Mona howled impatiently.

Harry's door flew open, and his mother hurried in. "What's all this shouting?" she asked. "Harry, get in your pajamas, and Mona, I thought you were going to the fair?"

"She is," Harry said. "She was just telling me goodbye."

"Such a sweet girl," their mother smiled. She turned to Harry and handed him a glass of water to take his medicine with. "I'm sure Mona will bring you back a little something from the fair. Right, Mona?"

Harry's eyes widened behind his mother's back in a last-ditch effort to convince his sister of his idea.

"Fine," Mona sighed. "I'll do my best to, um, remember."

Their mother smiled and told Harry to get some rest and she'd be back in to check on him soon. As soon as her footsteps rounded the corner, Mona shook her head as Harry started in on her again.

"No one is going to believe this!" Mona howled. "You can't be serious!"

"Please," Harry begged. "I'll do anything! I'll do your homework for the rest of the year. I'll do all of your chores! All work your shifts at the diner. Please, Mona! Please!"

Mona pursed her lips and thought long and hard about what Harry was offering. He already did her homework most of the time, so that wasn't a viable promise. She didn't mind working at the diner, so that too was out of the question. "Anything?" she asked.

He nodded earnestly. "What do you have in mind?"

"I'm not sure yet," Mona admitted. "I'm going to sit on it for a bit. But you have to promise that no matter what, no matter when, I can cash this in."

"I promise!" Harry blurted out.

"Even in a hundred years," Mona said sternly.

"Fine," Harry promised.

"Ok," Mona shrugged. "Give me your boots and that ugly hat."

"Thank you!" Harry howled. He crushed Mona in a bear hug as she squealed, "get off me! Don't make me change my mind!"

Harry helped her pull back her hair in a high bun and shoved his trademark cowboy hat over her eyes. He tossed her his lucky long-sleeve button-down shirt and jeans. It took a few minutes to get her to wear the boots once she realized they were covered in cow manure, but she eventually relented. She held her nose and gagged a little before frowning in the mirror above Harry's dresser.

"You smell too nice," Harry frowned as he sized her up in front of him.

"I smell like cow crap," Mona sighed. "How do you do this every day?"

"You smell like girl perfume," Harry said. "Hold on a minute." He snuck out of his bedroom window and grabbed a handful of Alabama clay from the front drive. Before Mona could protest, he wiped some of the dusty clay onto her neck and the bottom of the jeans. Then he sprayed her with enough of his cologne to ward off evil spirits, or any woman in the tri-county area.

"I can't breathe!" Mona gagged. She coughed and sputtered in the fog of cheap cologne.

"That's better," Harry said appreciatively. "Now, you can't carry on like that in there. You've seen how I do things. Be respectful but keep your head down. Don't talk, and if you do, talk like me. And no flirting with any boys."

Mona rolled her eyes and shoved her hands in her pocket. "I know how to mock you. Hi, I'm Harry. This is my cow," she sighed.

"Mona! This is serious," Harry whined.

"Oh, fine!" Mona huffed. "Get back in bed before mama comes back in." She snatched Harry's sunglasses off his dresser and put them on to complete the look.

If Harry crossed his eyes and looked into the light over Mona's left shoulder, he could barely decipher his twin sister under his clothes. He was pretty sure that this plan was never going to work, but he had to try. He tossed Mona one of his jackets and she slipped out of the open window without a backwards glance. His future was in the hands of his twin sister who had never even fed his cow, let alone worked with her. He watched her hop into their shared car and drive off. Thankfully, Lola was already at the fair in her own stall waiting. There was no way Mona could drive their dad's truck and trailer all the way to Junction.

Even if he was having second thoughts, there was nothing he could do about it now. The medicine began to work, and Harry drifted off to a fitful sleep.

"And the rest was history," Mona said to Wilbur and Mavis who looked awestruck.

"What?" Wilbur gasped.

"Mona!" Mavis giggled. "I can't believe you won!"

Harry could feel his cheeks turning redder by the minute. He and Mona had taken turns explaining what had happened that fateful day more than twenty years ago. It had changed his life. Mona had come home later that night with a belt buckle the size of Texas, as well as a full ride scholarship and trip. All in Harry's name, of course. Harry wasn't sure how she had done it, but she had blown the rest of the competition out of the water. He was amazed at her resolve, and he had crushed her in another hug. Their parents had not been thrilled with their deceit, but they didn't say anything to anyone. They were proud of both of their children, like always, and maybe a little awestruck at Mona's sudden interest in showmanship.

The following summer, Harry went to National's in Texas and won again. He went on to graduate college and even had a brief stint in Texas as a semi-professional bull rider. When his parents died in a head on collision when he was twenty-seven, he moved back to Rhinestone and ran the Starlight Cafe with Mona, whom he owed all of his success to. Not that Mona had ever asked him to, but Harry had not hesitated. Rhinestone was his home, and the diner was his refuge, even after a lifetime of eight second rides.

"Did you ever cash in on your end of the bargain?" Mavis asked. Her question once again shook Harry out of his memories.

Harry scowled and playfully rolled his eyes.

"I'll take that as a yes," Wilbur said. He was just as interested in this tale as Mavis.

"Well, you see what had happened," Mona began. Wilbur and Mavis waited with bated breath. "y'all remember when Earl tried to take over the diner last year?" Mona asked.

Wilbur and Harry both groaned at the mention of Earl's name. Mavis nodded and begged Mona to continue.

"Well, remember when we hatched that plan to catch him on his schemes? I had to get Harry out of there before he killed him. He and Earl didn't exactly get along, you see," Mona explained.

"I can't imagine why," Wilbur laughed.

"Oh hush," Mona said. "Anyway, Harry wouldn't budge. So, after all that time, I knew the only thing that would get him out of the way was our old agreement."

"Mona!" Mavis whimpered. "You had to waste your special chip on that old idiot Earl?"

"It worked though," Mona said triumphantly. "Come to think of it, we kinda have Earl to thank for all this."

"What?" Mavis coughed.

"It wasn't until he mentioned selling the diner and causing all that drama that me and Harry really did think about it seriously," Mona explained. "Obviously not with him involved," she followed up.

Mavis and Wilbur looked sheepishly at each other, and Mona's heart sank. "Wait a minute? What was that look for?"

"Nope," Wilbur said. He shook his head and pointed at Mavis. "You get to be the one to ruin this sweet moment."

"What is it?" Mona asked. She and Harry looked at each other apprehensively and turned back towards Mavis and Wilbur.

"He's back," Mavis sighed. "Earl's back in town."

Harry crushed the plastic soda bottle in his beefy hand. He was generally pretty laid back, but something about Earl boiled his blood. He couldn't get over the way that Earl had rolled in and tried to steal the restaurant from them, or the way that he could never get his name correct. For some reason, Earl had been convinced that Harry was Mona's ailing father, and Earl was half a mind to take him out back and shoot him or throw him in a nursing home. Either way, Harry's blood boiled any time that snake in the grass was brought up.

"What do you mean?" Mona asked.

"He's here, literally here," Wilbur sighed. He jerked his finger over his shoulder towards the midway and shook his head. "We don't know how or why."

"But we don't reckon he's seen us," Mavis interjected. "Probably best to keep it that way."

"Best for his sake," Harry nodded.

Mona sighed heavily and shook her head. She had been so glad to get rid of that man last year. How in the world was he back? "You don't think he escaped from jail or the asylum, do you?" she asked.

"Probably," Mavis nodded.

"I wouldn't put it past him," Wilbur sighed. "He may not be the brightest crayon in the box, but he's as slippery as an eel."

"You got that right," Mona sighed. "What's the plan?"

Mavis and Wilbur laughed. They knew Mona would be gung-ho to catch Earl once and for all, but unfortunately neither of them had a plan in mind. "I say we let it go," Wilbur said. "The fair will be over soon enough, and he'll move on. God willing."

"It's strange that he's back here near Rhinestone though," Harry added.

"That's what has me worried," Wilbur admitted. "But I hope he just moves on with the creek."

"I'll have my eye on him," Mona sighed.

"We all will," Harry nodded.

[Chapter Eleven]

"How about we go try our luck on the midway to get this frustration out?" Mona suggested. She wasn't exactly wanting to run into Earl, but she did want to keep her eye on him. It was better to remain many steps ahead of his schemes.

"Afraid I can't," Mavis frowned. She checked her watch and grimaced again. "It's my turn to run Opal's booth. And Wilbur has to help me. I swear, that dang booth is the most popular one here."

"She's right," Wilbur chuckled. "I knew Opal was a legend in this county, but I swear I didn't know she'd be this popular."

"I'm sorry we couldn't celebrate longer," Mavis fretted.

"And I hate that we had to tell you the bad news about Earl," Wilbur added.

"As soon as he's gone and this fair mess is wrapped up, let's the four of us go out to the steakhouse. My treat!" Mavis smiled.

"Deal!" Mona agreed.

"And maybe we can go on vacation together!" Mavis continued. She and Mona squealed in delight as Harry and Wilbur looked at each other.

"Don't worry boys, we'll take care of all the details."

"That's what I'm afraid of," Wilbur whispered to Harry. He shook his hand and patted Mona on the back. "Come on, Mavis, let's go rescue Ms. Maude and let these two win a few prizes over yonder. Just keep your eyes peeled. He's running a kissing booth last we saw."

Mona gagged at the thought of anyone lining up to kiss Earl. She hugged Mavis goodbye and promised to let her know the minute she saw Earl. She hurried to catch up to Harry whose stride beat hers by a mile. Mavis watched them hurry off and turned to Wilbur and asked, "You think we'll all make it out of this week without him seeing us?"

Wilbur shook his head and then shrugged. "I hope so, but where Earl is concerned, I can't be sure." They walked off towards the towering tent where Maude and Opal were waiting for them to relieve them.

"It's about time," Maude growled when they walked up. There were only a few people in line in front of Opal who was regaling one young woman in particular about a tale that involved Italian yarn and lime sherbet. "Don't ask," Maude shook her head. "That one is a particularly hard case to crack. I tried, but Opal said I had it all wrong. Anyway, as soon as she's done, we're going to get something to eat and then I want to play some of those games. I bet I can show those young'uns how it's done."

Ten minutes later, Opal had cleared the line and put a sign on the table letting the crowd know that she would be back in two hours for the final shift, but Madame Mavis would be there in her stead. She knocked back an entire bottle of water and took off the sweaty wig and cloak, revealing a tight purple jumpsuit underneath.

"That sure is some outfit!" Mavis whistled.

"I may be old, but I'm not dead yet," Opal said proudly. "Let's go Maude." They linked arms and made their way out of the tent into the cool afternoon air.

After Maude ate two footlong hotdogs and a basket of cheese fries, she felt full enough to try her hand at some of the throwing games close by. After her third try to no avail, she cursed the man behind the counter and yanked Opal over to the next booth that involved tossing small white balls into small goldfish bowls. If you sank three in a row, you won the goldfish inside. Maude didn't particularly have any use for any goldfish, but she was determined to win something. Opal, on the other hand, was perfectly content to sit on the edge of the counter and feed the pitiful goldfish in their small bowls.

"Uh, ma'am, you can't feed them crackers," the game worker frowned.

Maude grabbed Opal by the neck and pulled her off of the counter with a grunt. "Here, you try and win one of those blasted bowls," Maude huffed.

Opal shook the dust and dirt from the counter off of her behind and stood up straight. She squinted her eyes and took the bucket of balls Maude had purchased and began to toss them over the counter towards the many rows of goldfish bowls. She sank fifteen in a row as the crowd around her cheered in awe. The man behind the counter gathered up five of the nearest goldfish bowls and handed them over to Maude who looked both frustrated and proud.

"And that's how you do it," Opal shrugged.

"We can't carry all those around," Maude said. "We should've brought that danged wagon after all."

"Well, you go get it and I'll wait right here with my new friends," Opal smiled.

Maude cussed under her breath, but dutifully shuffled back to the main tent to retrieve the wagon. Wilbur and Mavis were busy entertaining what looked to be one of the local football teams when Maude clamored behind the booth to empty the wagon.

"What's going on?" Wilbur asked.

"Opal won a school of fish," Maude coughed. "I gotta get the wagon to haul them!"

"Fish? Live ones?" Wilbur asked.

"Of course, they're alive," Maude snapped. "I think they're alive. Well hell, I don't know. They're in little bowls. She's probably got them all named by now."

"How many of them would you say?" Wilbur asked.

"I don't know. Didn't stop to count them, Wilbur," Maude snapped.

Wilbur looked over at Mavis and saw that she was still mesmerizing the group of teens, so he leaned in behind her and whispered that he needed to help Maude with something, and he'd be back directly. She nodded and shooed him away so he wouldn't distract her from her act. Wilbur turned back to see Maude already stomping away from the booth pulling the wagon behind her. He had to jog for a bit to catch up to her.

"I can manage, Wilbur," Maude said when he caught up to her.

"Oh, I know," he chuckled. "I just want to see for myself about these fish." His eyes bulged out of his head when he saw Opal sitting on the counter surrounded by fishbowls.

"Hey Wilbur!" Opal waved. "Meet my new friends!" She waved her hands over the nearest few bowls and grinned.

"How many times did you win?" Wilbur asked.

"Thirteen times!" the young man next her shrieked. "She won thirteen times in a row. What's that? Thirteen times three is um, well, a lot!"

"Thirty-nine," Opal smiled proudly. "Thirteen fish in thirteen bowls. Might need some help getting them all home."

"I can see that," Wilbur nodded as Maude grabbed the closest fishbowl and plopped it in the wagon. "I don't think they're all going to fit."

"Can't we put all the fish in one bowl?" Maude asked.

"They won't have room to breathe!" Opal howled.

"Ain't you got a cooler or something in your truck?" Maude asked Wilbur.

"Yes ma'am, I do," he nodded. "Let me run go get it!" He hurried to the parking lot and wrestled the cooler from the truck bed and dumped the melted ice water out of it. Thankfully, it was pretty clean. By the time he got back to the older women,

Opal had won two more fishbowls, much to Maude's protesting.

"You don't need fifteen goldfish, Opal!" she howled.

"I'm going to give them to Mavis so Clivey can have a friend," Opal said solemnly.

Wilbur frowned at the idea. Clive would swallow those little goldfish whole, but he didn't share that notion with Opal. One by one, he helped Opal gently pour the contents of each bowl into the cooler. Fifteen goldfish took up more room than he thought they would. He handed the bowls back to Maude who tossed them to the man behind the counter.

"We don't need the bowls," she said. "Keep them for the next winner."

Wilbur picked up the heavy cooler and set it in the wagon. Maude put in to pull it, but he convinced her that he really wanted to be the one to pull it while she guided him through the crowd. Opal decided she wanted to play a few more games, so Maude shrugged and told Wilbur to go back to the tent and she would follow Opal to see what kind of prizes she could win next. "No more live ones though," she promised as she tagged after Opal who was already at the next booth in line.

Opal was on a hot streak! She threw a perfect football spiral through a tire and won a stuffed teddy-bear. She handed it over to Maude and walked to the next booth where the object of the game was to sink a free throw at a basketball hoop. She sank two shots in a row, and the young woman behind the counter told her if she hit the next one, she could choose one of the life-size stuffed animals behind the counter.

Opal gritted her teeth and squinted her eyes. To no one's surprise, the ball flew through the hoop effortlessly. Opal chose a delightful life-size stuffed dolphin that was neon pink. Maude flat out refused to carry it. She should have kept the wagon and let Wilbur carry the cooler back to the tent, but it was too late for that. She looked around and spotted Harry and Mona at the next booth trying to match the numbers on the bottom of some rubber ducks and failing miserably.

"Hey!" Maude shouted. She waved her arms over her head and shouted until she caught their attention. They rushed over and asked if she was alright. "I'm fine," she said. "I just need you to tote this mess over to Wilbur in that tent over yonder." She pointed at the giant dolphin and then looked around for Opal who was already two booths over holding a stack of plastic rings in her hand. "Opal, wait for me!" She ran off leaving Harry any Mona staring at the discarded teddy bear and dolphin at their feet.

Mona and Harry knew better than to protest. Mona took the small teddy bear and left Harry to struggle with the six-foot-long pink dolphin. She couldn't help but giggle as he stumbled behind her on the way to the big tent. As they approached the booth, Wilbur and Mavis both laughed at the sight. "Looks like y'all won big!" Wilbur called out. "Congratulations!"

"Wasn't us," Harry yelled from behind the stuffed animal.

Wilbur and Mavis looked confused, but Mona explained what had happened through her bits of laughter.

"We should have known," Wilbur laughed. "Thanks for taking care of that." He took the larger-than-life prize from Harry and set it on the ground next to the wagon. "Any idea what those two are up to now?"

"Ms. Opal was already winning some more goodies when we walked away," Mona said with a smile. "I don't know how she does it!"

Wilbur shrugged and shook his head. "I don't know how she does half the stuff she does, to tell you the truth. I'm sure there's books written about her all over the world. She sure is something." His face swelled with pride whenever he talked about Opal Tyler. She kept him on his toes, for sure, but he idolized that woman and always had. She had been the first person to ever really see him for who he was as a youngster. He remembered watching her in the woods a few times before she had spotted him. He hadn't meant to step on the broken twig, but somehow, he had. She had been alerted to his presence, and instead of getting mad like his father always had, she calmly and gently got to know him and invited him back to Magnolia Manor for lunch. That was where he had first met the Montgomery family, Opal's best friends, who owned the Manor. As fate would have it, they soon adopted Wilbur and the rest was history. One chance meeting in the forest with Opal had directly changed the trajectory of his life. He wasn't sure where he would be without her.

"How about I tell you your fortune?" Mavis offered. Mona shook with delight and plopped down on the stool in front of the counter. Mavis took her hand and examined the lines and veins on her palms. She smiled and said in a low voice, "Mona, I see many riches in your future. And a handsome man. Maybe more than one! Perhaps three or four!"

Wilbur and Harry rolled their eyes as their sisters giggled and joked around about Mona's love life. Mona had been married a few times already and wasn't looking for her next husband, but who was she to tempt fate.

"Your turn!" Mavis chirped to Harry who begrudgingly sat down on the stool that Mona had just vacated. She took his rough hands and flipped them over to see his palms. "Oh Harry, I see a beautiful beach in your future. A weeklong trip with two of your best friends and your lovely sister. I see a buffet full of crab legs and shrimp cocktail. How delightful!"

Harry laughed and stood up from the stool. He knew that Mona and Mavis definitely had something up their sleeve. It had been decades since he had been to a beach. He wasn't sure that he had ever eaten crab legs either. He reckoned now that they had sold the diner, he could start to venture out a little bit more. Maybe a vacation with Mavis, Mona, and Wilbur wouldn't be so bad after all.

"Here comes trouble!" Mona said. She jerked her head to the side where Opal and Maude were walking in. Maude's arms were stuffed full of cheap carnival midway prizes. Opal had racked up!

Maude dropped piles of stuffed animals, plastic flowers, bags of candy, and bouncing balls at Wilbur's feet. He reached out to grab them as they went in all directions. Harry and Mona dove after the stragglers and helped Wilbur pile the loot in the wagon next to the cooler of fish.

"Wow!" Mavis said. "You sure won a lot!"

"It's all in the wrist," Opal nodded. She disappeared behind the counter and put on her infamous wig and cloak. She checked her watch and sat down in her comfortable chair and entered her signature trance without another word.

"Did y'all stop and get anything to eat?" Wilbur asked Maude.

"Sure did," she nodded. She opened her purse and pulled out two giant turkey legs wrapped in foil. "I'm going to prop my feet up and eat this sucker before the evening crowd arrives. Y'all go on out and have some fun. Opal didn't leave many prizes left but go ride some of those contraptions if you're brave enough."

"Yes ma'am!" Mavis cheered, right as Wilbur said, "no thanks!"

[Chapter Twelve]

"There's always the Ferris wheel!" Mona suggested. "It's already lit up for the evening!"

"No way," Harry and Wilbur said together. "We'll watch y'all from down here," Wilbur continued. There was no way he was going to step foot on that contraption. Just thinking about it hurt his stomach.

"Suit yourself," Mavis shrugged. She and Mona handed over two ride tickets each to the ride worker and climbed into the empty cart. The worker secured the lap bar and pressed the button to send them up. They waved at Wilbur and Harry who had found a wooden bench to sit on. They waved back heartily and laughed as Mavis blew fake kisses to the ride worker whose cheeks blushed crimson.

"What about the bumper cars next?" Mavis called out as they came back around again.

Wilbur nodded and looked at Harry to see if he agreed. "Sounds good," Harry smiled.

The bumper cars were more their speed. Any excuse to wreck into Mavis was fun. She was intense when it came to any contest or game, and bumper cars were no exception. She took any and every opportunity to ram her car into anyone she came close to. Wilbur remembered as a teenager trying to dodge her as best he could. But she always found a way to crash into him. Her high-pitched giggle could be heard over all of the screeching tires and crashes around them. Even though Mavis was six years his junior, she had always been a force to be reckoned with.

Wilbur and Harry began to talk strategy on how to best avoid Mavis' rage on the bumper cars. Wilbur told Harry about one time a few years back when she dragged him to a vacation town that had bumper boats set up. He swore she was trying to drown him. Somehow, he ended up being drenched and she didn't have a single droplet of water on her. His story was interrupted by a loud crash behind them. Someone or something had toppled over a stack of crates ten feet high. Wilbur and Harry shrugged it off and turned back around to face the Ferris wheel in front of them. As the women came around for a third time, Mavis didn't bother to wave. She looked like she had seen a ghost.

"Oh my God," Mavis whispered to Mona. "Don't look."

"Don't look where?" Mona asked loudly.

Mavis jerked her head to the right of the box and sighed deeply. "He's like a durn magnet!"

"Who?" Mona asked. She stood up as best she could behind the lap bar and looked around.

"Sit down!" Mavis wailed. She tugged on Mona's shirt and felt the rickety box start to move. "You're gonna fall out!"

Mona shook her head, but dutifully sat down. She kept looking as the wheel moved closer to the ground. "Mavis, what's got you all freaked out?"

"Earl," Mavis whispered. She had shrunk down as much as she could next to Mona, but the closer she got to the ground, the more he came into view.

"Earl? Where?" Mona gasped. Mavis had taken up most of the room in the cramped box in an effort to hide herself.

"MAVIS!" Earl bellowed, much like Marlon Brando's famous line from Tennessee Williams' "A Streetcar Named Desire" from 1951. Only Earl wasn't as handsome. His wail sounded more like a cat that got its tail caught up under an old wooden rocking chair.

Harry and Wilbur nearly jumped out of their skin at Earl's screech. Earl pushed past them and scrambled past the ride worker who controlled the giant wheel.

"Was that?" Harry started to say, but Wilbur answered for him. "Earl!" Wilbur yipped.

"Can't this thing go any faster?" Mavis yelled as Earl clambered onto the platform and leapt towards Mona and Mavis' box. He clung tightly to the lap bar that held Mavis and Mona in place and refused to let go.

"Stop the ride!" Wilbur yelled, but the worker looked utterly confused. "Stop the ride!" Wilbur repeated. He lunged for the controls as Harry reached for Earl. His fingers barely grasped the loose material of Earl's shirt, and he snatched him backwards.

"Get off me!" Earl screeched. He hissed and flailed like a cat that was covered in fleas. Harry let him go and Earl toppled to the ground in a heap of dirt and oversized clothing. "Suga bear!" he drawled as he stood up and wiped the dust and dirt from his pants. He looked at Harry and sneered. "I rememba you, Larry. Nice to see you's out of the home me and Mona Lisa put you in."

Harry growled low and looked at Mona who had not moved from the ride cart. Mavis had tried to shield her face with her purse, but Earl was already like a hound on the hunt. "Suga! You know you can't hide from me!" he continued.

"That's enough, Earl," Wilbur said loudly. At the mention of his name, Earl shrunk down and scowled. "Don't know who dis Earl fella is, but he sound mighty fine." He patted the embroidered name tag on his too big shirt that said "Ernest, Maintenance Worker."

"What in the world are you talking about, Earl?" Mavis shouted. She wasn't sure where her sudden gumption had come from, but the ride cart began to sway as she pushed the lap bar up and stumbled onto the platform. Harry grabbed her arm and kept her steady so she wouldn't fall.

"Hey Larry! Don't touch my woman!" Earl scowled.

"I am not your woman, Earl!" Mavis shouted.

"Suga bear, don't be like dat. You know how much you always meant to me," Earl put his hand on his heart to demonstrate his sincerity.

"Go away, Earl!" Mavis yelled, but Earl merely smiled his signature creepy smile. Mavis could see that he had lost a few more teeth since their last encounter, as well as a significant amount of weight.

"Get on now," Wilbur said again. He stood in between Earl and Mavis as a crowd began to gather around. He knew that Earl liked to make a scene, but he was clearly outnumbered in this situation.

Earl looked around and sighed heavily. "Y'all came on by my booth over yonder. I be set up all day tomorra," he smiled. He blew Mavis a long kiss and skedaddled off without another word. "I give you a free sample an' everything. Dat way you can rememba what you been missing all dis time," he called over his shoulder.

Mavis shuddered and turned back to help Mona off the ride. "Thanks Mavis. Thank God he's gone," Mona said.

"Doubtful," Mavis sighed. "Come on, let's get out of here. We need to find Ms. Maude and Opal anyway. It's about time to wrap things up for the night."

"Let's grab something to eat on the way," Mona suggested.

"How can you eat after that?" Wilbur said. Earl soured his stomach.

"He's not the first leech I've ever encountered," Mona shrugged.

The four of them regrouped and walked towards the food truck to get a snack before the trucks and booths shut down for the night.

"That man!" Mavis fumed as she ordered a turkey leg for each of them. She was so upset with Earl she ordered a large basket of fries as well. "Throw in four colas as well," she added to her order hastily.

"Sorry, ran out of drinks about an hour ago," the woman grunted as she handed the drumsticks out of the window.

They found an empty picnic table further down the lane. Harry went to buy some sodas for each of them to wash down the hunks of meat.

"You said he was running a kissing booth?" Mona asked Mavis.

Mavis nodded. "Not sure why in the world he thought that was a good idea."

"The thought alone is enough to turn your stomach," Wilbur said.

"You're right about that," Mona nodded. She held her hand to her mouth as if her earlier meal was attempting to make a daring escape. The turkey leg sat before her uneaten.

Wilbur ate the drumstick with a watchful eye on everything around him. He would have been much happier if they had gone the entire time without running into Earl Thibodeaux Boudreaux and all his shenanigans.

Harry returned with four sodas and four large funnel cakes. He hoped the dessert would lighten the mood and get their minds off the irritating canker sore that was Earl.

"So, what are we going to do about this? We can't sit around and wait until he starts some of his mess again," Mavis said. She picked a piece of funnel cake from the plate.

"Not sure there's anything we can do," Wilbur said. "As long as he leaves with the fair, we should be alright."

"You don't believe that for a minute," Mavis said.

She was right. Wilbur knew enough about Earl to know this was only the beginning, but he didn't want to admit that at the moment. "Come on, let's go check on Ms. Maude and Opal."

"But Mona hasn't finished her food yet," Mavis said.

"I'm not that hungry after all. Let's take this back with us. Maybe Ms Maude is hungry," Mona said.

They wrapped up what was left of their snacks and walked towards the big tent where Maude and Opal should be wrapping up their final shift of Madame Opalina. Harry led the way with Wilbur casually strolling a few feet behind in case Earl tried anything.

"You've got to be kidding me," Harry growled. He pointed at the mouth of the tent where Earl had dragged his makeshift kissing booth to. People poured out of the tent to head towards their cars in the parking lot since the fair was closing, not paying a lick of attention to the sleazeball catcalling the women who passed by.

"Just ignore him," Wilbur said to Mavis in particular. "Go get Maude and Opal and tell them to hurry."

"Suga!" Earl called out when he spotted her. "I knew you'd be back fo' mo'!"

"Ignore him," Wilbur whispered loudly.

Mavis gripped her purse and walked past Earl as Harry blocked her from Earl's line of sight as she passed under the tent flap. Earl hissed and called after them but didn't dare cross Harry or Wilbur who waited at the entrance to make sure he didn't follow behind her.

"You two mighty close to my suga," Earl said in a low voice. "Don't be thinkin' no kinda thoughts like dat."

"What kind of thoughts?" Harry asked dryly.

"Mavis belong to me," Earl crooned. "I'mma win her back. You'll see."

Wilbur rolled his eyes and wished that Mavis, Mona, Maude, and Opal would hurry up. He could feel his brain cells dying every second that he was exposed to Earl.

"She can't resist my charms," Earl continued. "I bet she ain't been on a single date without me."

Harry grunted and leaned down to see eye level with Earl. If Wilbur hadn't been standing next to him, he wouldn't have believed it. "She's on a date with me right now. What do you have to say about that?" Harry said in a gravelly tone.

"What?" Earl gasped.

"You heard me. Now leave us all alone if you know what's good for you," Harry continued. Wilbur stared as the large man spoke in an even tone and didn't blink. Harry was such a gentle guy, but he didn't look like one, especially when he was aggravated. Wilbur knew that Earl wouldn't dare lay a finger on any of them as long as Harry was around.

Harry turned towards Wilbur and winked ever so slightly so that Earl didn't see him.

"And what about Mona?" Earl breathed.

Wilbur chuckled slightly and said, "We're dating. You've ruined a perfectly good double date. Now scram!"

Earl swallowed hard and stumbled backwards into his rickety booth. He had not been expecting either of those bombs. His entire plan was now awry, but that had never stopped him before. Before he could muster up the nerve to retort to Wilbur, Maude and Opal bounded out of the tent and looked at Harry and Wilbur.

"Why are y'all standing around?" Maude asked. "The wagon ain't gonna pull itself."

Mavis and Mona followed behind them and ignored Earl's gawking eyes. "Suga! You datin' ol' Larry here? And Mona, you's wit da ol' handyman?"

Mavis and Mona both whirled around and looked at Earl who still looked aghast. They could see Wilbur and Harry nodding slightly behind him.

"Yes," Mona nodded. "Agreed," Mavis said with a fake smile plastered across her face.

"I can't believe it," Earl sighed.

"Neither can I," Mavis nodded. "Now shoo before I call the law on you again."

Earl looked over his shoulder and back at Mavis. "Dis ain't ova," he said sternly.

"Afraid it is," Wilbur said. He looped back in between Earl and the rest of the party and took the handle of the wagon from Maude. "Time for us to leave and for you to go back to wherever you came from." He ushered Mavis and Mona to walk ahead of him as Harry escorted Maude and Opal away from the tent. Neither of them had spoken to Earl or acknowledged his presence during this interchange. Wilbur wasn't sure they had even been paying attention. They were both reading the back of a cookbook they had bought at one of the booths earlier. As they all walked towards the parking lot, Earl made a sudden dash after them.

"Mavis! You know you still want me!" Earl screamed.

"Who's yelling at our Mavis girl?" Opal asked blankly. She turned to Maude and looked briefly concerned. "Is that?"

"It's Earl," Wilbur said. "Just keep walking."

Recognition flooded over Opal's face, and she frowned. Maude scowled in Earl's direction and shook her fist at him. "That's the old buffoon himself!" Maude howled. "Shoo fly! Get on out of here!"

Earl ignored the two old women and tried to push past them to get to Mavis who was still hurrying ahead. She was doing her best to ignore Earl, which only seemed to enrage him further. In his mad haste, he knocked over Maude who tumbled to the floor. Wilbur dropped the wagon handle and grabbed Earl's arm to keep him from reaching Mavis.

"Maude!" Opal gasped. She and Harry leaned down to help Maude up off the floor, but Maude dusted herself off and scowled. "Bop him one, Opal!" Maude directed.

Opal picked up the long wooden baseball bat from the wagon in front of her and walloped Earl across the bottom with it. He howled in pain and Maude yelled, "Hit him again!"

Earl yelped like a whipped dog and slunk off behind a row of dirty trailers before Opal could do more damage.

"Nobody picks on Maude but me!" Opal yelled. She started to run after him waving the bat wildly around in the air. "Come back here so I can give you one for Mavis!"

"I think he got the message," Wilbur laughed. He had to run to catch up with her. She was still waving the bat around and he barely missed getting him himself. "Come on now. Let's head home."

[Chapter Thirteen]

Maude was fine as wine after her tumble in the parking lot. Wilbur and Mavis made sure she got inside her house safely once they got back to Rhinestone. "Y'all worry too much! I've never been described as delicate!" Maude huffed as she locked the front door behind her.

Opal was still fit to be tied as Mavis walked her into her house. She had been mumbling to herself in the car the entire ride home. Mavis wasn't sure if she was muttering actual curses under her breath directed towards Earl or not. She knew it was better not to ask.

Wilbur stopped by the Manor before heading to his house for some peach cobbler that Mavis had bought at the fair earlier that day. They needed to discuss what had happened this evening.

"Maude could have seriously gotten hurt," Mavis fretted as she added another scoop of vanilla ice cream to her bowl of peach cobbler. She asked Wilbur if he wanted any ice cream, but he politely declined.

He poured them both a glass of iced sweet tea and said, "It would take more than Earl to hurt her.

That woman has seen some things over the years. I can't help but still think of her as indestructible."

"Indestructible or not, she is getting older, or at least not getting any younger," Mavis sighed. "I'd hate for something bad to happen to her or Opal. Or any of us for that matter. Oooh, that man!" Wilbur could see that Mavis was genuinely upset by their altercation with Earl. He understood exactly why. Earl seemed to be the thorn in their side that they couldn't remove.

"What if we never get rid of him?" Mavis asked tearfully. "Do you think he'll ever fully go away?"

Wilbur sat down at the table and picked at his cobbler with his fork. "I don't know," he admitted. "But I'm going to do everything in my power to make sure that we're all safe. Don't think for a minute I'll let him hurt any of y'all."

Mavis smiled and patted his hand. "I know you won't. I'm just so tired and mad at him. Honestly, I'm mad at myself. It's my fault he ever entered our lives. If I could turn back time, I'd do things so differently."

Wilbur ate a bite of cobbler and nodded. "I think we'd all do some things differently, but then who knows where any of us would be in life. Changing one small detail could unravel everything." He checked his watch and chuckled, "But it's too late for that deep of a thread. Let's get a few hours of sleep and then I'll be over here bright and early so we can go fetch Opal and Maude. I'll bring over my new waffle iron and we can make us a good breakfast to start off the day."

He rinsed his bowl and spoon and placed them in the dishwasher before draining his glass of tea.

"When did you get a new waffle iron?" Mavis asked.

"Ms. Maude gave it to me last week. She said she had won it in some church raffle. It was still in the box unopened," Wilbur shrugged.

Mavis laughed and cleaned up her dishes. "I'll be up around eight. That should give us plenty of time. I've got bacon and plenty of eggs."

"Sounds good," Wilbur said. "Goodnight, Mavis. And don't worry about Earl. Things have a way of working out. We'll get through it." He locked the front door behind him, and Mavis watched him walk down the porch steps to his truck. Once he was out of sight, Mavis turned off all the lights downstairs and went upstairs to take a shower and go to bed.

She had a fitful night of sleep. She kept dreaming about a bayou full of alligators that kept trying to kiss her. When the sun began to shine though her curtains, she threw the blankets off and decided to start her day early. She had already gotten dressed, made the waffle batter, and fried the bacon when Wilbur knocked on the front door two hours later.

"Surprised to see you so awake," he mused.

"I couldn't sleep," Mavis sighed.

"I couldn't either," Wilbur admitted. "But today's a new day. Let's move forward. We may not even see him today."

"Fingers crossed," Mavis agreed. She knew Wilbur wouldn't let anything happen to them, but she still felt responsible for bringing Earl's nonsense into their family.

Wilbur waited for the new waffle iron to heat up before he added Mavis' batter to it. Once the first waffle was done, he added some fresh cut up strawberries to the top and dusted it with powdered sugar just the way Mavis liked it. He set it in front of her and poured more batter into the iron for his waffle. Once it was ready, he put the finished waffle on his plate and sat down across from Mavis. She was already finished with her waffle and stood up to make another one.

They ate their breakfast in relative silence and quickly cleaned up the kitchen. Mavis started the dishwasher and grabbed her purse from the counter. She and Wilbur walked out of the Manor and climbed into her car to go pick up Maude and Opal. As expected, both women were waiting for them on Opal's porch. Opal was holding a small doll that Mavis hadn't seen before. It didn't seem to matter that she and Wilbur were ten minutes early. Maude was halfway down the porch steps when Mavis put the car in park. Wilbur got out of the passenger door to help them down the steps, but Maude pushed past him and climbed into the passenger seat, leaving him and Opal to sit in the middle row. Mavis couldn't help but laugh as Wilbur helped Opal buckle her seat belt and then secure himself.

"Alright, let's head out," Mavis said cheerfully.

Opal hissed under her breath and made funny gestures at the doll.

"Oh my, that's an interesting doll you have. Is it new?" Mavis asked.

Opal continued to mumble, but Maude answered. "Don't worry about that one. She's had it for years. Only brings it out for special occasions."

"Oh, is that right?" Mavis looked over at Wilbur who shrugged.

"Honestly, after what happened the last time I saw her with it, I thought she'd got rid of the durn thing, but I guess she found it amongst some of her," Maude cleared her throat. "Collections."

"What happened after the last time she had it?" Wilbur asked. He looked over at Ms Opal sitting next to him.

"Oh nothing," Maude said with a distant, far away air. "No use in bringing all that up, especially since they never could prove anything."

Mavis looked at Wilbur through the rear-view mirror. When their eyes met, they both had a look of concern on their faces. With these two, you could never tell if their stories were real or not, no matter how farfetched they seemed.

"What do you mean?" Wilbur coughed. He wasn't sure he wanted to know, but at the same time, he was curious.

"That was a long time ago. You were just a little thing, Wilbur. It was before you came to live with Ruby and Jameson, as a matter of fact," Maude continued absentmindedly.

"Wait, what happened?" Mavis asked.

Wilbur was ashen. "It didn't have anything to do with my dad, did it? When he died?" He was looking directly at Opal. To their knowledge,

Wilbur had never once mentioned the night his father had died, and rarely, if ever, mentioned his father at all.

Opal stopped talking and looked at him. "Wilbur, I would never do anything that would hurt you like that. I promise," Opal patted his hand.

"Oh Lord. It was nothing like that. She, uh, took care of a personal matter for me," Maude said.

"Personal matter?" Mavis asked.

"Maude had a stalker," Opal announced dryly.

"Ms. Maude, you didn't!" Mavis gasped.

"You had a stalker?" Wilbur asked.

"She always makes it sound so dramatic. It wasn't a stalker like you see on those shows. Larry's ex-wife hadn't figured out that we were getting married yet, that's all," Maude explained, trying to be as diplomatic as possible, which was unusual in and of itself.

"Brenda was crazy as a loon," Opal added.

"Larry was your first husband?" Mavis asked.

"My second. We were only married for about a year. Turned out he wasn't my type after all," Maude shrugged.

"Who was your first husband?" Mavis asked.

"Allan," Maude answered. "He wasn't my type either. We were all better as friends."

"I still think you could have figured that out before you were married, but you never have been a fast learner," Opal muttered.

"Hush up! Who's telling this story?" Maude huffed.

"Well, you're not telling it very fast," Opal said.

"Anyway," Maude said loudly, "Brenda didn't like the fact that Larry and I were together, so she started making a fuss.

"Threw a hissy fit right in the middle of the street. Right in front of the house." Opal said. "With firecrackers. Near about burned her house down."

"Buford had a fit!" Maude said.

"That's okay. You held your own with her," Opal said proudly. She looked at Mavis and Wilbur. "Maude stood out there and told her the, you know, was about to hit the fan!"

"They're old enough to say shit in front of, Opal. Anyway, I just didn't know it was going to be so literal," Maude said.

"What do you mean?" Mavis asked.

"Well, two days later, Brenda's septic tank exploded. Covered her whole yard," Maude explained. "Could smell it across town."

"Really made her grass look good though," Opal shrugged.

"But what in the world did that have to do with you two?" Wilbur asked.

"Some folks thought I had something to do with it. Thought I might have gotten a hold of some fireworks myself," Maude said. "But I never even thought about blowing up her septic tank. Kinda wish I was that imaginative."

"I'm so confused," Mavis shook her head. "What does that have to do with the doll?"

"After that day with Brenda out in front of my house, I saw Opal with that doll. She started muttering just like she's been doing now. And then Brenda's septic tank blew up," Maude shrugged.

"Are you trying to tell me that this doll caused the septic tank to explode?" Wilbur looked at Maude. He looked over at Opal and scooted over a few inches just to be safe.

"All I know is she told me that next day that Brenda was going to get what was coming to her, and then the next thing I know, her yard was covered in shit," Maude said.

Wilbur looked up to see Mavis staring at him again from the mirror.

"Nobody messes with Maude but me," Opal said firmly. She smiled at Wilbur and then looked out the window at the cow pastures they were rolling by.

"But they could never prove anything?" Mavis said.

Maude shook her head. "No. Thank goodness we were all over at Ruby and Jameson's playing cards when it happened. Nobody in the world would have questioned Jameson about an exploding septic tank. But Brenda told anybody who would listen that I had done it."

"Did they ever figure out what caused it?" Wilbur asked.

"Just one of those freak accidents that you hear about every now and again," Opal said with a shrug.

They pulled into the grassy lot full of cars and parked. Wilbur unloaded the wagon and followed behind Maude and Opal who led the way to the tent where Opal's booth was. Mavis nudged Wilbur in the ribs and pointed out the doll that

Opal had left behind in the backseat. Wilbur shook his head and said it was best to keep walking, just to be on the safe side. Mavis agreed and together they followed behind the two women.

Once Maude and Opal were set up and ready, Mavis and Wilbur ventured out of the tent and walked towards the line of food trucks that were open for business. Mavis had wanted to try the steak tips and fried mozzarella bites, which sounded good to Wilbur. As they passed the pizza truck, Wilbur caught something out of the corner of his eye near the giant clock tower.

"Oh, Lordy. Take a look at what he's gotten into today," Wilbur sighed. He pointed over at Earl who was drawing something on his handmade sign in front of his duct taped booth made out of scrap wood and boxes.

Mavis stood on her tiptoes and looked over to where Earl was standing behind his raggedy booth. The handwritten sign had the previous words scratched out. It now had something else written on it, but his handwriting was too illegible to make out.

"What does it say?" Mavis asked.

"Beats me," Wilbur shrugged. "Let's just walk away and let him be."

About that time, Earl stood on top of an upside-down bucket and yelled out to whoever was listening, "I can know yo' weight and age off the toppa my head. Come 'round here and see my great mind at work!"

"Oh, dear God," Wilbur sighed.

"Ten dollas a person," Earl continued. "If I don't know then you only owe me five. Can't beat dat deal!"

Mavis' eyes bulged out and she grabbed Wilbur's hand. "Did I hear him right?"

Wilbur shook his head and sighed. "He's going to tangle up with the wrong person one of these days. Goodness gracious!" He was rooted to the spot as a small line formed in front of Earl.

"I'm getting in line for food," Mavis said. She left Wilbur standing there while she placed her order.

A scrawny teenager handed over a fistful of cash and stood in front of Earl with his arms crossed. Earl squinted his eyes and walked around him in a circle to size him up. The kid couldn't weigh more than a hundred pounds soaking wet, but Earl stomped around him multiple times like a cock-eyed rooster. "Hmm," he muttered. "Yous a lil' fella, ain't ya?"

The teenager frowned and stood up straighter. "I'm big enough!"

"You's about eighty pounds," Earl concluded. He misled proudly and gave himself a round of applause.

"I ain't done it!" the boy shouted back. "I'm one twenty!"

Both Earl and the boy were clearly out of their minds, but Wilbur was not about to get involved. Earl pocketed the money and shook his head. "Nex' in line!"

"I want my money back!" the boy shouted.

"No refund," Earl said loudly. "Yous ain't got a scale, do ya? Nope. Now get on and let someone else have a turn." He patted the boy on the back and Wilbur saw him silently grab the boy's wallet from his back pocket.

"Mavis! He just stole that kid's wallet!" Wilbur hissed. He turned around and saw Mavis eating the fried mozzarella bites even though they were smoking hot. Before Mavis could speak, Wilbur marched himself over to the booth and snatched the wallet from Earl. "That doesn't belong to you!" he huffed.

Earl went instantly pale and stuttered, "My mistake," he swallowed hard.

Wilbur handed the wallet back to the teenager who hadn't even noticed it was missing. "Go and get out of here, Earl. It's one thing for you to be out bothering people, but it's another thing to be a thief!"

"I ain't no thief," Earl bellowed, as he scrambled back behind the booth and grabbed the five-gallon bucket he had been sitting on. It was full of something, but Earl wouldn't let Wilbur see into it. "I best be on my way," he told the few people left in line. Before anyone could respond, he hightailed it out of there.

Wilbur shook his head and walked back over to where Mavis was still standing. "He's up to something," Wilbur frowned. "He had a bucket full of something that he didn't want me to see. I'm willing to bet it's stuff he stole. I'm going to call Harlan over at the police department. Something's not right here."

He walked over to a patch of grass where no one was and pulled out his cell phone. Mavis continued to eat her lunch and looked around to see where Earl had slunk off to, but she couldn't see hide nor hair of him.

[Chapter Fourteen[

As soon as Wilbur mentioned Earl's name, Harlan had sighed on the other end of the telephone. It was hard for Harlan to forget the swindler that came into town a year ago and caused so much fuss. He promised Wilbur that he would take care of things in a jiffy. The conversation with Harlan made Wilbur feel much better about things. He wandered back over to Mavis and filled her in. She listened intently and nodded along. She trusted Harlan and knew that if he was on the case, justice would be served swiftly. He had been the one to arrest Earl at Magnolia Manor almost two years ago. She had been certain that Earl would from then on be a memory, but here he was again. The only thing that Mavis struggled with was waiting on other people's timeline. She wanted Earl carted out of Rhinestone as soon as possible, but she knew that things like this would take time.

"Should we follow him and see what he's up to?" Mavis asked Wilbur.

"I thought we agreed that we were going to stay out of things?" Wilbur frowned.

"You're the one who just jumped in and yelled at him," Mavis said with a wry smile.

Wilbur rolled his eyes. "I had to. He's robbing people in plain sight," he explained.

"And I bet there's more funny stuff going on," Mavis added.

"I'm not some private investigator, and neither are you," Wilbur pointed out.

"But how fun would that be!" Mavis chirped. "You could use a little fun in your life, Wilbur!"

"Fun?" Wilbur stared at her.

"Can you imagine!" Mavis continued. "We could be like those people on television who go around and solve crimes!"

"No thanks," Wilbur shook his head. Trailing after people like Earl day in and day out did not sound remotely fun.

Mavis started to pout. "I think I'd be great on my own television show!"

"We are not going to follow him around," Wilbur told her. "I mean it. We're not investigators. I know you. With your luck, you'd end up in some sort of hairbrained scheme again. We're not doing it."

"Now you're just being ugly," Mavis frowned.

"I mean it. Let Harlan handle it," Wilbur continued.

"Okay," Mavis said.

There was something in the innocent way that she agreed with him that unnerved him greatly. "What do you mean, okay?" he asked.

"Okay. What else is that supposed to mean?" Mavis smiled.

"Okay," Wilbur mumbled. For some reason he couldn't quite explain, he was more worried now than ever before. Mavis had never been one to listen to anyone else, especially when she set her mind to something. It had often gotten her into trouble, and Wilbur was usually the one who had to fix her ventures. He couldn't help but think of the broken joist at the Manor last year or the aquarium fiasco or the time she signed him up for a recreational volleyball league for senior citizens. He had been the best player on the team once Patsy had fallen and broken her hip. She couldn't believe that he refused to sign up for the next season, but he held his ground on that one.

"Go get yourself something to eat. I'm going to pick up something for Opal and Ms. Maude," Mavis said.

"You're not going to do anything foolish, are you?" Wilbur asked.

Mavis smiled at him. "Wilbur, I would never do anything foolish!" She scampered off before he could stop her.

"Here we go again," he sighed to himself. He felt his stomach growl and decided to get a barbeque sandwich from the nearby food truck before he had to find Mavis and deal with whatever drama she was about to get them all into. He knew he needed something fairly quick to eat if he was going to keep up with her shenanigans.

Mavis, true to her word to Wilbur, had set off toward the line at the taco truck. The mozzarella bites had been good, but she needed something with a little more substance to finish off the meal. Wilbur watched her get in line as he stood in his own line not far away. He lost track of her as her line moved much faster than his. The afternoon sun bore down on him, and he looked around for a table in some shade to cool off. As soon as he got his order, he grabbed a bottle of water and walked over to the empty lot of picnic tables in the shade to relax. He hadn't sat down for two minutes when he heard it.

Wilbur would know that snarl anywhere. Very few things got Mavis' dander up, but he knew instantly it had to involve Earl. He had just sat down to eat his lunch. She had only been gone for fifteen minutes before he heard her and saw a rush of color rush past him.

"I swear!" Mavis snapped as she flew by him. "He's like a durn cockroach that just won't give it up!" She looked around and saw the only way to escape him. At the end of the lane was a haunted house with spooky noises emitting from the entrance. She knew that Earl was terrified of anything remotely haunted and hoped that that fear extended to cheap carnival attractions. She made a beeline for the building that had flashing lights and a sound machine that played rattling chains and werewolf howls in between screeches that sounded worse than a broken record.

"Suga! Don't go in dere! Deys spooks and haunts all in dere!" Earl fretted. He pushed past Maude and Opal who had appeared out of nowhere. Wilbur wasn't sure who was watching their booth, but he didn't have time to ask them as he watched Earl running like a maniac after Mavis.

"Did he say his aunt was in there?" Opal asked loudly.

"No, he said haunt," Maude replied. "The only scary thing in there is the moldy costumes that haven't been washed in God knows when."

"Mavis!" Earl cried out, but she ducked into the haunted house and disappeared quickly.

Wilbur was sure that Earl would be too afraid to follow her, but Earl cut the line and chased after Mavis down the dark hallway that marked the entrance. Wilbur had no desire to follow either of them. He knew that Mavis could hold her own in some place like that, especially with Earl afraid of his own shadow. He looked at his watch and made a mental note to give them ten to fifteen minutes before he would start worrying. He swallowed the last few bites of his sandwich and turned to Maude and Opal who had found a nearby bench where they continued their squabbling.

"Did y'all tell me one time that y'all ran a haunted house once?" Wilbur asked them.

Opal nodded and smiled widely. "Sure did!"

"It was awful," Maude added.

"No!" Opal shook her head. "You were awful. Didn't scare a single child. Just yourself!"

Wilbur laughed along with Opal and waited to hear the full story. He knew it had to be a good one to get Opal this tickled.

"She put on the costume backwards and got stuck," Opal began.

"Because you wouldn't help me!" Maude interjected. "This big ol' flour sack looking thing that didn't have a zipper or the right buttons. I don't know where she found it!"

"Made it myself," Opal said proudly.

"That explains it!" Maude sighed. "My head got stuck and I couldn't see in the dark."

"I may have forgotten to put eye holes in it," Opal winked at Wilbur.

"Opal, I swear!" Maude snapped. Even though the haunted house for a local charity had been over forty years ago, Maude had still not forgiven Opal for the pure bedlam that occurred that weekend.

Wilbur needed to change the subject quickly before Maude stormed off. "Um, who is watching your booth while we're all out here?" he asked.

"Nobody," Opal shrugged. "Maude had wandered off to look at some of those birdhouses that a man a few booths down had made, and I didn't have anyone lined up, so I put up a sign saying we'd be back by three."

Maude checked her watch and remarked that they had plenty of time. Wilbur couldn't help but smile at them. It must be nice to be that old and confident where you could do anything you wanted. "Then we saw that bird looking man and decided to follow him. You know, we could have a show where we follow criminals on the loose. I'll carry the gun though!" Maude said.

Wilbur shook his head and sighed. The last thing Maude needed was a loaded weapon. What was it about the women in this group who had a deep desire to be on television?

"Wilbur, I need a favor," Opal said.

"What's that?" he asked. Knowing Opal, it could be anything.

"I still have those goldfish in the cooler," she reminded him.

He had forgotten completely about the prized goldfish that Opal had won. "How are they doing?" he asked.

"They're fine as wine," she shrugged. "At least they were when I fed them this morning."

He knew better than to ask what she had fed them. Some things were better left unsaid. "What exactly do you want to do with them?"

"I think Clive is lonely," Opal frowned. "He could use some friends."

"It's called enrichment," Maude interrupted to explain. "I saw a show about zoos and the way they offer enrichment to the animals. Keeps them young and feisty, or something like that."

Enrichment with young and feisty carnival fish. That's exactly what Clive needed. If Wilbur had to guess, Clive was probably about sixty pounds at least. He was the biggest catfish Wilbur had ever seen, even before Mavis had nursed him back to health after Wilbur had caught him one afternoon. He knew that Clive would swallow those goldfish whole in a heartbeat, but there was no use arguing with Opal about it. He nodded along as they trailed down a new path about what a cross between a zebra and a giraffe might be. Opal argued that it was impossible, but Maude was certain that she had seen an episode about it on one of her late-night television shows.

"I told you to stop watching cable," Opal said. "It rots your brain."

"Then what's your excuse? You don't even have a tv!" Maude countered.

"That's why my mind is still sharp as a tack," Opal said.

Wilbur listened to the two ladies bicker while he continued to scan the area for any sign of Mavis. Hopefully, she had lost Earl somewhere in the haunted house.

Maude saw him looking in that direction. "Don't guess we'll be lucky enough for a ghost to get him."

"Probably not," Wilbur said.

"Don't worry," Opal said. "We'll be rid of him soon enough."

Maude and Wilbur both looked over at Opal before meeting each other's eyes. They never really knew what Opal had up her sleeve. Wilbur wondered if the doll from this morning had anything to do with it, but again, he knew better than to ask. He stood up and walked towards the haunted house exit to ask a worker to maybe check on them inside. Before he could ask the attendant, he heard Mavis holler.

"Earl! Will you get off of me!" Mavis yelled as she tumbled out of the carnival exit.

"What in the world!" Maude yelled.

"He's attacking her!" Wilbur said. He jumped over the small fence that separated the public from the attraction and leaned down to pull Earl off of Mavis, but they were both caught up in the fake wispy spider web. Somehow, they had knocked over the smoke machine from the wall in their fuss.

"Don't worry! I've got my bat!" Opal said as she followed the other two.

"Suga bear. That thing almost ate you!" Earl shouted. He was half wrapped in a black curtain so that only his legs appeared flailing around in midair. Mavis was partially buried underneath him. She was trying to push him off to no avail. They seemed to be fighting against one another.

"Get off of me, you ol' fool!" Mavis said.

"But suga!" Earl yelled back. "I gots to save you!"

"Will you get off of her!" Wilbur grabbed the curtain and yanked it off of Earl's head.

"He said get off of Mavis!" Opal shouted. She raised the bat over her head and swung wildly. Wilbur ducked but wasn't quite fast enough for Opal. He fell on top of Earl, who was now flinging for dear life with the stained heavy curtain.

"Hit him again, Wilbur!" Maude called out. "Whack him good, Opal!" She was thankful that Opal had insisted on bringing her new bat with her.

"Stop Ms. Opal!" Wilbur yelled. He reached up and grabbed the end of the bat before Opal could swing again and seriously injure him. He tossed the bat as far as he could so that she couldn't easily retrieve it and finish him off.

"Hey now!" Maude snapped. She grabbed Opal's hand and they toddled away to retrieve the bat before anyone else could snatch it up.

"Suga, dey's attackin' us! Da ghosts after us!" Earl yelled.

"Shut up!" Wilbur snapped. He grabbed Earl by the nape of his scrawny neck and set him down on his feet before reaching down to help unwrap Mavis from the fake decor and curtain.

"If you don't get off of me!" Mavis yelled. She was still flailing and trying her best to hit Earl anywhere she could. She didn't realize that Wilbur was now trying to help her up, and she punched him on the side of the face. Mavis knew how to pack a punch. Wilbur keeled over and held his face

"Oops! Sorry, Wilbur!" Mavis flinched.

Wilbur shook his head. He had been punched in the face and hit with a bat all within thirty seconds of each other. For someone who liked the peaceful life, this day had gone drastically off course. His eye was already swelling, and he was still seeing stars.

"Wilbur, what are you doing on the floor?" Maude asked. She held Opal's bat in her hand and looked down at him. "Let me handle this." She turned towards Earl who was making kissy faces at Mavis. "You look here, you scrawny looking vulture! You better not lay another hand on Mavis or Wilbur, or you'll be dealing with me! You understand me!" Maude waved the bat menacingly.

"I ain't never touched that ol' handyman. He's the one that attacked me!" Earl said.

Technically, Earl was correct. He hadn't been the one to hit Wilbur, but Wilbur was not in the mood to discuss technicalities at the moment. He got to his feet as quickly as he could. "Get on out of here, Earl."

"Let's go," Maude commanded. She turned towards Opal and whispered something so only she could hear.

"Don't be telling me what to do!" Earl yelled with a bit of gusto. "And don't let those crazy ol' bats loose either or I'll fix 'em up good."

"Is that a threat?" Mavis snapped. She had had enough of Earl personally, but it was another thing to threaten her family directly.

"Get out of here, Earl," Wilbur said. "For your own safety."

Maude was not to be outdone. She had pushed past Wilbur and Mavis to confront Earl once again, but Wilbur grabbed her before she could do anything. "Let's go, Ms. Maude."

Earl slid closer to them and reached out slyly for Maude's purse.

"Don't you dare!" Wilbur yelled. He slapped at Earl's outstretched hand and leaned on Mavis who helped support him.

"I's just sayin' bye," Earl shrugged. He took one last look at Mavis and blew her a kiss. The hair on the back of Wilbur's neck stiffened and he sighed deeply. He only had one good eye to see out of, but he knew this adventure with Earl wasn't over just yet.

[Chapter Fifteen]

Wilbur's eye was swollen shut by the time they made it back to Opal's booth. Mavis found him some ice from one of the nearby vendors and wrapped the ice in one of Opal's colorful scarves. He held it to his face and grimaced in pain. Mavis apologized again and remarked that she really could've hurt him if she had used her full force. Wilbur was lucky to have made it out of the melee without any broken bones.

"That man should be ashamed of himself acting that way!" Opal sighed. She muttered something about her bat that was now resting by her feet behind the counter. She pulled on her wig and cloak and settled into her chair. She tossed the sign behind her, narrowly missing Wilbur's head, and said she was ready for customers.

Mavis kept control of the line that had formed while Maude sat down next to Wilbur. "Don't worry about him no more. I've got a plan," Maude explained.

Her words did very little to calm Wilbur's mood. "What do you mean?" he asked hesitantly.

"I said don't worry about it," Maude repeated. She eyed Wilbur warily and shook her head.

"You're already maimed. The less you know the better."

Wilbur groaned and held the ice pack closer to his injured eye. He was going to end up in the funny farm before too long when it came to the three women in his life. He had a sneaking suspicion that Mavis was in on the plan as well, but he was in too much pain to go down that rabbit trail.

"You want me to run you over to the doctor?" Maude asked.

"No ma'am," Wilbur answered. "This ice should take the sting out of it soon enough."

"I can walk over yonder and get you one of those steaks to slap on it. Raw meat will draw that swelling right on out," she replied. "Nothing like a good ribeye right on that bruise."

"No, no, I'm fine," Wilbur stammered. He did not want to put any kind of raw meat on his face. Especially not anything Maude scrounged up at the county fair.

"Come to think of it, I bet Opal has some plant powdery stuff she can put on it later," Maude continued.

"I do," Opal replied over her shoulder.

Wilbur felt better about using one of Opal's salves. At least he was pretty confident that it wouldn't have any raw meat juice in it.

The afternoon passed quickly as Opal's fortune telling booth once again became the most popular attraction. Wilbur only got up from his chair to put the mounds of money in the portable safe every time the donation jar began to overflow. When the line died down early on in the evening, Opal pulled her wig off and said that she was too tired to continue.

"Good. I'm hungry," Maude said. "Plus, we got to go to Nadine's."

Mavis and Wilbur turned to look at Maude. "Ms. Nadine?" Mavis asked.

Maude nodded. "We're going to take her dinner. She loves the fair and can't make it this year." She was very matter of fact and neither Mavis nor Wilbur knew what to say in response.

"That's very sweet of you," Mavis said finally. "Opal, what are you doing?"

Opal dug around and found the sign she had made earlier. She crossed out the previous message and wrote a new one thanking everyone for their donations. Mavis walked around to the front of the booth and read the sign. "You're retiring?" she gasped. "But you're so popular!"

"You have to always leave them wanting more," Opal nodded. She began to pack up her costumes and arranged everything neatly in her ancient trunk. Her wigs were placed carefully into their bags, and she folded the long cloaks into compact squares.

"Are you sure?" Mavis asked.

"I'm always sure," Opal smiled. She walked over to the man with the booth next to them and chatted for a few minutes while Maude, Mavis, and Wilbur finished packing. She returned with an armful of wooden birdhouses and set them down in the wagon. "Morris said he'd be happy to move some of his products over here after we clear out. He was happy as a lark! Gave us these to say thanks." She gestured to the birdhouses and shrugged. "We about ready to head out?"

Wilbur nodded and reached for the wagon's handle. "I'll pull the wagon," Mavis said. "Hey, maybe we could get you a pirate eye patch!"

"I've got one at home you can borrow," Maude said quickly.

"I'm good, but thanks," Wilbur grimaced. He picked up the heavy safe and followed Mavis to the parking lot. Maude and Opal drug the remainder of Opal's things behind them. Wilbur loaded everything into Mavis' trunk and held the door for Opal and Maude, but they shook their heads. "We've got to get food for Nadine," Maude reminded him.

Wilbur shut the door and dutifully followed Maude, Opal, and Mavis back towards the vendors. Wilbur sat down on the bench in front of the pizza truck while Maude and Opal scurried between the different trucks to get a nice variety. Mavis sat down next to Wilbur and picked at the funnel cake she had just bought. "Want some?" she offered him.

He shook his head and asked if that was her supper. "No," she laughed. "How about after I drop them off, I'll make something at the Manor. They can come by after Nadine's and we can eat a late supper and just relax after this eventful day."

"Eventful?" Wilbur asked. "I'll say!"

As soon as Maude and Opal were satisfied with their haul, they all walked back towards the parking lot. Opal and Maude agreed to have a late dinner at the Manor after their visit with Nadine. They didn't think it would be wise to stay at

Nadine's for too long so she could eat her food in peace and continue to get better.

Once they were all situated in the car, Mavis pulled out of the field and got on the highway towards Rhinestone.

"What all are you bringing her?" Wilbur asked.

"A slice of pizza and a funnel cake," Maude said.

"And a pecan pie and ear of corn," Opal added.

"That sounds nice," Wilbur said. "I'm sure she'll like that. I hope you all have a nice visit."

"Yep," Maude nodded. She had gone a bit pale at the mention of Nadine.

"You ok?" Mavis asked from the driver's seat.

"I'm good," Maude nodded, but it was clear that she wasn't.

"Are you worried about Ms. Nadine?" Mavis asked.

In the passenger seat, Maude shook her head. "She'll be fine," she said quietly.

Wilbur looked at Opal who was seated next to him in the middle row. She shook her head slightly and avoided his stare. Wilbur's heart sank. The rest of the ride was silent as sadness hung in the air. Wilbur helped Maude and Opal out of the car and into Maude's car. He barely stepped out of the way as Maude threw her car in reverse and backed out of the driveway. Nadine lived across the street, but Maude insisted on driving so they could head to the Manor when their visit was over.

Wilbur climbed into Mavis' car and buckled his seatbelt. "She's sure worried about Ms.

Nadine," he told Mavis as she backed out of the driveway a bit more carefully than Maude had.

"Ms. Nadine isn't doing well," Mavis admitted. "I meant to tell you that I ran into Michael from church yesterday. You know he's dating Ms. Nadine's niece, and, well Wilbur, the news isn't good."

"I'm sorry to hear that," Wilbur nodded. "She's always been a real sweet lady."

Mavis nodded in agreement. It was true. Nadine had always been lovely to the both of them from the time they were children. It was hard to see the people they cared about age in front of them.

"Do you think Maude knows?" he asked.

"I think so," Mavis nodded. She pulled into her usual spot at the Manor in front of the signature magnolia tree and sighed. "She heard what Michael said. She acted like she wasn't eavesdropping, but I could tell she heard. He said the cancer was back and it's spread all over. They aren't giving her long at all."

"I really hate to hear that," Wilbur said. "Is she home or are they having to keep her at the hospital?"

"She's home, or at least she was yesterday, according to Michael. They don't know for how long though. I just didn't have the heart to tell Maude and Opal that Nadine can't eat any of that food they're bringing her. Michael told me after Maude walked away that she can hardly swallow. They found a mass in her esophagus and another in her lung. I just don't understand it all, Wilbur. Cancer is such a terrible disease," Mavis said tearfully.

Wilbur handed Mavis her purse and followed her up the front porch steps to the Manor. It was already dark outside, and he hadn't bothered to ask Mavis if they should have stopped by a grocery store on their way in. "What did you have in mind to cook?" he asked.

"I've got a casserole in the freezer that I can pop in the oven right quick," Mavis said. "And I bought a pumpkin pie yesterday from the high school booth yesterday, too. Just need some whipped cream on top and it'll be perfect."

"That sounds good," Wilbur agreed. He turned on the oven and unwrapped the chicken and rice casserole that Mavis pulled from the freezer and placed it in the oven as Mavis made sweet tea on the stove.

"Can you grab the stack of mail from the hallway?" Mavis asked.

Wilbur nodded and walked to the hallway to the small table besides the front door where Mavis usually kept her purse. There was a small stack of unopened envelopes next other car keys. Something moved out of this corner of his eye, and he turned towards the wall length aquarium where Clive, Mavis' catfish, lived.

"Good Lord, Mavis!" Wilbur howled.

"What?" Mavis squeaked.

"Clive's about to bust out of that tank!" he gasped.

Clive had been larger than normal for quite some time, but it was like he had gained even more weight in the last few weeks since Wilbur had paid much attention to him. "What are you feeding him?"

"He eats what I eat," Mavis shrugged.

"You mean to tell me that you cook for a fish?" Wilbur wheezed.

"Of course not," Mavis said. "I just cook extra for him when I cook for me. It makes perfect sense."

"Perfect sense? When did you start this mess?" Wilbur asked.

"I don't know, but he's happy thank you very much!" Mavis said. "He was looking tired and wasn't swimming around like he normally does. I think he's bored."

"He's a wild animal, Mavis. He should be working on catching his own food, not eating filet mignon!" Wilbur gruffed.

"He prefers macaroni and cheese," Mavis sassed.

"Oh dear God," Wilbur sighed. "We need to get together a plan to release him back into the wild."

"He's too cultured for the wild!" Mavis gasped. "He'd die out in the elements."

"He's bigger than anything out there in the pond," Wilbur countered.

"An alligator or bigger fish could hurt him. He doesn't know he's a fish," Mavis shook her head.

"He's near about as big as my jon boat," Wilbur said flatly.

Mavis shook her head and refused to talk about it any longer. Clive was her most favorite pet of all time. She would make sure that he got an extra helping of chicken and rice casserole and a slice of pumpkin pie tonight. She changed the subject back to Maude and Opal. "Do you think we ought to call and check on Maude and Opal? The casserole will be ready soon."

"I think they're having a nice time visiting," Wilbur said. "If it's ready before they get here, we can go ahead and eat and just keep it warm for them."

Mavs agreed. When the timer on the oven went off, she put on her oven mitts and pulled the casserole dish out of the oven with ease. She doled them each out a heaping portion into a bowl and they dug in. They were halfway through their slice of pumpkin pie for dessert when Maude and Opal walked through the front door.

"How was your visit?" Wilbur asked. He stood up and got them each a bowl of casserole and a glass of sweet tea.

"Thank you, Wilbur," Opal said. She drank some iced tea and shook her head. "It's pretty bad with Nadine."

Mavis and Wilbur looked instinctively at Maude who nodded. "She fell asleep when we were leaving. She looks really sick."

"Oh no," Wilbur lamented. "I'm sorry. I hope they can keep her comfortable. I know she was glad to see you both."

Maude nodded and picked at her casserole. "Oh, Wilbur, can you get that cooler from my car? Those fish are in it, and I think it's too heavy for us to get up the steps."

"Yes ma'am," Wilbur said. He took Maude's car keys and walked outside to her car to retrieve the cooler. It was indeed heavy. He could hear water sloshing around as he carried it up the steps.

Opal met him at the front door and held it open for him. He set it down on the floor in front of the aquarium and peeked inside. He hoped that they were still alive inside. Several fish were swimming around the cool water, but a few others had already begun to float. "You want me to dump them in the tank? The tank with Clive?" Wilbur clarified.

"Yes," Opal nodded. "For his richness or whatever it was that Maude said. He won't be bored with new friends. When you're done, I brought some salve with me for your eye."

Wilbur looked at her like she was crazy, and maybe she was, but he did as he was told. Thankfully, Opal had walked back to the kitchen to finish her supper before Clive began to swallow every last fish, both alive and dead, whole.

Wilbur took the now empty cooler back to the porch so it could dry out. He washed his hands in the half bathroom and returned to the kitchen where the three women were speaking in hushed whispers.

"Everything ok?" he asked.

"We were just discussing your eye," Mavis said a little too quickly.

Opal rummaged through her purse and found a small tin jar. She handed it to Wilbur and instructed him on how to use its contents. "Smear a thin layer of the salve onto your bruise. Careful not to get it in your eye though. That'll burn like the devil if you do."

Wilbur opened the small jar and almost gagged at the smell. "What is this?" he asked.

"I make it myself from natural herbs," Opal explained.

"What's that awful smell?" Maude coughed.

"The smell of healing. Now go put some on it before it's too late," Opal ordered.

[Chapter Sixteen]

Wilbur could still hear them talking from the downstairs bathroom. None of them knew how to properly whisper.

He looked in the mirror and sighed. His eye was a sickly shade of purple. Mavis had connected at the perfect angle. If she had hit Earl like she intended, he would probably have sailed backwards a few feet. It was probably for the best that she missed him after all. Mavis didn't need her own criminal record.

Wilbur washed his hands and opened the small jar. It was a pale yellow with bits of crushed up green and brown bits. He dabbed the foul-smelling salve onto his bruised eye and felt immediate relief. Whatever it was would surely work, but he'd also be able to ward off every animal and human in the county at the same time. He washed his hands again and stood outside the kitchen as the three women chatted. He wasn't trying to eavesdrop, but they had clearly been trying to get rid of him so that they could hatch their plan.

"I'm gonna rope him like a calf," Maude boasted. "The trick is catching them off guard and snatching them up by their feet. I know just how to do it! Won't be my first rodeo!"

"You've never been in a rodeo," Opal corrected.

"It's a figure of speech," Maude replied. She stuck out her tongue at Opal who then flung a spoonful of rice onto her.

"Y'all quit!" Mavis chastised. "We've got to be serious about this!"

"I am serious," Maude said. "My daddy used to rope cows and I watched him enough. And if he carries on like he did today, Opal's got her bat. It's foolproof."

"Then you've never met a fool quite like Earl," Mavis sighed. "No, we've got to trap him again. If I could only figure out how he got back here in the first place!"

"It's going to be fine," Opal said. "Trust me. He'll get what's coming to him."

"Is that you or Madame Opalina speaking?" Mavis smiled.

"We are one and the same," Opal shrugged. She finished her slice of pie and took another sip of her iced tea. "You can come back in now, Wilbur."

Wilbur felt his cheeks flush as he stepped inside the kitchen. "How do you always do that?" he chuckled.

Opal winked and whispered, "I could smell you from a mile away. You know, you might want to only use that at night away from people."

"Good plan," he nodded. "Anyway, let me get these dishes started and y'all go on home if y'all want. I know it's late."

"I rarely sleep anymore," Opal mused. She stretched her arms over her head and walked towards the hallway.

"Me either," Maude said.

Opal shot her a look and shook her head. "You sleep all the time. You're always nodding off."

"That's because you're boring," Maude replied. "Hey, look at Clive go!"

They all peered around the corner and watched as Clive swam to the top of the tank and blew bubbles.

"Didn't you put those goldfish in there, Wilbur?" Maude asked.

"Yes ma'am," Wilbur nodded.

"Reckon he ate them," Maude suggested.

Wilbur looked at Mavis who was trying to hide a smile. There had never been any doubt that Clive wouldn't go after the fish right away.

"Guess that's why they call it enrichment," Maude continued.

"He's a big fella," Opal said. "Maybe a little too big."

"I think it's time he moves back out to the pond," Wilbur agreed.

"He's just a baby!" Mavis squealed.

"Maybe a baby elephant," Maude said. "You've had him for years. He needs to be with his own kind."

"He's gonna eat his own kind," Wilbur muttered. "But I think it's time. You think about it, Mavis, and maybe we can get him moved before it gets too cold outside. He can get settled in and um, make new friends before the winter."

Mavis was unsure. "But what if the other fish are mean to him? Do you really think he'll fit in and make new friends?"

"I don't think there's much chance of the other fish picking on him," Wilbur assured her.

"But he's my pet," Mavis sighed.

"You can get a new pet," Wilbur reminded her. "There's all kinds of animals that need good homes. We can always go down to the shelter and find you a nice puppy or a kitten."

"I'll think about it," Mavis finally agreed.

"That's all I'm asking," Wilbur said.

He stepped back into the kitchen and began cleaning up after dinner. He hoped to God that Maude didn't bring her roping gear to the fair. That was the last thing he needed to worry about. He also made a mental note to conveniently misplace Opal's bat until the fair was over. He couldn't afford anymore bumps and bruises for that matter. Between Opal and Mavis, he was getting walloped pretty good already.

When the kitchen was clean, he walked over to the living room and found the three ladies looking over the wooden bird houses that Opal had brought over. They instantly reminded him of the ones that he and Jameson used to build for Ruby. Those precious birdhouses were still scattered across the grounds of the Manor all these years later. He loved walking in the woods and seeing sweet little reminders of Jameson and Ruby long after they've been gone.

He sat down on the couch next to Opal and they began to discuss the plans for the next day.

"Since you aren't setting up a booth, we don't have to go to the fair tomorrow," Wilbur said.

"Yes, we do!" Mavis said. "It only comes once a year! It'll be a whole year before the fair comes back!"

"And it'll be too soon," Wilbur said as he rubbed his eye.

"Opal and I want to ride those contraptions tomorrow. Not all of them," Maude explained. "I saw that car ride and I'm going to tear some up. You can crash into people, and they won't give you a ticket for it!"

"I'm going to sit that one out," Opal said.

"Me, too," Wilbur nodded. "And the haunted house."

Mavis winced and smiled apologetically at Wilbur. "Your eye is looking much better!" she remarked.

"Just a thin layer before bed every night for the next day or so and you'll be back to normal," Opal confirmed.

"Well, as normal as you've ever been," remarked Mavis. Wilbur rolled his eyes at her, and she giggled.

"Well, I'm going to head out since it's been such a busy day. Y'all sure you're ok to drive this late?" Wilbur asked.

"Fine as wine," Maude said. She turned to Opal and whispered loudly, "the youngins never could hang with us."

"Never will either," Opal agreed. "Kinda sad actually."

"Alright, y'all be safe and I'll see y'all tomorrow. Want to meet here or should Mavis or I pick y'all up?" he inquired.

"I'm going to pick them up around one. Want me to come get you?" Mavis asked.

"Then I'll be here a little after noon," Wilbur answered. "I've got some errands to run. I'll put that money from the fair in your account, Opal. Then you can decide what to do with it. Then I need to look at those beams out in the barn. Then we can all ride over to Junction together. Apparently, I need to keep my eyes on y'all."

"More like eye," Maude laughed heartily.

Wilbur chuckled with them and then walked outside to his truck. He knew they were planning something, but he also knew that if they didn't want to tell him, he'd have quite the time trying to get it out of them. He'd have to be extra vigilant.

When his alarm went off the next morning, he awoke with a start. The swelling in his eye had come down significantly. He got ready and ate a quick breakfast and headed into town. There wasn't much traffic for a Thursday, but he reckoned most people were already at the fair. All of the towns pretty much shut down when it came to the fair. He decided to stop by the Starlight Café but saw that there was a sign in the window saying it would be closed for the rest of the week for minor repairs and updates.

"Good for them," Wilbur said out loud to nobody in particular.

He drove down the street to the bank and deposited the large sum of money into Opal's account. She had raised over two thousand dollars during her time as Madame Opalina. He put the deposit slip in his wallet and drove over to the hardware store and picked up his new drill that he had ordered online and a few scraps of lumber. There was a faulty beam in Jameson's old barn that was starting to split. Since he had a bit of time before going to the fair with Mavis, Maude, and Opal, he decided to go ahead and take care of it before it fell completely. He loaded the new tools and wood into his truck and drove out to the Manor much earlier than expected. Mavis' car wasn't in its spot, so he headed straight for the barn and got to work. After an hour in the dusty barn, he hopped off the ladder and admired his work. Keeping up Jameson's barn had been a labor of love over the years. He had spent a great deal of his teenage years working in the barn and attached wood shop with Jameson when he was younger. It had been ages since he had built anything, and he yearned to get back at it once things died down with the fair. Seeing those birdhouses, the man from the fair made had relit the spark in his heart. He loved being creative and looked forward to making more time for that.

He put up the tools and stored the remaining wood pieces in the loft before walking back to his truck. He had just enough time to shower back at his house before he needed to come back to the Manor and meet Mavis. She still wasn't home, so he drove down the dirt road through the woods to his custom-built log cabin. It was nestled underneath the pine trees that he had used to build it. He loved his home and felt so much at peace out there in the woods that he had spent so much of his youth exploring.

After a quick shower, he made a sandwich and ate it on the way back to the Manor. He pulled up at the same time as Mavis. She opened her car door and he saw that she had two bags of what he knew to be her favorite fish tacos.

"Have you eaten lunch?" she asked.

He held up the last bite of his sandwich and popped it into his mouth. "Well, I brought you some just in case," she shrugged. "Nobody makes tacos as good as these!"

They walked inside the Manor and sat down at the kitchen table. Wilbur ate a taco and had to agree that they were the best. After Mavis put away four fish tacos, she wiped her mouth with her napkin and sighed happily. "I ate light so I could get me one of those funnel cakes. I just can't say no to them!"

"You know you can make them at home, right? I know there's bound to be a cookbook around here with a recipe for fried dough in it," Wilbur said.

"I've tried and it's just not the same," Mavis shook her head. "There's something about eating it on a paper plate with all that powdered sugar at the fair." She unwrapped the final taco and dumped it into the tank. Clive gobbled it up as soon as it touched the water. "Let me change my shirt and we can go get Maude and Opal. I told Mona and Harry we'd be there, too. I think they're going to meet us later this afternoon!"

"Speaking of them, I drove by the Starlight on the way here. There's a sign in the window that says it's closed for repairs and updates. I wonder what all the new owners are going to do to it?" Wilbur said.

"Ooh, I wonder!" Mavis replied. "We'll have to check it out once they open back up." She disappeared upstairs and came back a few minutes later wearing jeans and a bright purple t-shirt. She threw a light sweater over her arm and grabbed the keys and her purse. "Ready?" she asked Wilbur.

He nodded and locked the front door behind him. He climbed into the passenger seat, and they listened to the radio on the short drive over to Maude's. They passed Nadine's house and noticed her sitting in a rocking chair on the porch with a group of people. She had a blanket over her lap and looked eerily thin. "She doesn't look well at all," Mavis frowned. They both waved and pulled into Maude's driveway across the street. "I wish there was something we could do."

"We'll ask Maude if there's a signup sheet for meals or something. If there's anything she needs, we can take care of it," Wilbur nodded.

Maude and Opal hurried down the front steps to the car as soon as Mavis pulled in. Maude frowned at Wilbur in the front seat, but she held her tongue. She climbed into the middle row next to Opal and mumbled something about needing more leg room, even though there was more than enough room in Mavis' vehicle. By the time that they pulled into the familiar field parking lot, Wilbur and Mavis had been caught up on all the local gossip.

"Where did you hear about all these things?" Mavis asked.

"We're old," Maude shrugged. "People don't think we're listening, but we are. Plus, we're bored. I don't need to watch soap operas. There's plenty of drama in real life."

"I don't have any drama," Opal said.

"You don't call taking a bat after a strange man drama?" Wilbur laughed.

"That's not the first person she's taken a bat to," Maude said.

"It's just another day for Opal," Mavis laughed. "Anyway, where to first?"

"To that car ride you were telling us about!" Maude said. She linked her arm through Mavis' arm, and they walked off in search of the bumper cars.

Wilbur wasn't sure that the bumper cars were the safest fit for Maude who was in her eighties, but she had her heart set on it. He should probably be more worried for the people she rammed. She had always been a pretty reckless driver in real life.

"I guess that leaves us," Opal said cheerfully. She linked her arm through Wilbur's, and they followed Maude and Mavis at a slower pace.

"How's Ms. Nadine really?" Wilbur asked. He made sure that Maude was too far ahead of them to hear.

"They told us last night that she was going to hospice Friday morning. She couldn't eat any of the food that we brought her, but I could tell that it made her happy that we were there. Even Maude," Opal admitted.

"Ms. Maude's not taking it well, is she?" Wilbur asked.

Opal shook her head. "No," she said. "It isn't easy seeing your friends suffer. I think it brings up bad memories of Ruby for her. For us both."

Wilbur understood completely.

"We said our goodbyes last night. I think we all know it'll be the last time we're together. I wish I had written down all the crazy things those two had done over the years," Opal smiled.

"I've heard quite a few that were doozies," Wilbur chuckled.

Opal patted his hand. They had finally reached the entrance to the bumper cars. They leaned against the railing and watched as the ride attendant helped strap Maude into her car. Mavis settled into the one next to her and gripped the wheel tightly.

"Take it easy on them," Wilbur called out playfully.

Maude shook her head and stepped on the gas pedal as soon as the music began to play over the loudspeakers. She rammed everyone who came close to her, including Mavis who tried her best to steer clear of her.

"She's going to feel that one in the morning," Wilbur winced as Maude rammed the back of Mavis' car for the third or fourth time.

"And that's exactly why I'm on this side of the fence," Opal nodded.

[Chapter Seventeen]

"They're going to outlive us both," Mavis whispered to Wilbur as she walked through the exit of the bumper car ride. The bumper cars experience wasn't as much fun with Maude at the wheel next to her.

Maude didn't seem any worse for the wear as she bounded off the ride. She wanted to ride it again, but Mavis refused. "Fine," Maude huffed. She looked at her watch and gasped, "the cakewalk starts in five minutes! We have to hurry!" Without another word, she turned and scuttled off towards one of the buildings on the other side of the midway. Mavis, Opal, and Wilbur hurried off behind her.

"Always thinking about food," Opal shook her head.

"She must have a hidden motor or something!" Mavis breathed heavily. "There are times where she just slap wears me out!"

By the time they caught up to her, Maude was already in line. Mavis, Opal, and Wilbur decided to forgo the walk and sat down in some empty chairs near the table that was piled high with cakes, pies, platters of brownies, and plates of cookies. It took a few rounds, but Maude's number was finally called. She made a beeline for the table and chose the butternut cake that she had been eyeing. She carried it around proudly and refused to set it down as they walked around the various merchant booths. She told Wilbur that it was such a beautiful cake that someone might try and steal it. She couldn't wait to get home and eat it later.

Wilbur found a booth selling homemade jams that offered free samples. He and Maude tasted the different jellies and jams and settled on a few different jars while Mavis browsed the racks of purses across the aisle. Opal found a stand selling honey. They had several different types of honey that she didn't have in her garden. She was particularly fond of the orange blossom samples which both differed greatly in taste from the blueberry and wildflower batches she normally got from her hives. She bought two jars and grabbed a few brochures for bee keeping supplies.

After they had all bought a few different trinkets, Wilbur went and put their purchases in the car. Maude had still not relinquished hold of the cake, so he crammed the shopping bags into the trunk and walked back towards the entrance. He ran into Mona and Harry along the way. "I was just about to call y'all!" Mona exclaimed.

They found Mavis, Opal, and Maude watching people try their luck at riding the mechanical bull. The padded flooring around the base of the bucking machine was scuffed and looked like it had been well worn. They watched numerous drunk college aged kids give it try and fail miserably.

"You care to give it a go?" Wilbur asked Harry.

"Not a chance," Harry grinned. "I've had too much of the real thing to hop up there."

"Who in their right mind would do something like that?" Mavis asked out loud.

"I could do it," Opal said. She watched as the woman flew off the mechanical bull and landed on her back.

"That's so dangerous!" Mavis squealed. "Opal! No!"

"Opal, where are you going?" Maude called to her.

Opal had walked over to the man by the gate and handed him cash. He looked her up and down and finally nodded and opened the gate to let her in. The mechanical bull was too tall for her to climb onto, so he lifted her easily onto it and showed her where to put her hands.

"She's going to hurt herself," Mavis fretted.

"Have you ever tried to tell Opal not to do something?" Maude asked. "Let me tell you, it does no good."

"Seems to be a trend," Wilbur whispered to Mavis.

"But she's going to break a hip or something," Mavis said.

"She's been in worse spots than this before," Maude countered. "There was that one time with the alligator in south Florida when, well, never mind."

Wilbur shook his head and looked over at Mavis. "I can't watch," Mavis said. She covered her eyes and peered through the slits of her fingers.

The buzzer sounded and Opal looped her fingers tightly through the rope and held on with all her might. The bull started off slowly rocking back and forth. Opal leaned left and leaned right to steady herself. She hung on as it rose off the ground and rested backwards in an attempt to buck her off. At the very last second, she slid off and landed on her feet like a cat. The timer next to the gate flashed her time in bright red letters.

"Seven seconds?" Maude cheered. "She almost did it!

Opal bowed and walked over towards them as they all clapped and cheered. "That was amazing!" Mavis said.

"You're a real professional!" Harry agreed.

"Are you going to try next?" Mona asked Maude.

"Do I look crazy?" Maude shouted over the noise of the blaring music on the stage behind them.

"Well, um," Mona stuttered.

"Yes," Opal answered Maude's question loudly.

Thankfully, Mavis launched into a new conversation about the band who had taken the stage behind them. "Their new album is hideous," she mouthed. "Let's get out of here."

"Who are they?" Maude yelled.

"You wouldn't know them, Ms. Maude," Wilbur said. "They're trying to bring techno back."

"I don't think that's disco, Wilbur," Opal corrected him.

The group walked further down the path towards the giant clock tower in the center of the

186

complex. "My ears are still ringing," Mona complained. "What should we see next?"

"I heard there was a hypnotizing thingy going on soon," Mavis said.

"Oh! The nightly hypnotist show is the best!" Mona exclaimed. "They choose a few volunteers and, let me tell you, it's hilarious! We saw it a few nights ago, but I'm game to go again." Harry nodded in agreement, and they all decided that it sounded like fun. They stopped for a few snacks along the way and walked towards the outdoor amphitheater where the hypnotist held his show each evening.

"How do they choose the people to come up on stage?" Mavis asked Mona.

Mona pointed to a table to the left of the stage where a small line had formed. "You can sign up right there. Are you wanting to volunteer?"

"God no!" Mavis laughed. "I don't need my secrets spilled all over town. Are you?"

"Never in a million years," Mona said. "But it looks like Ms. Opal is."

"Oh Lordy, here we go again," Mavis said. She tapped Wilbur on the shoulder and pointed out Opal and explained what she was doing.

"She would be highly entertaining," Wilbur smiled.

They found seats a few rows back from the front of the stage and sat down. Opal came over a few minutes later and grinned at them all. The show couldn't start soon enough!

Right on cue, a man wearing all black stepped on stage and spoke into a microphone. He introduced himself as Aaron and bowed as the crowd applauded him. He gestured to the three empty chairs behind him and announced that his assistant, a beautiful dark-haired woman holding a clipboard, had chosen the three volunteers for the night. She stepped closer to the microphone and announced with a booming voice, "Matthew Morgan, Sally Jeffries, and Maude Cooper."

"What?" Maude yelled.

"I thought you signed yourself up?" Mavis gasped at Opal who merely shrugged. "Why would I volunteer to get hypnotized?" Opal asked.

"So, you volunteered me instead?" Maude snapped.

Opal nodded and smiled widely. "I can't be hypnotized, you know that. But I reckon you can. Go on up there."

"No way," Maude said with sudden ferocity. "I ain't gonna do it."

"Maude Cooper?" the woman called out again.

"She's right here!" Opal called out loudly. She grabbed Maude's arm and raised it high in the air.

"I'm gonna kill you one of these days!" Maude howled.

"But not tonight, now go!" Opal cackled. She was tickled pink over the fact that Maude's name had been called. The twenty-dollar bill bribe she had given the assistant had probably not hurt her chances either, but Maude didn't need to know all that.

"Don't let anybody eat my cake," she told Wilbur as she set the cake down on the chair she vacated.

Maude walked to the steps near the stage and climbed them slowly. She could feel every pair of eyes from the crowd on her as she took the empty seat on the far right.

"Welcome!" the hypnotist bellowed. "This is a time of relaxation. Let your mind go at ease on this journey that I will facilitate!"

Maude rolled her eyes and stared daggers at Opal who looked enthralled. Mavis, Mona, Harry, and Wilbur watched with bated breath as the hypnotist walked across the stage explaining what the show was about. He said he could have the participants spill their deepest, darkest secrets or do acrobatics across the stage at his will with just a few simple commands. They all knew that Maude did not believe in hypnotists and thought everyone on the television shows were paid actors, so this was going to be extra interesting.

Aaron had the first volunteer stand up and introduce himself. He was a local chiropractor who was single. The next volunteer was a married woman from Mississippi who was in town for the fair with her family. When it came Maude's turn to introduce herself, she sighed into the microphone and said she had better places to be. Aaron laughed and said that she was right where she needed to be and that he didn't believe in coincidences. She rolled her eyes which seemed to delight him further.

"Alright, we'll start with you, Matthew. Close your eyes and tell us about your most favorite vacation spot. Tell us about a time that you were completely relaxed there," Aaron driveled on.

Matthew closed his eyes tightly and began to talk about the time he took a cruise to Bora Bora and fell asleep in one of the hammocks on the island. Before the crowd knew it, Aaron had Matthew standing up in his chair honking like a goose every time he heard the sound of a bell. At one point Matthew jumped down to the stage and flapped his arms and tried to fly. Every time he heard the sound of a bell ring, he honked louder.

The crowd roared in laughter and clapped their hands. Matthew was released back to his seat on stage, but throughout the rest of the show, any time a random bell would ring, he would jump up in his seat and honk like a feral goose.

Sally was up next. Aaron asked her to close her eyes and talk about her favorite smell. She closed her eyes and explained that as a little girl, she loved the smell of fresh coffee brewing in the morning as her parents got ready for the day. Aaron said that the next time he said anything about coffee, Sally would stand up and pour him a cup. Like clockwork, he asked for a coffee, and Sally popped up in a trance and filled his imaginary coffee cup. The crowd went wild again! Aaron instructed her to fill his assistant's imaginary coffee mug, and Sally did as she was told. Aaron released her back to her seat next to Matthew. That left Maude next.

"Now Maude, it's your turn. Stand on up," Aaron motioned for her to stand up from her chair and walk closer to where he stood.

Maude glared back over at Opal, but begrudgingly made her way over to Aaron who was centerstage with a microphone.

"Isn't this exciting!" Aaron asked.

"No," Maude grumbled.

"Aren't you ready for a little adventure?" Aaron asked.

"I have enough adventure on my own, thank you very much," Maude said firmly.

"So, what would you rather be doing?" Aaron asked.

"I'd rather be at home eating my cake!" Maude said gruffly.

"What cake is that?" Aaron asked.

"This one!" Opal yelled out. She held up the cake before Wilbur could stop her.

Wilbur put his hand to his forehead. "Oh Lord. Maude's going to be mad as a hornet."

"Are you hungry right now?" Aaron asked Maude.

"Little bit. Haven't had my snack yet," Maude said.

"She's always hungry," Opal smirked.

"Why don't you close your eyes and envision how good that cake smells. Think about how good it tastes. How moist and delicious it surely is. It's the best tasting cake in the entire world. The best you've ever had! Wouldn't you like to have a piece of that cake?" Aaron suggested.

"Alright," Maude agreed. She closed her eyes and took a deep breath as Aaron repeated his earlier statements about how good the cake was.

Aaron's assistant was at Opal's side in a second. She picked up the cake and marched it onstage. She sat it down on a small table that she wheeled onto the stage and uncovered the beautifully decorated cake.

"Now, Maude, I want you to have a piece of your cake. The best tasting cake there ever was. Don't stop until I tell you to," Aaron instructed her.

He turned his attention to the audience and began to chat with them for a few minutes, pausing every now and again to check on Maude who was still eating the cake before her. It didn't take her long to work her way through it.

"He's making her eat the whole thing! She's going to be mad as fire when she realizes what she's doing," Mona said.

"And she's going to be mad at me," Wilbur grumbled.

"Why will she be mad at you?" Mavis asked. She frowned and her shoulders slumped. She had been hoping for at least a slice of that cake after supper.

"Because she told me to watch it," Wilbur reminded Mavis. "Now, I've got to go back over to that booth and see if I can sweet talk them into selling me another cake just like it."

"She ate the entire cake in one sitting! That's the power of the mind for you!" Aaron whistled.

Opal looked over at Wilbur and shrugged. "That's nothing new for Maude. She eats whole cakes daily."

"Now, Maude, when you sit back down, I want you to completely forget that you ate that cake. You won't remember having a single bite. You'll still think you're going to have cake tonight for dessert," Aaron explained.

Maude returned to her chair and Aaron waited for the cheers to quiet down before he continued.

"When I snap my fingers, you will forget what happened on stage tonight. When I snap my fingers, Matthew, Sally, and Maude will forget everything. They will have no memories of anything. On the count of three. One, two, three!" He snapped his fingers loudly and Matthew, Sally, and Maude looked around.

"Are we going to get this over with or not?" Maude snapped. She looked around and suddenly noticed the table with the plastic cake container full of crumbs. "What's going on?" She stood up angrily and looked down at Wilbur, Mavis, Opal, Harry, and Mona who were staring back up at her. "Where's my cake?"

"I'm going to have to leave town," Wilbur mumbled.

Opal beamed with laughter and pointed to what was left of the cake on the table.

"Opal Tyler, I'm going to kill you," Maude grumbled. "You let somebody eat my cake."

Opal, Mona, and Harry began to laugh, but Wilbur and Mavis tried to shush them quickly. There was no need to get on Maude's bad side, especially when she was already ticked off. Aaron bowed low and waved as he walked off the stage. The crowd began to disperse as Maude's face turned crimson.

"Opal!" Maude stormed off the stage back to where they all were still sitting in their seats.

"You were great, although I thought you'd do something out of the ordinary," Opal told her.

"I'm about to do something out of the ordinary! I'm about to really kill you like I've been promising for seventy years!" Maude fumed.

"Only seventy?" Harry asked, but not loud enough for Maude to hear him.

"Why'd you let them eat my cake?" Maude bellowed.

"They didn't eat your cake. We'd never let someone else eat it," Mavis explained timidly.

"Then who ate my cake? Was it one of y'all?" Maude continued.

"I didn't even get a bite and it looked so good," Mavis sighed.

"Well, someone did!" Maude snapped. She walked up to each of them in turn and began to sniff at their faces.

"What are you doing?" Mavis gasped.

"I'm like a bloodhound!" Maude replied. "I'll find the evidence."

Opal howled in laughter and slapped Mona's knee. "She's crazier than a loon," she cackled.

"Was it you, Opal?" Maude shouted when she got back to her.

"No, but the evidence is everywhere," Opal smiled. That twenty-dollar bribe had been worth every penny.

"What do you mean by that?" Maude grumbled. She rubbed her stomach that had started to hurt but continued to look around for any shred of evidence concerning the cake thief.

"Ms. Maude, you have something on your shirt," Mavis said timidly.

"What?" Maude barked. She looked down at her shirt to see icing from her cake crumbled down the front. Her hands had flecks of icing underneath her fingernails. "Who did this?" she asked suspiciously.

194

"You did, you ol' goat!" Opal cackled. "You always would eat anything." She was tickled pink at the entire scene.

"Come on, Ms. Maude, let's go see if they have another cake," Wilbur said.

"What if they don't have another one?" Mavis asked Wilbur quietly.

"Then we better get to baking," Wilbur said.

[Chapter Eighteen]

They had thankfully found Maude not one, but two butternut cakes for her to take home with her. Mavis and Wilbur were exhausted when they finally dropped Maude and Opal off at their homes.

"I still didn't get a piece of cake," Mavis frowned. She hadn't wanted to poke the bear anymore by asking Maude to share.

"You can look for one tomorrow night when we go back. I can't believe the fair is about to wrap up," Wilbur said. Just two more days of it and then life can go back to normal."

"We still have Earl to deal with," Mavis reminded him.

"Harlan's got it taken care of," Wilbur assured her. "He's never let us down before."

Mavis pulled up at the Manor and watched as Wilbur pulled out his truck keys from his pocket. "I'm going to take a shower and fall into bed. I've got a free morning tomorrow, so if you need anything, like maybe moving Clive to the pond, let me know."

Mavis shrugged and said she would call him in the morning. She knew that Clive had long outgrown the tank, but he was special to her, and she wasn't sure how he would fare if she released him back into the wild. He had long been domesticated and Mavis was sure that he was a tame pet, even though Wilbur said Clive would sooner bite any of their hands off if given the chance.

The next morning, Mavis fed Clive an extra helping of scrambled eggs and sausage links. He didn't have much room in the tank to turn around like he used to when he was younger. She sighed heavily and picked up the phone to call Wilbur. "Fine," she breathed into the phone. "We can put him in the pond on a trial basis, but if he starts to look unhappy or gets picked on by the other fish, we have to bring him back!"

Wilbur didn't waste any time once Mavis finally agreed to release Clive. He called Harry and asked him to come over as quickly as he could to the Manor. Thankfully, Harry wasn't one to ask too many questions about things. It was exceptionally humid that morning and hopefully between the two of them, they'd be able to wrangle Clive without any of them getting hurt, or worse, breaking Ruby's prized ceiling to floor aquarium.

"Are you really sure I'm doing the right thing?" Mavis asked once Wilbur pulled up a few minutes later.

"Yes," Wilbur comforted her. "It's for the best.

They waited on the front porch for Harry to arrive in his truck. They didn't have to wait long. Harry pulled up about fifteen minutes later with Mona in the passenger seat.

"What's this adventure we're having?" Harry asked.

Mavis was near tears. "It's time for Clive to go home to be with the other fish."

"Oh Mavis! He died?" Mona asked.

"What! No, don't say that!" Mavis cried.

Mona looked at Wilbur for an explanation.

"We're rehoming him. He's moving back to the pond," Wilbur nodded. He patted Mavis on the back to try to calm her down.

"Oh, now I understand. Well, that's for the best, even though I know you'll miss him," Mona said. She turned to Wilbur and whispered, "I wondered how you were going to flush him down the toilet if he had died."

Harry nodded. "Let's get to it." He knew that it wasn't going to be an easy job. The way that Mona talked about the fish made it sound like Clive was as big as a calf.

"Let me say goodbye one last time," Mavis said. She walked inside and spoke to Clive for a few minutes while the others waited outside on the porch.

"How big is this thing?" Harry asked Wilbur.

"Big," Mona said. She spread her arms far apart and repeated, "Very big."

"He's sizable," said Wilbur.

"Do you have a plan?" Harry asked.

"I've thought about it, and honestly, no," Wilbur admitted. "I don't know how we're going to do it, but I think it's best that Mavis does not help us, if you know what I mean."

"I'll take care of Mavis," Mona stated.

"I think he understands that it's for the best," Mavis said through tears as she walked back out onto the porch. "I told him that he'd get to see his family again and make some new friends."

"He'll probably eat them the minute he sees them," Wilbur whispered to Harry.

"Come on, let's go sit down on the swing while we let the guys take care of getting Clive out of the tank," Mona said.

"Okay. Wilbur, the cooler is in the hall closet if you need it," Mavis sighed. She turned and walked with Mona down the steps to the swing underneath the oak tree.

"Thanks," Wilbur said.

Harry and Wilbur walked inside to view the tank. Harry took one look at Clive and then turned to Wilbur. "How big is that cooler?"

"I don't think it's big enough," Wilbur said. "But we can check."

He walked to the hall closet to search for the cooler Mavis had told him about. He returned a few minutes later with a picnic cooler barely big enough to hold a few casserole dishes.

"Yeah, that ain't gonna do it," Harry agreed.

"I don't know that they make a cooler big enough for him," Wilbur said.

They pondered the situation for a few minutes more before deciding the best course of action was simply to put the beast in the bed of Wilbur's pickup truck and drive him directly to the pond for release.

Wilbur went outside and backed his truck up as close to the porch steps as possible while Harry began moving the decorative paneling above the tank piece by piece. He was careful not to break any part of it.

"We need to siphon a good bit of this water out before we start. Otherwise, it's going to make a mess," Wilbur told Harry. He was carrying a couple of buckets with him

"Mona knows a good bit about that," Harry said. "She used to steal gas from her ex-boyfriend's Charger back in the day."

"Well, she's otherwise occupied right now consoling Mavis," Wilbur laughed.

Wilbur hurried outside and found some plastic tubing from the backseat and put one end in one of the buckets.

"You just happened to have plastic tubing in your truck?" Harry asked him.

"I've been hoping Mavis would let me move Clive for two years now," Wilbur admitted. "When she called this morning, I threw whatever I could find in the truck and hurried over before she could change her mind."

They watched as the water from the tank began to drain out into the buckets. It only took a few minutes to fill up Wilbur's buckets, Mavis' mop bucket, and the cooler from the hallway. He and Harry carefully carried the buckets outside and dumped them by the magnolia tree. Wilbur made sure not to get any drops of pond water on Mavis' prized rose bushes by the porch.

"I think you made a wise decision," Mona said when she saw Wilbur and Harry carrying the buckets of pond scum. "Harry and Wilbur will take care of things. Once it's all cleaned out, you can get some new fish. I remember you telling me how

Mrs. Ruby had all those beautiful exotic fish. Maybe you can get some more of those."

Mavis nodded. It might be fun to have all the brightly colored fish and corals back in the Manor again.

Mona decided to change the subject away from fish for the time being. "Only two more nights for the fair. It's sure been an interesting one, hasn't it?"

"Sure has," Mavis lamented. "I hope Earl moves on with it once they pack up, but I've got this nagging feeling in my gut, Mona."

"Yea, he makes me sick to my stomach, too," Mona agreed. "Honestly, I'm a bit surprised he hasn't tried to make more contact with you than he has. There's something a little fishy about that."

"Fishy," Mavis said tearfully.

"Damn't," Mona sighed. She looked over at the porch where Wilbur was wringing out his sopping wet shirt. Mavis looked over and screeched. "What are you doing with all that water?" Before Mona could stop her, she raced over to the porch and pushed past Harry who was walking out of the door with another full bucket.

Harry stumbled and sent water flying in all directions. Wilbur, who had been following close behind Harry, slipped and fell. The bucket he was carrying turned upside down and drenched him and the living room carpet with murky water and bits of scrambled egg.

"Clive won't be able to breathe!" Mavis howled. She ignored the chaos around her and pressed her face against the glass tank that was still filled a little over halfway with water. Mona burst

202

through the front door and looked aghast. There was pond slime on the walls, and she couldn't hear her own thoughts over Mavis' wailing and Wilbur's hollering.

"Get her out of here!" Wilbur said sternly.

"I'm trying," Mona pleaded. "Come on, Mavis. They've got it under control."

"You call this under control? Clive! Are you okay?" Mavis yelled.

"I swear if you don't get her out of here," Harry bellowed. Somehow the bucket had landed on his head. Slime dripped down his face past his mouth.

"Come on Mavis. The guys will take care of everything," Mona said. She took Mavis by the arm and tugged.

"But Clive will suffocate!" Mavis yelled.

"If he hasn't suffocated from all that mess in there, he'll be fine!" Harry countered.

"Yoo-hoo!" Opal called out from the porch.

"Oh God no!" Wilbur sighed. The last thing he needed was for Opal and Maude to get involved.

"We're just seeing what y'all are up to," Opal continued. She looked around the fiasco and turned back to Maude. "I don't like this new decorating technique."

"Ruby would have a fit if she saw this," Maude agreed. "She never did like the all-natural look that some of those houses have. Green does not look good on the walls."

Opal nodded and sniffed the green moss that was slowly sliding down the front wall. "Not good," she said sagely. "It'll take more than bleach to remove that."

"If you don't get them out of here," Harry mumbled to Mona.

"How am I supposed to get them all out of here?" Mona asked him

"Would you rather wrestle Moby Dick over there?" Harry asked.

Mona studied the situation for a minute and weighed her options. It might be easier to deal with Clive than handle Maude, Opal, and Mavis, but she saw the look of frustration on Wilbur and Harry's faces and sighed. She turned to Maude and Opal and asked if they'd like to join her and Mavis on the swing.

"Mavis is right there," Opal pointed out.

"Well, yes, but we need to get her back outside," Mona said carefully. "She's having a hard time letting go of Clive."

"I'll handle this," Maude said. She walked over to Mavis and patted her on the back. "Come on, Mavis girl. Things like this happen. He went out with a bang, I'm sure."

"He passed on?" Opal asked Mona.

"That's what I thought!" Mona said, but Mavis interrupted her conversation. "Why does everyone think he died? He's alive and happy!"

"Then what's going on?" Maude asked.

"We're moving him to the pond," Wilbur interjected. "Now if you four could go outside and give us some peace and quiet!"

"Well, I'll be!" Maude said. "Someone needs a snack." She ushered Mavis and Opal towards the door and raised her eyebrows at Mona. "Men!"

Wilbur watched the four women close the front door behind them and looked around the linen closet for some towels so he and Harry could dry off. They cleaned up some of the mess as best they could. "Probably ought to leave the towels out in case we spill any more water during this operation," Harry said.

"I think that's a good idea," Wilbur agreed.

They continued to siphon water for another twenty minutes until it looked like the majority of the water was gone.

"Now comes the fun part," Harry said.

Wilbur looked at him. "Yep."

"Mavis wouldn't happen to have any step ladders to make this easier, would she?" Harry asked.

"That would be too simple," Wilbur muttered. He went and grabbed two chairs from the kitchen table for them to stand on.

"Guess we just reach in and grab him?" Harry asked, a little unsure that they were going to be able to get Clive out of his home. "Unless you have a net?"

Wilbur shook his head. He didn't have one nearly big enough. "I've got this rope though. On the count of three then," Wilbur said.

"One," Harry said.

"Two," Wilbur continued.

"Three!" they both yelled together. Wilbur flung the rope with a large loop around the wiggling catfish and pulled tight as soon as Clive was encircled.

Mona could hear a great deal of noise coming from inside the house, but she tried to keep Mavis' attention focused on other things like old pecan pie recipes and some of her favorite vacations. A few minutes later, the four women turned and saw Wilbur and Harry dragging a tarp down the porch steps. They were both soaked head to toe and covered in a fresh coating of slime. They heaved and lifted Clive who was wrapped in the tarp and tied with dog leashes into the bed of the truck.

"How'd you get him out of the tank?" Mona asked incredulously.

"Don't ask," Wilbur replied through gritted teeth. He had inhaled more water than any man ever should.

Wilbur refused to let Mavis accompany them on the trip to the pond. Mavis was already fit to be tied with the way they had Clive wrapped in a tarp. She was convinced that he would suffocate during the two-minute trip it would take Wilbur to drive through the woods towards his pond. Harry leapt in the truck bed and promised Mavis that he would keep an eye on him as Wilbur drove.

"You better hurry," Harry called through the open back glass. "If this thing dies, I'm not telling her."

Wilbur drove faster than he ever had before through the winding path in the woods. He spun the truck around at the edge of the lake and backed it as far in as he dared without getting stuck in the thick mud.

"Let's get this dang thing in the pond before I kill him myself," Harry said, wiping slime off the side of his face. "He'd make a nice mount."

"Mavis and her pets, I swear!" Wilbur mumbled.

They waded into the pond and pulled on the tarp holding Clive into the water. Once he was unbuckled and finally clear of his makeshift enclosure that resembled a straight jacket, Clive floated for a minute before finally swimming to freedom once and for all.

Mavis had waved until she couldn't see Wilbur's truck anymore. She sank back into the swing, narrowly missing Mona in the process. The swing shook as she kicked off the ground and pushed the swing to its limits. Maude and Opal sat back down in their respective wire chairs.

"Let's go over this plan one more time," Mona said.

[Chapter Nineteen]

"I done told y'all that I'm going to handle it," Maude said. "I brought my rope with me. It's over in the car."

"Your rope?" Mona asked. She wasn't sure what Maude was capable of.

"Won't be hard at all," Maude continued. "Opal's got her bat, too. We're ready when y'all are."

"Now, Ms. Maude, you can't go around roping people," Mavis sighed. She was worried sick about Clive, and now that she knew Maude was serious about her plan that contained elements of violence, she had that to worry about, too.

"Trust me," Opal began. "This Earl man will be out of your hair soon enough."

"Yea, whatever she said," Maude agreed. "Opal's never been wrong about a prediction yet. Right, Opal?"

Opal nodded sagely and looked at Mona. "Just like I knew you'd sell the cafe. Good move."

"But how did you know?" Mona asked.

"We rode by the cafe earlier and saw where they said they were doing things to it. Met the new owners out front. Told us how you and Harry sold it. You know me and Opal had to investigate. We remember when your mama and daddy opened it years ago. Great people. Great food. But I'll give these new ones a chance to see if it lives up to the standards I'm used to," Maude continued. "I've got some cookbooks if they need them."

Mona couldn't help but laugh. She had to admit that she was anxious to see the upgrades that the new owners had promised. Harry had stopped worrying about it as soon as the check deposited, but it was hard for Mona to let go. Though the new sports car she had ordered online made it a little easier.

"You two are a mess," Mona said to Maude and Opal.

"You have no idea!" Mavis said.

"Like I was saying, it'll all come out in the wash," Opal said.

"But we need a real plan just in case," Mavis reiterated.

"Well, I have an idea, but you ain't going to like it," Mona started.

"You want me to bop him on the head and Opal to lasso him?" Maude asked. "I don't think that'll work as good."

"Not exactly," Mona began.

"I can hogtie somebody just as good as you can," Opal said.

"Nobody is hogtying anyone," Mavis said. "This is serious. We need to figure out how to catch Earl before anything else happens."

"I've got an old beaver trap in the shed somewhere," Maude offered.

"That'll fix him," Opal agreed.

"Oh, dear God!" Mona gasped. She howled with laughter. She needed to spend more time around Opal and Maude. Laughing at them was good for her soul.

"Ms. Maude, we are not going to physically maim Earl no matter how inviting that idea might be," Mavis said. "Mona, what are you thinking?"

"You're going to have to see him," Mona said.

"I have seen him," Mavis said. "He looked horrible. You saw him, too!"

"I saw him! Right before I walloped him one!" Opal added.

"No, I mean you're going to have to actually go spend some time with him and figure out what he's up to," Mona told her. "Try to figure out how he got out of jail so soon."

"Sweet talk him," Maude nodded. "Good plan."

"Not to me it isn't," Mavis said. Y'all don't know Earl like I know him."

"And no one wants to know him like that," Mona gagged as she spoke.

"Don't you start on that," Mavis frowned. "I just meant he's a bit more deceptive than y'all realize."

"He did look pretty decrepit," Maude agreed.

"No, well, anyway," Mavis groaned. "Mona, I don't think this is going to work. I hoodwinked him last time. He's not going to suddenly forget about that."

"I think he will," Mona disagreed. "Earl clearly has a soft spot for you. Tell him you broke up with Harry, and hell, tell him last time was all my fault. Blame it all on me, and Wilbur, too. He hates

Wilbur," Mona laughed. "Tell him we forced you to take part in that sting operation and you've been so depressed ever since."

"Why did you break up with Harry?" Opal asked.

"Which one's Harry again?" Maude asked.

"The big one working on Clive. The other one is Wilbur," Opal explained.

"I know who the hell Wilbur is!" Maude said.

"I know how your mind gets sometimes," Opal shrugged.

"I didn't know you were dating Harry. Nobody tells me nothing anymore," Maude frowned.

"Ms. Maude, Harry and I have never dated each other. That was all a misunderstanding," Mavis explained.

"More like a ruse to get away from Earl," Mona added.

"Booze? No, Mavis, that stuff will get you in trouble," Opal sighed.

"Got me in trouble once or twice," Maude agreed.

"Like that time you got the tattoo to prove it," Opal nodded.

"Hush up," Maude said.

"Or the time you got drunk on our flight to Italy and we ended up in Nepal," Opal said.

"That was your fault, you old bat!" Maude said.

"Or the time," Opal began, but Maude clamped her hand over Opal's mouth to silence her.

"I know how it goes," Mona agreed. "The booze is how I ended up married the first time. What happens in Vegas does not stay in Vegas."

"So, no booze for you, Mavis. You can't end up married to that fool," Maude said sternly. "Leave the drinking to us."

"Well," Mona started to say, but she quickly changed her train of thought. "Never mind!"

If looks could kill, Mona would be buried six feet in the ground. Mavis' face had turned a bright shade of red and she shook her head vigorously. "I don't like this one bit," Mavis pouted.

"I already said it'll all come out in the wash," Opal repeated for what felt like the thousandth time.

"Yea, but that ain't," Mona winced. Harry and Wilbur had pulled back up to the house. They were both drenched and covered in mud and pond scum. "How'd it go?"

"Is Clive ok?" Mavis begged to know.

"He's fine," Harry waved her off. "I've got to get showered off. I'm trying not to gag."

"Then we're going out for a steak," Wilbur said. "A big one."

"Oh, that sounds good! What time are we leaving?" Mavis asked. A nice steak dinner would be sure to take her mind of Clive.

"No. Not as in you and I are going to dinner. Harry and I are going to dinner," Wilbur explained.

"But what about Mona and me? Why can't we come, too?" Mavis asked.

"Because you didn't get several buckets of pond scum poured over your head today. Harry and I deserve a nice steak dinner before you all get us trapped in some other hairbrained idea," Wilbur told her.

"First of all, moving Clive was your idea," Mavis began. She had her hands on her hips and pursed her lips.

"You shouldn't have rescued a catfish to begin with," Wilbur countered.

"Second of all, you and Harry would be bored without us," Mavis continued.

"You mean we would have a little peace and quiet," Wilbur said.

"And third of all," Mavis waved her finger in the air. "If you'd listen to me more often, you probably wouldn't get into these kind of messes! Smelling like a used sewer drain."

"I wouldn't get into these messes?" Wilbur replied. "What in the world? I'm always cleaning up after you!"

"Well, I never," Mavis began.

"And you ain't never either. I'm going to get a nice steak with Harry before you get me mixed up in any more of your mess," Wilbur finished.

"Mavis, we already have plans, remember?" Mona smiled innocently. She turned to Wilbur and Harry and shooed them away. "Y'all go shower and get on with your plans. We'll just hang out together tonight here, or wherever," Mona added under her breath.

Wilbur didn't wait for Mavis to interject. He hopped back in his truck and drove home to get cleaned up. Harry did the same. They didn't want to be around when Mavis discovered the mess they had left behind in the Manor. They made plans to meet at the nicest steakhouse in Junction in two hours, Wilbur's treat to Harry for him dropping everything to help with catfish.

"I'm thirsty," Maude said. "This humidity isn't good for my lungs."

"Neither is smoking two packs a day," Opal muttered.

"Ms. Maude! You still smoke?" Mona gasped. She had kicked the nasty habit after her rekindled friendship with Mavis who was a genius when it came to being a life coach. "Mavis can help you get off that drug."

Maude looked at Mona like she had three heads. Mavis giggled and pulled Mona out of the swing. "She's been smoking since Jesus himself was a toddler. It's best to let her be," she whispered.

"But at her age," Mona said.

Mavis shook her head at Mona who got the hint and dropped the subject. It was best not to get Maude riled up unnecessarily. She got herself riled up well enough.

Maude and Opal were the first to walk into the house. They were standing at the doorway when Mona and Mavis entered the room.

"What in the world?" Mona said. She looked around at the sopping wet carpet, the drenched towels scattered about, the slime and gunk which made a large trail from the tank to the front door, and the overturned kitchen chairs. But worst of all was the large scrape and five-inch diameter hole in the sheetrock above the fish tank.

"I'm going to whoop both of them for leaving my house in this kind of fix!" Mavis said.

"Now Mavis, I'm sure they probably didn't realize it was this bad," Mona said.

"Neither one of them were raised in a barn. They both know how to clean up after themselves," Mavis said. "I know for a fact that Wilbur knows to act better than this."

"It smells like a fish," Opal gagged.

"I wonder why," Mona laughed sarcastically.

"Probably because there was a fish in here," Opal replied. Sometimes it amazed her how dumb the younger generation could be. She shook her head and tried to step over the mounds of grass and dirt on the floor.

"I can't believe Wilbur left it like this," Mavis seethed. "Oooh, when I get a hold of him!"

There was another hole in the wall the size of a circle of bologna on the wall across from the tank. Mavis gasped in horror when she saw it. "My wall!" she wailed.

"That's about the size of someone's head. You don't reckon one of them went through the wall, do you?" Mona asked.

"Wilbur wouldn't poke his head through the wall," Opal said. "Not on purpose."

"I can fix that," Maude said.

Mona started to say that maybe they should call a professional to help fix the wall, but Maude didn't listen. She hastened past Mona and grabbed one of the picture frames off the hallway table and held it up over the hole. "Yep, that should cover it completely."

Opal grabbed the picture frame from her and stared at the occupants in the picture. "Who are these people?" she asked.

Maude sighed and took the picture back. "That's Ruby's cousin, Edwin, you old fool!"

"It ain't done it! I dated Edwin once or twice and he wasn't black when I knew him," Opal countered.

Mavis walked over and snatched the picture from them. "I never put a picture in there! I don't know who these folks are, they came with the frame," she explained.

"Well, it'll still cover this hole nicely," Maude continued.

"No!" Mavis yelped. She put the picture back on the table and looked around to survey the damage. "We're going to clean this mess up and let Wilbur come back in here later and fix the holes. He's the one who fixes this kind of stuff, not me!"

"Where's your mop at?" Mona asked. "And bleach. We're going to need lots of it." The Manor looked like a scene straight out of a science-fiction film.

Mavis showed her where the cleaning supplies were, and they all got to work. Opal spent most of the time looking around the dining room and living room while Maude rummaged through some drawers in Jameson's old study. There was no telling what she would find in there. Thankfully, Mona knew how to clean. The years spent owning her own restaurant made her a professional when it came to cleaning up messes.

Mona picked up the wet towels and headed to the washing machine. She held them out at an arm's length to avoid getting contaminated by the smell herself. She found some bleach and a box of borax. She poured liberal amounts of both in the machine. One of them was bound to take the smell out. Then she washed her hands in the sink before returning to the living room for the next project.

"You wouldn't happen to have a steam cleaner, would you?" Mona asked. "You know, one of those things for the carpet?"

"No, but there's a shop vac that Wilbur keeps out in the barn. That might get up some of this water from the carpet," Mavis said. She was too busy scrubbing the contents of the aquarium from the wall to worry about the carpet just yet.

Mona returned a few minutes later with the shop vac. It took several attempts, but she finally made progress cleaning up the water out of the carpet. "I think most of it will be up after the next time or two," she told Mavis as she went to empty the vat of dirty water.

Mavis was wiping off the side of the tank. "Thanks, hopefully, we've got most of it by now."

"I do think you're going to need to have the carpet professionally cleaned though," Mona added.

Mavis picked up some papers that had fallen to the floor and wiped off the end table that had been splashed with water. Honestly, from the state of this mess, it looked like they had waged war on a killer whale, not moved a sweet little pet like Clive. She would have to go check on him frequently and make sure to feed him more so that he wouldn't starve out in the wild.

Now that the hallway looked much cleaner, they all sat down at the kitchen table to catch their breath. Mavis poured them all glasses of water and handed out cookies from her cookie jar. After they settled down, Opal and Maude showed them what they had each found on their treasure hunt. Opal had accumulated a pile of what looked to be old recipe cards scrawled in Ruby's handwriting, while Maude had found a plastic bag full of old keys to who knew what. Mavis almost let her keep them, but the last thing she needed was Maude showing up in the dead of night trying to find which locks they fit.

"I need a shower before we hit the fair this evening," Mona declared. "And so do you," she pointed at Mavis. "Let's go upstairs and pick an outfit for you to wear before I head home."

"Do we have to do this?" Mavis pouted.

Maude and Opal bounded off towards the stairs and disappeared. "Oh God, come on!" Mavis frowned. "They can't be left unattended."

Mona and Mavis found them upstairs in Mavis' room browsing through her closet. Opal had pulled an old floor length dress from the 1990s over her head and was dwarfed by the sheer size of it. "I like this one," she marveled at herself in the mirror. The sparkles on the dress really brought out her eyes.

"No, this one will get his attention," Maude said. She tossed Mavis a pair of neon pink spandex shorts and a matching crop top with bedazzled rhinestones on it.

"Oh goodness," Mavis mumbled. "This really will be a night to remember."

[Chapter Twenty]

Mona had hurried home and showered and changed clothes quickly. She didn't want to leave Mavis alone with Maude and Opal for too long, not when the plan was about to be put into action. While she was gone, Mavis finally agreed to wear the skintight navy-blue dress that Mona found in the back of her closet, but she drew the line at Maude and Opal doing her makeup. She knew she would end up looking like a clown on an acid trip.

"But if we just put a little bit of pizzazz here," Maude brought the brush closer to Mavis' face.

"No, Ms. Maude," Mavis shook her head. "No ma'am. You know you can't see without your glasses."

"You can trust her, Mavis. Maude knows a thing or two about the face paint. She used to have suitors lined up around the corner," Opal said. "Well, before they all died, that is."

But Mavis was firm. She would not allow Maude or Opal anywhere near her face. She finally did concede and allowed Mona to add some eyeliner to her tired eyes and rouge to her cheeks. She brushed her thick hair and made sure it looked perfect. Tonight was going to take a lot of effort on her part and she was not looking forward to it at all.

She spritzed her favorite perfume and tossed Mona the keys to her car. The tight dress made it difficult to drive. Maude offered to drive, but Mavis nearly popped out of her dress when she shook head from side to side. She would never in a million years let Maude behind the wheel of her new vehicle.

"These kids don't think we can do anything," Opal said.

"If they only knew," Maude agreed. "They'll never have half the adventures we've had."

Mavis had to admit that that was true. She learned something new about them every single day. While Maude and Opal chatted about the time they took a riverboat cruise, Mona made Mavis go over the plan again. They rehearsed the plan the entire ride to the fair. As soon as Mona pulled up into the parking lot, Mavis began to feel sick to her stomach. She wasn't convinced that this plan would even work. They didn't have any idea where Earl would be or if he was even still in town.

"I told you, we aren't lucky enough for him to leave town that easily," Mona told her as Mavis repeated this argument for the third time.

"Maybe not, but a girl can hope," Mavis said.

"He's dating Hope?" Opal said, from the back seat.

"Who's Hope?" Maude asked.

"Mona's new friend," Opal explained. "I don't know why she's keeping her friend from us. We're nice folks."

"What's she got to do with tonight?" Maude was confused.

Opal shrugged. "I don't know. I guess she's the one who went out with Wilbur and Harry to get them out of the way," Opal reasoned.

"Well, good for her. We didn't need them out here messing things up," Maude nodded. "They get too emotional about things."

Mona and Mavis listened to the conversation coming from the backseat. They tried not to giggle as the two older ladies completely made up a person and dinner date. Wilbur and Harry were going to love hearing about that in the morning.

"Where should we start looking for him?" Mavis said once they had all walked through the fair entrance.

"Maybe we should split up," Maude suggested. "We can cover more ground that way."

"Yeah, Maude and I can go this way," Opal pointed to her right, "And you and Mona can go that way." Opal indicated the opposite direction in case the two young people didn't understand. They were generally slow on the uptake.

Mavis didn't like that plan. Maude and Opal were hard enough to keep up with when she knew where they were. When they were out of sight, there was no telling what kind of tomfoolery they could get up to. They were worse than two toddlers in a glassware store.

"We'll all meet back here in exactly one hour," Mona suggested.

"Perfect! We can do that," Maude agreed.

"See you in an hour!" Opal said. She scampered off before they could stop her in the direction that she had indicated Mona and Mavis should go.

"Did she even look to see what time it was so she'd know when to be back?" Mavis asked.

"Were either one of them even wearing a watch?" Mona asked.

"Oh, dear Lord in heaven," Mavis said. This was already starting off on the wrong foot, but it was too late to worry about that. "They have cell phones. We can always call them. God, why didn't I put that tracer on their phones!" She sounded like a helicopter mom parenting two teenagers.

"Come on, let's go," Mona said. They headed off toward the carnival games and booths where they had seen Earl most frequently. They hoped he would be there causing his usual mischief.

The fair was more crowded than they'd seen it before. People jostled left and right. The lines for the rides snaked around several times over. It seemed that the final Friday night was the evening everyone in the county had decided to come out and enjoy the festivities.

"I don't know how we're going to find him in all these people," Mavis said. She was seriously regretting the shoes Mona had picked out for her to wear. The heels were the tallest pair she owned. They had been wrapped in paper in the fancy box from the shoe store when Mona found them. They were what Mavis had referred to as an impulse buy. They certainly weren't practical for a county fair.

"Well, we have to find him," Mona said. "Let's look down this way." She pulled Mavis down a somewhat less crowded section that held the games that were considered less popular. Earl tended to dwell primarily in the outskirts of everything, but he was nowhere to be found. Mona and Mavis walked around the fairgrounds for almost an hour with no luck. They had searched under every scrap of lumber and kicked aside every milk crate. They had even ducked into the haunted house to see if he was hiding out there, but there was no creepy man in there besides the carnival worker.

"We're going to have to meet with Maude and Opal in a few minutes," Mavis said, looking at her watch.

"Let's give it a few minutes before we go back and try to find them," Mona suggested. "You know as well as I do that those two can handle themselves. They're probably back at the mechanical bull or the hypnotist show." Mavis didn't find either of those options funny. "Oh, lighten up," Mona smiled when she saw Mavis' grumpy look.

Mavis didn't like it, but she continued to follow Mona as she meandered through the crowd. As they circled back to the front of the midway, Mavis heard a voice that made her skin crawl.

"Oh, looky dere at dat fine lookin' lass dere!" Earl shouted. "I knowed you come back, and you lookin' mighty fine in da process."

Mona slipped away so that Earl wouldn't readily see her, but he seemed to only have eyes for Mavis. He picked at what few teeth he had left with a toothpick and eyed Mavis up and down.

"Hello Earl," Mavis croaked.

"You alone?" Earl asked. He looked around behind him to see who was all around.

"I am," Mavis swallowed hard.

"Where's dat handy man of yours dat tried to beat up ol' Earl da last time I was tryin' to be polite?" Earl asked.

Mavis wasn't sure why Earl had a propensity to refer to himself in the third person, but it was even more annoying than his other habits.

"Oh, that was just a simple misunderstanding, Earl," Mavis said. She batted her eyelashes for effect. "You didn't take that seriously, did you?"

"He sho' put a hurtin' on me over a simple misunder, well, whateva," Earl rubbed his cheek.

Mavis knew that Wilbur hadn't hurt Earl nearly as much as he wanted to, but she played along. "Were you hurt really bad?" she gasped.

"I'm too strong for him," Earl sassed. "I had to fight for my life my whole life," Earl continued.

"Oh, you poor thing,' Mavis swallowed back bile. "Tell me all about it."

"How I know you ain't recordin' me like last time?" Earl sneered. He inched closer to her and sniffed the air around her.

He had a point. The last time Mavis tricked him at the Manor, she had hidden multiple tape recorders around her living room to tape his confession. That plan had worked then, but she was certain that it couldn't work twice.

"I'm so sorry about that," she said.

"Dat cut me real deep, suga," Earl said. "Real deep."

"I can't, uh, imagine," Mavis said. She looked around to make sure that no one she knew was around. This was one of the most pathetic things she had ever done. She was sweating in places that she had long forgotten about, and it wasn't in a good way.

"So, what made you have dis change of heart?" Earl crooned. He was putting his best moves forward and it was nauseating.

"I, um, didn't want to hurt you in the first place," Mavis swallowed hard.

"Den why'd you do it?" Earl scowled. His face flushed red, and he crossed his arms across his chest.

This was the moment she had been practicing for. It was make or break in this moment. "Well, Earl, I, um. Well, it was all Mona's fault!" she wailed.

"Mona Lisa?" Earl frowned. "I knew it. I always inspected!"

"Inspected? Oh, expected, right," Mavis said.

"She always had it out for me," Earl continued. "She couldn't handle my charms. Or my mind. You know what they say! Big mind, more money!"

"That's right," Mavis nodded. She had no earthly idea what he was talking about, but she needed to get on his good side.

"And she knowed da only way to get me outta your life was to crisscross applesauce me," he continued.

"Oh, well, maybe," Mavis said.

"I knew dis day would come soon enough," Earl said. "All day I sat out dere on the roadside just thinkin' about it."

"On the roadside?" Mavis asked.

"Yea," Earl shrugged. "On da chain gang. I wadn't cut out for da gang life, ya know. Not wit dese strong arms and my brain."

227

"Of course," Mavis nodded. She was trying her best not to gag.

"Oh, suga bear, dis yo' lucky day," Earl grinned. "I have so much to tell you."

"That was my plan!" Mavis squealed. "I mean, I hoped."

Earl looked at her suspiciously for a second, but shrugged off any qualms he had. He launched into his tale full of woes. When he was finally arrested in Rhinestone in the early part of 2020, he was extradited back to Baton Rouge on multiple charges of theft, battery, stalking, and arson. Mavis tried her best not to look shocked at Earl's ramblings, but the more he spoke, the more she became frightened. She had known that Earl was a criminal, but he had never gotten overtly dangerous with her. There were times he would get angry and lose his temper, but he had never hurt her physically. He had made her life a living hell the entire time she had lived in Louisiana with him in the slums of an unpronounceable bayou, but she never feared for her life.

"Are you listening to me?" Earl asked.

"Of course," Mavis lied. She hadn't heard a word he said, but she needed to continue to play it cool.

"And dat's why I came here to dis town fair. Dey needed my expertise and I needed da money," Earl continued. "Unless you know somewheres I could find some fast money." He batted his eyes and grinned at her. Mavis was unmoved, so he turned on the charm even harder. He grabbed her hand and mistook her jump for affection. "Oh suga, why didn't you come visit me at my kissin' booth when you first seen me?"

"I, well, Harry wouldn't let me," she lied through her teeth. Earl cut her off and sneered. "I knew Larry be involved in dis somehow. He always had dose sneaky eyes. Like dat gaytuh out behind our ol' house. Rememba?"

Mavis nodded. There were a ton of alligators behind their old trailer. How could she forget! She couldn't walk ten feet without hearing or seeing one. Their eyes followed her when she walked to the dumpster at the end of the pathway. The only good thing about them was that they tasted like chicken if you knew how to deep fry them.

"So, you got any money?" Earl asked quickly.

"Uh huh," Mavis nodded, still not paying any attention to him. The dress was starting to ride up and she hadn't brought a change of clothes with her.

"And da handyman still around? Of course, he is. He was with you da otha day wit yo' new man!" Earl gasped.

"Wilbur?" Mavis asked. "Oh, yes, he still works for me. And as for Harry, we broke up," Mavis said. "When I saw you, that is."

"Oh, really?" Earl asked.

"Yes, really," Mavis nodded. "He couldn't, um, measure up." She swallowed quickly to keep her lunch down.

"I could tell by lookin' at him," Earl nodded. "I know what you're applyin.'"

"Implying? No, I'm saying he wasn't you," she said. Where in the world was Mona? Mavis wasn't sure she could keep this whole ruse up for much longer.

"Too old fo' you," Earl agreed. "Not as strong as Earl T, huh?"

Mavis nodded and tried her best to not roll her eyes.

"How's about we go someplace a little quieter so we can talk about this proper?" Earl moved closer to her and tried to wrap his arm around her waist. She shook him off and saw his reaction, so she quickly bent over and picked up a piece of trash on the ground and walked to the nearby trashcan to throw it away. She felt his eyes follow her every move.

"Not here Earl. I didn't come alone you see," Mavis said over her shoulder.

"I knowed you were fooling me," Earl snarled. He looked over his shoulder again to see if Harry or Wilbur was nearby.

"No, you don't understand," Mavis explained. "I came with a group of elderly women. They don't get out much and wanted me to bring them. I gave them the slip so I could come and find you, but I've got to get back to them. Let's meet again in the morning," Mavis finished.

Earl eyed her suspiciously. He knew she kept company with some crazy old bats, but he wasn't sure that he believed her. On the other hand, she was looking too good to be lying. She knew that dark blue was his favorite color and she had chosen the perfect outfit to woo him. If his plan was going to work, then he needed to make sure she was on board. She had always been the key to his ultimate plan.

"What time tomorra?" he asked. "We supposed to be done tomorra night. Dey 'spect me to take down all da rides and box them up, ya know. I got lots of stuff to do before den."

"I can imagine," Mavis nodded. "You're a real busy man."

"Yea, I am," Earl said proudly. He puffed out his chest and thumped it hard. "I'm gonna be da best real estate mongrol in da game."

"Real estate?" Mavis coughed.

"Dat's right!" Earl said. "I'll tell ya more about it tomorra. One o'clock at the Ferris wheel. You and me. We can ride if off into da sunset!"

"I'm not sure that's how it works, but ok, yea," Mavis said.

"You'll see. Ol' Earl has got plans. We gonna be rich and powerful," Earl said. He kissed her cheek before she could pull away. "Now go on and take care of your grandmama."

Something about the mention of her grandmother made Mavis' blood boil worse than before. "Don't worry. I'll take care of everything," she said with a smile as she waved goodbye and headed off in the direction she hoped Mona was waiting.

[Chapter Twenty-One]

Earl wondered if he should have told Mavis the truth about jail. She should have to listen to all the hard things she had put him through. After all, if it weren't for her trickery, he would have never been caught. She would just have to find a way to make it all up to him. Giving him the deed to Magnolia Manor would just be the beginning. After that, they could probably get married for real this time and he'd have her family all carted off to the loony bin where they belonged. Now that he had money again, it'd be an easy bribe to pay. Money talked and he knew exactly h ow to make it work in his favor. Mavis would be thanking him for coming in and saving the day.

He had been through so much during their time apart. As soon as he was extradited back to Louisiana last year, things had continued to go downhill for him. He had acted as his own attorney, which didn't go so well. He couldn't help that the judge and jury were all corrupt. They sent him straight to jail for ten years with no possibility of parole. They said something about him being too good of a criminal, or something like that. Earl had not been paying too much attention.

His cell in the county jail had been sparse to say the least. The bed was uncomfortable, and the toilet constantly smelled like sulfur. He was bored, so he decided to make some new friends. Unfortunately, no one seemed to want to be friends with Earl. He couldn't imagine why! He was so charming and simply delightful, but these men were either too stupid or jealous to get close to him.

Earl had not done well in solitary confinement the first or second time. He lost track of all time while he sat there in the small dark room for hours on end. He felt like it had been two hundred years, but it had really only been twenty-one days. Earl vowed to himself that he would do whatever it took to never have to go back inside that box ever again.

When he was finally released from solitary and taken back to his cell, he found that he had a new roommate waiting for him. Lester was short, stubby, and had a bright red beard that covered half of his face. He only came up to Earl's chest, but he looked tough enough. He must have heard all about Earl because he didn't make idle chit chat or even acknowledge his presence once. Earl planned on rifling through his things while Lester went to the showers or outside. It was easy to learn about people by the way they kept their personal belongings. Not that Earl had any personal belongings with him in the beginning. He picked them up the longer he stayed. Stealing from his fellow inmates was what landed him in solitary the first time.

He landed in solitary confinement the second time due to a simple misunderstanding. Lester had tried to dig a tunnel underneath the bottom bunk through the wall. It did not work at all, but Lester was on his last strike. He was ornery and had a temper that rivaled anything Earl had ever seen before. Earl didn't like him, and he wanted the cell all to himself, so he snitched to the guard one evening and he and Lester both ended up in solitary. Even though Earl had not been a part of the escape attempt, he was guilty by association. Life was not fair!

He had only been in jail for a total of nine months when the bright idea came to him. He would have to radically change his ways and be on his best behavior for it his new plan to work. He was going to be good enough to join the prisoners who worked to keep the city of Baton Rouge beautiful.

It took six months of perfect behavior before he finally convinced the powers that be to give him a chance. On his first day of work detail, he shuffled out behind the man in front of him and worked himself to the bone. It was hot, sweltering hot, under the unforgiving sun. He picked up trash, mowed the grass, cut the weeds, and planted trees along the roadside. He worked day in and day out for three weeks before the opportunity presented itself.

As soon as the warden turned his back, Earl made a break for it. He hopped in the bed of a passing pickup truck and buried himself under the tires that were piled high. He wasn't sure how far he rode in the back of the truck, but as soon as it stopped, Earl tumbled out onto the side of the road. He didn't dare stand up and bring further attention himself, so he rolled down the embankment towards the edge of the river. In the distance he heard sirens and panicked.

He stripped out of his jumpsuit down to his thin cotton underwear. His socks were full of holes, but his boots were in pretty good condition. He could swim faster without them, but he would need them once he found civilization again. He tossed the black and white jumpsuit over a branch of the nearest tree and took a deep breath to settle his nerves.

Earl jumped into the head high water and took a deep breath. He pushed his way to the very bottom of the swamp water where the mud was thick enough to suck a man under. He swam as fast as his spindly legs could carry him, making sure he didn't thrash around like he'd seen others do in the water. That was a sure way to attract an alligator or snake. The key was to make sure that no one could track him, not an animal or person. He swam towards a large bush near the middle of the bayou and chanced a quick breath. He could hear the baying of the hounds behind him and the firing of rifle shots in the air. There was no way they could have tracked him here this quickly. Maybe he shouldn't have left his jumpsuit out in plain sight. Without another thought, he took another deep breath and sank back under the surface. He had no idea where he was at or where he was going, but he had always managed to find a way out when it came down to the wire. The sun was starting to set in the night sky, but he couldn't chance being found.

After hours in the murky water, Earl felt safe enough to swim towards the bank. He shook off the water and thick grass and weeds that had become glued to his skin. His underwear had fallen off somewhere in the middle of the underbrush. He was stark naked, except for his muddy boots that were full of water and slime. His first priority would be to find some dry clothes.

He slunk towards the railroad tracks and leaned his ear down towards the ground to listen for a rumbling noise. Unfortunately, there was no sign of an incoming train. It was too hot outside to walk, and he was already exhausted from swimming for so long. He didn't have any way of telling the time, but it was early morning. He had stayed hidden in the cool water all night long. He walked along the side of the river until the overhead sun began to burn his exposed skin. He wandered over to the tree line and climbed some of the low hanging branches to get a better look of his surroundings. About a mile away, he saw what looked like a traveling carnival. That was the answer to all of his problems!

He scurried out of the tree and ran as fast as he could through the wide-open field towards the midway. The gates were locked, but he managed to slip through the cattle gate and walked around until he found a tent with booths of all sizes set up. On the nearest one, he saw a stack of terry cloth robes and took the one on top. He slipped it onto his damp skin and marveled at how soft it felt. Now that he was clothed, he needed to see what kind of food he could rustle up. He was simply famished.

He exited the tent and followed his nose towards the rows of food trucks. In their fury to get everything setup, the workers didn't seem to notice the robed visitor filling his pockets with food. He grabbed a water bottle and drained it in one gulp. He grabbed two more just to be on the safe side.

"Hey! Get out of here!" a man covered in flour howled when he saw Earl stuffing his face with a slice of pizza.

Earl lumbered away and ran headfirst into a man in a dark jumpsuit with the word maintenance embroidered across the back.

"Hey you!" Earl crooned.

"Do you mind?" the man asked. He grimaced as he turned away from Earl who knew nothing of modesty.

Earl looked down and saw that his robe had come undone. "Can I help you with something?" the man asked.

Earl nodded and put his hand son his hips and stretched side to side. "I need a job fo' a bit."

"Uh, did Sheryl send you over here by chance?" the man grunted. Sheryl was in charge of hiring locals in every town they traveled to. She was indiscriminate in her picking, too. Earl nodded and sized up the man in front of him. He had no idea who Sheryl was, but he figured it was best to agree. The man's name tag said he was called Johnny. "She said she had one or two more guys she would send over my way today. Ok, well, you know how to cut grass?" Johnny spit his tobacco at Earl's feet.

"I got experience," Earl nodded. The angels in heaven were surely looking out for him!

"Good. My company travels this circuit and does all the landscaping for each setup and tear down. Sometimes we get called to work on one of the rides if it goes down. You know anything about that?" Johnny asked.

"I know a good bit," Earl nodded. He had ridden on many a carnival ride in his life. How hard could fixing one really be?

"Right," Johnny said warily. "You sure you just want to up and travel like that? Being a carnival worker ain't for the faint of heart."

Earl thumped himself on the chest and ginned wickedly. "My ticka jus' fine."

"Ok," Johnny shrugged. "Go on in there and get you a maintenance uniform." He pointed to one of the closest portable trailers behind him. "We need to get this patch cut and ready before the fair opens to the public tomorrow."

Earl nodded and looked around at the waist high weeds in front of him. It was not going to be an easy job.

"What'd you say your name was again?" the man asked.

"Uh, Ben," Earl lied.

"Alright," the man shrugged. He honestly didn't care what his name was, as long as he did what he needed him to do. "You from around here in Lafayette?"

Earl nodded and chewed on the inside of his cheek. He'd been to Lafayette plenty of times in his traveling salesman days. He wasn't exactly supposed to be back around these parts, but according to the schedule the man handed him, they'd be gone in ten days' time towards the next destination: Jackson, Mississippi. He scanned the entire list and his heart near about jumped out of his chest. In three and a half months, he'd be back to where it had all begun. The fair was set to land in Junction in October and if he knew Mavis, she'd be the first one through the gates.

Earl took to the traveling carnival life like a duck to water. The work was easy, not that he ever worked per say. He spent the majority of his time practicing his pickpocketing skills on unsuspecting fairgoers. Before he knew it, he had more money than he knew how to count. He bought a portable cash box from a local pawnshop and returned a few days later to pawn some jewelry he had lifted from the lost-and-found booth at the fair. It was like a treasure trove waiting for him at the end of each day. People were not careful with their wedding rings, cell phones, jeweled necklaces, and wallets, which made it easy for Earl. He scooped them up and pawned them with ease. Before anyone could suspect him, the fair would be over in that city, and they'd pack up and head on to the next venue. Life was good!

As soon as they arrived in Junction, Earl knew he had to keep his cool. He couldn't show up at Magnolia Manor unannounced. He needed to take things slowly and woo Mavis like he used to. As luck would have it, Mavis ending up finding him! Not long after he had discovered the honey hole of wealth itself, the old fortune telling lady at one of the booths. He had overheard a group of men at one of the food trucks talking about the amount of money the woman was raking in. Apparently, the old woman was loaded down with money and was nothing but an old kook. That was Earl's specialty. He'd be the wealthiest man in all the parishes before too long.

After making plans with Mavis for the next day, Earl hurried off in search of a place to shower. Behind the barns were rows of campers and RVs that were frequently left unattended. He found an unlocked door and checked to make sure that it was unoccupied. After a relaxing shower, he exited the camper smelling like lavender and chamomile. He had styled his hair with gel and borrowed a couple of nice-looking button-down shirts for the occasion. The man who owned the camper was two sizes larger than Earl, so the pants didn't fit, but Earl would just have to find a belt in one of the booths later on once everyone was gone for the night.

He found a bunch of wildflowers and snatched them up. He shoved them in his pocket and smiled at himself. He was so romantic. Any woman would be so lucky to have him! Mavis really was lucky. Earl had mostly forgiven her for all that she had done. When she left him in Louisiana all those years ago, it had been the handyman's fault. Then her grandmother or grandfather had passed away not long after. Earl couldn't exactly keep up with all the details of it all. He was a busy man and had met so many people throughout his journey.

[Chapter Twenty-Two]

Wilbur barreled into the kitchen of Magnolia Manor early the next morning without knocking. He had seen the kitchen lights on and knew Mavis was already awake. "Do you want to tell me what in the world is going on?" he demanded.

Mavis was sitting at the breakfast table with a towel wrapped around her wet hair as she sipped hot coffee.

"Good morning to you, too," she said.

"Mavis, why did I wake up to a text message from the deputy sheriff telling me that you're interfering with an active investigation?" Wilbur seethed. His face was a deep shade of crimson. Mavis could see that he was really riled up this time. She would need to come clean about the plan and her run-in with Earl the night before, but first she needed to calm him down.

"Let me get you a cup of coffee," she smiled. To be safe, she cut him a thick slice of banana bread that she had just pulled out of the oven. She knew Wilbur couldn't say no to homemade banana bread. She set the warm plate and hot mug at the seat across from her at the table and ushered him to sit down.

"Mavis," Wilbur said. "What's going on?"

"Well, first we need to discuss the hole in the ceiling and the wall," she smiled politely.

"We'll get to that later," Wilbur countered. "What in the world is Harlan talking about?"

"Oh Wilbur, are you sure you want to get involved with all that mumbo jumbo," she giggled innocently.

"Cut the crap, Mavis," Wilbur said directly.

That was almost like cursing for Wilbur. She knew that there would be no other way around it. She asked for him to sit down and try to eat breakfast while she explained what was going on. He sighed heavily and sat down in the empty seat across from her. The banana bread smelled good, and he picked at it with his fork while Mavis shuffled back to her seat after refilling her coffee cup.

"Well, you see what had happened was," Mavis began.

"Mavis, every time you start a story like this, I end up either in a lot of pain, covered in pond slime, or up the creek in one of your latest shenanigans," Wilbur interrupted.

"Sounds like you should be used to it then," Mavis smiled.

"I'm getting too old for this. And so are you." Wilbur dug into the bread with his fork and began to eat. "Just come out with it," he said in between mouthfuls.

"Well, after you and Harry left here last night, without fixing the holes in the wall, might I add. But I digress," she began. "We cleaned up and went upstairs to change clothes. We decided that we needed to catch Earl in the act. And before you start, let me finish. We came up with the perfect plan to get Earl to spill the beans!"

"Mavis!" Wilbur howled.

"You know, I'm starting to see why he doesn't like you very much," she shrugged.

Wilbur rolled his eyes and snorted. "I'd hate myself if he did like me," he retorted.

"Anyway," Mavis continued. "Our plan worked. I got him to confess to lots of different things."

"And?" Wilbur asked.

"And what?" Mavis looked at him like he was crazy. "I told you it worked. I threw that dress and those shoes out though. They were such a pain."

"What dress? What shoes? Oh, never mind! Tell me what happened next!" Wilbur exclaimed.

"Well, that was it," Mavis frowned. "I found Mona and it took us a while to find Maude and Opal. They were on the swings; you know those high ones that whip you around. I'm not sure how Opal got Maude on them, but she did. Probably kicking and screaming the whole time. That's actually how we found them."

Wilbur looked at her in amazement. "So, it sounds like nothing was accomplished," he sighed.

"Well, that's because we aren't done yet!" Mavis replied. As usual, Wilbur was being a spoilsport and jumping the gun. This was mainly his fault. He had been the one who hadn't let them tag along to dinner last night. If he had, then they could have all discussed the plan together.

"Mavis, yes you are done! Harlan has it covered. I called him as soon as his text came through. He said you were there with Earl batting your eyes and cooing at him like a durned pigeon! What in the world has gotten into you!" Wilbur cried.

"I had to sweet talk him!" she declared. "I had to go undercover!"

"You what?" Wilbur gasped. "Harlan didn't go into that little detail!" Wilbur covered his ears with his hands and shook his head. Mavis did not need to be so committed to her role. She was the sole reason Wilbur had graying hair.

"What?" Mavis asked, then realization hit her. "No, not like that! You're disgusting, Wilbur. I meant that I had to go undercover and try to get on his good side by listening to him! You men always thinking with, well, not your God given brain!"

"Mavis! Harlan's got plain clothes officers already following him! Don't you go getting back involved with a scoundrel like Earl!" Wilbur chastised.

"I'd rather a bear gnaw off my foot than get back with Earl," Mavis hissed.

"Then why are you doing this?" Wilbur demanded to know.

"Because I can't let anyone else handle my problems!" Mavis exclaimed. "I started this mess years ago and it's high time it ended. I'm meeting him after lunch today and I planned on making a scene, which you know I'm real good at, and Earl finally getting arrested for good. No more work release or gangs or whatever he escaped from. I was so sure it had been the loony bin, but he said no."

Wilbur softened at Mavis' explosion. He knew that her heart had been in the right place. He couldn't imagine how hard it had been on her seeing him again at the fair when she least expected it. Seeing Earl was a nightmare in and of itself. Maybe she and Harlan could work together. Maybe if they combined all the plans, Earl could finally be caught and detained for good. Stranger things had happened, but it still felt dangerous. Especially if Earl had escaped from some kind of gang. Wilbur had no idea what kind of gang would accept a man like Earl, but that subject was not something he knew too much about.

Mavis stood up and washed her plate in the sink while Wilbur finished his breakfast.

Wilbur finished the last bite of his banana bread and drained his cup of coffee. "Mavis, Harlan's got people tracking him. Stay out their way and let them handle it. Just be careful, please," he said.

"I'm always careful," Mavis shrugged.

"You're about as careful as a bull in a china shop," Wilbur chuckled. "Do I dare ask the rest of your brilliant plan?"

"I'm meeting him after lunch," Mavis said. "And if Harlan's people are tracking him, then they can snatch him up!"

"I'm not sure it works like that," Wilbur said. "Just let them handle it."

"Ok," Mavis smiled, but Wilbur knew better. Mavis had never been careful in her entire life. That's why he had to keep an eye on things.

"What time are you headed up there?" Wilbur asked.

"Mona's coming to get me at eleven," Mavis said. "I need you to get Maude and Opal. After you get those holes fixed," she added.

"I'd planned on getting those patched up this morning," Wilbur nodded. "I've got the tools in my truck, and I can get the rest from the hardware store. What time am I supposed to get Maude and Opal?" He hoped he had enough time for repairs, pick up Maude and Opal, and still beat Mavis and Mona to the fair.

"Whenever you call them and let them know," Mavis shrugged. She saw the look on Wilbur's face. "I can't have them coming with me today. It took an hour to find them last night, and this was well after we had planned to meet up. You know how they are." This afternoon with Earl had to go swimmingly, and she couldn't afford to have Maude and Opal mess it up.

Wilbur nodded and picked up on what she wasn't telling him. He had his work cut out for him. He checked his watch and sighed. It was already later than he had intended on getting started. He rinsed out his mug and washed his plate before putting them in the dishwasher. Mavis had already gone upstairs to blow dry her hair and do her makeup. She needed to look radiant when meeting Earl. "I'm planning on ripping out that wet carpet, too!" she called down the stairs.

Of course, she was. Wilbur made a mental note to discuss that later. He knew he would end up being the one who tore out the carpet and replace it with whatever she saw fit. He headed to the hardware store and got the items he needed to fix the hallway wall and ceiling. Mavis was still upstairs getting ready when he returned to the Manor. Thankfully, the holes were minor, and he patched them up quickly. Once they were dry, he would add a coat of paint over them, and no one would be the wiser.

"I'll see you at the fair in an hour!" he called upstairs. "Call me when you get there."

"We'll see!" Mavis called down.

"Mavis," Wilbur sighed.

"Fine, fine. Drive safe!" she replied.

Mavis was going to be the death of him one of these days. He called over to Maude's house, but she didn't answer. He tried Opal next, but her phone also went to voicemail. He decided it would be best to drive over anyway to check on them. He drove a little faster than normal. It wasn't unusual for them to not answer their phone, but with all the drama going on, he needed to be sure.

He pulled up into Opal's yard a few minutes later and saw them poking around Opal's side garden. Opal had a basket full of what looked like peppers while Maude sat on a flipped over five-gallon bucket eating a cookie. "Howdy Wilbur" she called out when he opened his truck door.

"How's it going?" he asked.

"Opal's gardening," Maude said very matter-of-factly.

"I can see that," he chuckled. He waited for any further conversation, but Opal nor Maude offered any more words. "Mavis said I was supposed to come over and ferry y'all over to the fair this afternoon."

"Yes, that's the plan," Maude nodded. "I mean, not that there was a plan. It's a figure of speech, Wilbur."

"I already know about the plan,' he sighed. "And I'm not on board, if you must know."

"I told them it will all work out," Opal shrugged. She handed Wilbur her basket that was full of sweet peppers and okra. "Maude, go get your rope. I got my you know what packed already."

"Now wait a minute," Wilbur said. No one had mentioned anything about a rope or whatever it was Opal had packed.

"Don't you worry, Wilbur, it'll all work out," Opal repeated. "Let's get these inside before the weather rolls in."

Wilbur looked up at the cloudless sky. The sun was shining and there wasn't a hint of a storm on the horizon. "Weather?" he asked.

"Oh yes," she nodded. "It's going to rain something awful this afternoon."

"I don't remember the weatherman predicting rain," he muttered.

Opal looked over at Maude who shook her head. "She's never wrong," Maude told Wilbur. "You'll see."

He decided that it would be best to take their word for it. He carried the vegetables inside and set them on Opal's counter. He washed his hands and saw that they had not followed him. He found them both sitting inside his truck. Maude was in the driver's seat and Opal was in the passenger seat. There was no way that he was going to let either of them drive his truck all the way to Junction.

"Where are the keys?" Maude asked. "What good is leaving it unlocked if the keys aren't in it."

He fished the keys out of his pocket and grinned. Maude frowned and slid over to the passenger seat, squishing Opal against the window. "There's an entire backseat," he reminded them.

"We like to sit in the front," Maude said.

Wilbur shrugged and slid in the driver's seat. He looked in the backseat and saw that they had already thrown their purses and a giant sack in the floorboard behind the driver's seat. He hoped to God that the sack didn't contain any ropes or weapons. It was going to be an interesting ride to the last day of the fair. He knew it was going to be busting at the seams with people, and any wild antics the women in his life had in the sleeve was going to send him over the edge.

He tried to make idle conversation, but Opal and Maude were hyper focused on something else. They mumbled quietly to each other and even turned on the radio at one point, so Wilbur had a harder time hearing them. They were not going to be easy to crack. Mavis had been no help, so that left Mona. Wilbur realized he didn't have a chance in heaven of cracking their code. Those four women were tight-lipped when they wanted to be.

When he pulled into the parking lot, they hopped out of the truck quickly. Maude slung the sack over her shoulder and tossed Opal her purse. Opal skipped off and Maude shouted over her shoulder, "Have a great day with Hope!"

"Now wait a minute!" Wilbur called back. He jogged after them and got in front of them. "Are y'all going to tell me what's going on? And who is Hope?"

Opal shrugged and smiled up at him. "We're going to enjoy the fair. You have fun!"

"Right," Wilbur grunted. He turned to Maude already knowing that she wouldn't be any help. "Are y'all planning on meeting Mavis? I don't think she's here yet. Is she meeting Hope?" He was so confused. He had done his best to beat Mavis to the fair, and she had promised to call him when she arrived. Not that he necessarily believed her.

"Mavis? Mavis who?" Opal feigned ignorance.

"He's not that stupid," hissed Maude.

Wilbur wasn't sure if he should be offended or not. These two were really laying it on thick.

"We aren't meeting Mavis," Maude swore. "We have plans, I mean, we have our own agenda."

Wilbur eyed them warily as Opal crossed her heart and made the sign of the cross. "I'll be keeping my eye out."

"Speaking of which, your eye looks much better," Maude said appreciatively. "Good job, Opal."

Opal nodded and smiled back at Wilbur. "Catch you on the flipside!" she said. Without another word, she and Maude walked towards the food vendors. Opal looked over her shoulder a few times and saw Wilbur following them at a comfortable distance. He swore he heard her say, "We can lose him at the next turn."

[Chapter Twenty-Three]

It had been right under two hours and Mavis still hadn't called him. Wilbur had a sneaking suspicion that she was already here somewhere, but he had yet to find her. Worse still, he had lost Opal and Maude. For two senior citizens, those two ladies could scamper off faster than a toddler. He had kept up with them for a few turns, until they made the right into the main fairway and ditched him. It should have been easy to see them in such an open area, but he hadn't seen hide nor hair of them after that. They didn't exactly blend into a crowd. Maude was wearing comfortable joggers, tennis shoes, and an old fair t-shirt from 1979. She also carried a gunny sack over her back. Opal, on the other hand, was dressed in a floral pants suit and sandals. She had tied a silvery scarf around her head that clashed with her bright clothes.

Wilbur paced up and down each alleyway trying to find them in hopes of keeping them out of trouble. It was a full-time job, and he was already maxed out on overtime. There was no way he could focus on Mavis and Mona with Maude and Opal on the loose.

Mavis and Mona were indeed already at the fair. Mavis felt bad for not calling him, but he didn't exactly fit into her plan. Her perfectly styled hair, exquisite makeup, and knockout wardrobe was all going perfectly to plan. Mona had picked her up the minute that Wilbur had left for Opal's. She was counting on the two older women to slow him down.

"Are you sure he won't come busting up in there?" Mona asked when she pulled into the open field to park.

Mavis bit her bottom lip and frowned. "I'm hoping Maude and Opal keep him just busy enough that he forgets about little old me." She tugged at her skinny jeans and smoothed her button-down blue shirt. She had worn her best cowgirl boots that were bedazzled on the sides. They were sure to hold Earl's attention. He was like a cat when it came to anything with glitter and sparkles.

"Where are you meeting him again?" Mona asked. "I know we talked about it, but I'm nervous!"

"You're nervous?" Mavis asked. "I'm the one throwing myself to the dog."

"It has to be you," Mona reminded her.

"I know, but that doesn't mean I have to like it. He said one o'clock by the Ferris wheel," Mavis said. "We've got a little bit of time before I need to go over there."

Mona checked the time on her cell phone. "We've got more than a little bit of time. We've got over an hour. I hope Opal and Maude are good decoys."

Mavis nodded. "They've been known to keep more than one person guessing at a time."

"I want to be just like them when I grow up," Mona laughed. "Lord willing."

"Me too," Mavis agreed.

"How do they do it?" Mona laughed.

"They've been this way for as long as I've known them, well, my whole life!" Mavis said. "Opal has had a few strokes over the years, and they've slowed her down a lot at times, but she works harder than anyone I know and takes a lot of supplements, so thankfully she has bounced back every time."

"The fact that this is slow for her cracks me up," Mona said in awe. "They really are amazing."

Mavis couldn't help but agree. She was so blessed to have them in her life. However, she hoped they would stay far away today. That was critical for her plan to work. There was no telling what either of them would do or say to Earl if they ran across him.

They walked through the entrance and made their way to the booths they'd been visiting for the past week. Mavis found some delectable pecan and chocolate candy that would hopefully settle her nervous stomach. Mona was too nervous and excitable to eat, which surprised Mavis. How could someone who had been in the restaurant world her whole life not love to eat?

Every now and again, Mona would look at her phone and check the time. She updated Mavis every ten minutes or so in case Mavis didn't fully comprehend the passing of time.

"I know, Mona," Mavis said.

"I just want to make sure we're not late," Mona said.

"I swear! You need to calm down just a little bit," Mavis said.

"When has telling someone to calm down ever actually made someone calm down?" Mona asked.

"That's completely beside the point," Mavis muttered under her breath.

They walked a little further along and continued to look at the vendors who were trying to get rid of the last of their wares. Mavis found time to stop by the ice cream truck and get a little something to soothe her stomach. The pecan candy was good, but it wasn't enough. Undercover work always made her hungry. Mavis was carefully eating her vanilla ice cream cone so that it wouldn't drip onto her clothes when Mona jumped up and nearly knocked her over.

"It's time!" Mona shouted a little too loudly. She looked as white as a ghost.

"Ok, ok!" Mavis huffed. The closer it got to time, the more nervous she became. She looked down at the ice cream that had fallen out of her hand when Mona yelled. It landed upside down at her feet. Hopefully, she would have time to find that particular ice cream vendor later on. Their ice cream had been really good.

"You sure you're ready?" Mona asked again.

Mavis nodded. Even if she wasn't, it was time for the plan to be set in motion. She had told Mona about her conversation with Wilbur earlier that morning. Mona looked all around at everyone who passed by them and wondered aloud whether or not they were undercover cops or regular people enjoying the fair.

"Look at that haircut. He could definitely be the fuzz," Mona whispered to Mavis.

"Nobody says the fuzz," Mavis looked at her.

"Oh, whatever," Mona waved her off. "What about that one?"

"Mona! That's just a kid. He can barely read yet!" Mavis sighed.

"That's what they want you to think," Mona shook her head. "He'd be the perfect undercover."

Mavis shook her head and did her best to ignore her friend. Once the Ferris wheel was in sight, she waved goodbye to Mona who promised to lurk just out of sight the whole time. She sashayed over to the wheel to meet Earl. She looked around the ride and didn't see him. According to her watch, she was right on time. She had been certain that he would be waiting for her, but he was nowhere in sight. She looked high and low and even asked the ride attendant if he had seen him. She thought she had given a pretty adequate description of what he looked like, but the oily man merely shrugged.

Twenty minutes later she heard the screeching of her name from ten feet away. "Suga bear! My Lawd!" he crooned. She froze on the spot and Earl wrapped his spindly arms around her large waist. "I been missin you!"

"Oh really?" Mavis coughed. It felt like Earl was trying to give her the Heimlich maneuver. She did her best to breathe and not regurgitate the contents of her stomach.

"I been a real busy man!" Earl continued. He was wearing the same outfit from last night, but he had added some wildflowers to his pocket. Mavis looked down at the clearly dead flowers and Earl grinned heartily. "Dese are for you!" He handed her the brittle flowers and Mavis thanked him profusely. There was no amount of water or care that would revive them, but she needed to play along.

"Oh, my, these are nice. Where did you find them?" Mavis asked.

"Ova by da porta potties," Earl boasted. "Dats where all da nice flowas are."

Mavis nodded and wished she had a tissue to wrap them up in before she placed them in her expensive purse, but she didn't have one. Earl paid no mind to Mavis' inner war as he launched into his latest scheme.

"What was that?" Mavis asked. She suddenly realized that he hadn't been paying Earl's word any mind.

"Huh?" Earl said. "I'm tellin ya about my meetin dis mornin."

"Right," Mavis nodded. She batted her long fake eyelashes and pretended to listen intently. "It's just that the noise of the Ferris wheel is so loud. Shouldn't we go somewhere a little quieter?"

Earl's beady eyes lit up like a Christmas tree. He nodded and grabbed her hand. "I know da perfect place!"

He led Mavis past the wheel ride through a patch of waist high grass. "This grass is something!" Mavis coughed. "Shouldn't someone mow it?"

258

"Dats my job," Earl said with a shrug. "I just been too busy to get at it. Lots of meetins and fundraisin opportunities."

"Meetings? Fundraisers?" Mavis mumbled.

"Well, dey raise my funds," Earl cackled. He slapped himself on the knee and continued to laugh at his own joke. "Right dis way!" he said.

Mavis looked up and saw row after row of portable toilets along the fence line. The smell was unbearable. They were at the far boundary of the fairgrounds where the carnival workers lived during their off shifts.

"Earl, where are we?" Mavis gagged.

"You said we needed somewheres private, so here we are!" he explained.

She held her nose and gagged again at the smell emanating from the closest toilets. "Earl, I can't be here. We have to go somewhere else," she whispered while trying not to breathe in.

Earl looked dejected, but he took her hand and walked away from the portable toilets towards the giant barn that housed the horses. "Are you sure we gotta go in dere?" he croaked. Earl was afraid of horses. "Dose beasts sooner kill ya!"

"I want to see them," Mavis smiled sweetly. "They're so soft and warm and sweet."

"Dey monstas," Earl countered. "Dose big old feet'll squish ya and mash ya."

Mavis shook her head playfully and walked up to the nearest stall. A beautiful brown mare and her colt were behind the bars eating some hay on the ground. Mavis squealed in delight! "Look! It's a baby!"

"I don't like de way it's lookin at me," Earl said. He opened his eyes as wide as he could and peered through the barn door. "Whoa now!" he cried right as the mare kicked at the door. Earl flew backwards and landed on his rear end on the hard stone floor.

"Earl!" Mavis yelped. "What did you do?"

Earl clambered up and dusted himself off. "Not a dam thing!" he howled. "That one dere is rabid! I see it in da eyes!"

Mavis looked back at the horses who had returned to eating the hay without a care in the world. She knew that horses definitely had a sixth sense about them. They could probably sense that Earl was a rotten apple, and the mother horse wanted him away from her colt. "Let's walk on down a bit," Mavis offered.

Earl continued to mumble under his breath but followed Mavis, nonetheless. The next few stalls were empty, but the fifth one held a giant stallion that was solid black with a white star on his forehead. He was absolutely gorgeous. Without thinking, Mavis reached her hand through the bar and patted him on the nose. He sniffed her hand and nuzzled against it. If the gate had not been locked, Mavis would have happily gone inside and rubbed her face against his soft neck.

The moment was interrupted by Earl who sneered loudly. "Look at dat thing! Suga! He's tryin to maul you!" Earl climbed onto Mavis' back and swatted at the horse who snorted loudly and reared up on his hind legs.

"Earl! Stop!" Mavis cried. She flung Earl off her back and backed away from the agitated animal.

"What's going on here?" a voice yelled. A man raced over to the stall and began talking gently to the midnight black stallion who calmed at once. The man then turned his attention to Earl who stood back up for the second time swearing. "What did you do to my horse?"

"He tried to eat my woman!" Earl yelled.

"No, he didn't!" Mavis retorted. Earl was ruining everything. She apologized profusely to the man and snatched Earl's hand before he could protest. They walked quickly away from the horse barn back outside in the autumn breeze. She kept looking around for Mona, but she couldn't see her. Either Mona was doing an excellent job of hiding, or she had found something else to do in the meantime.

Mavis spotted an open picnic table by a donut truck and told Earl to sit still while she bought them some snacks. The line wasn't long, so she was able to keep an eye on Earl the whole time. He gobbled up two whole glazed donuts in one bite as soon as Mavis set the box on the table. She felt bad that he was so hungry, but then she remembered that he had done most of this drama to himself. He was a pathological thief and liar. He had scammed people of all ages out of their life's savings over the years. She was sure that there were situations and charges she would never even know about. It made her sick to her stomach knowing what she did know.

"Dese are good," Earl said as he ate his fourth donut. He rubbed his belly and sighed happily. "When we gets outta here, we can open our own donut shop. Ain't too hard to do.'

"When we get out of here?" Mavis questioned.

"Yea," Earl said. "Da carnival life is no life for me. I'm ready for my next adventure."

"And what adventure is that?" Mavis asked.

"Real estate," Earl grinned. "I got it all figured out! Investin all dat money I got. Take da Manor for instance, we about to turn dat place into a billion dolla vacation destination!"

"My Manor?" Mavis gasped.

"Our Manor," Earl nodded. "What's yours is mine and what's mine is mine. You know da sayin!"

Mavis had no idea what Earl was going on about. She had hoped that he was well over Magnolia Manor by now, but she had been wrong. That must be why Earl was back in this area. He was still after her beloved family home. He had no idea what lengths she would go to in order to protect the place where she was raised.

"What are your plans exactly?" she asked.

"Take my money and fix it up. Paint it. I think a lovely shade of purple will be good. And add a nice little bayou swamp in da back for some wildlife, ya know, and get some fan boats for da people. Open our own little waterpark right and people will come for miles! I knowed yall aint got no water park or what dey call a tourist destination around here, so I got it covered," Earl said proudly. He had clearly put a lot of thought into this project, but Mavis was fuming on the inside. No one was touching a single inch of her property. Especially not for some swamp creature water world.

[Chapter Twenty-Four]

Mavis stuffed donuts into her mouth to keep quiet. Earl had launched into his grand plans with no regard to anyone else. She listened intently and tried to keep quiet, but she had so many questions. When Mavis asked him where all the money had come from for his venture, he smiled slyly and leaned in closer to her. "I stoled it, of course," he whispered. "It was so easy if you know what you doin! And I do!"

Mavis had known or at least suspected it, but she still needed more information. She had to be careful not to raise his suspicions, so she smiled playfully and commented how expensive it all sounded. "I don't have much money," she lied. "The only thing I have left is my home."

"Don't worry bout dat," Earl said casually. "I gots plenty of money and I know where to get more."

"Oh really?" Mavis gushed. "Wow! You're such a great businessman!"

"Yea, dats true," Earl nodded.

Mavis almost choked on her soda when he confided that he had thousands of dollars hidden under a few of the portable toilets out in the fields.

"No one suspects me," Earl said proudly. "I'm just so good."

Mavis knew how to stroke his ego, even though it made her feel disgusting. Smiling and encouraging Earl while he talked about his unscrupulous dealings made her sick, but it was for a good cause. He told her how he had stolen from nearly everyone he worked with and how easy it was to pick the pockets and purses of the fairgoers. He had found a treasure trove of things in the lost-and-found booth as well. He had about fifty wallets and numerous credit cards that he had collected over the past week and a half. "But dere's one honey hole I haven't tapped into yet," he whispered.

"Oh?" Mavis asked. She felt the hairs on the back of her neck stand up.

"Dere's dis lady here at da fair, some voodoo woman. I been asking around about her and whoa suga! Let me tell ya! She is loaded! I'm talking big money. Real big money. And she's old, too," Earl smiled. "Dose ol' ladies, dey always love ol' Earl!"

Mavis felt her heart sink in her stomach. He had to be talking about Opal. Of course, he wouldn't have recognized her the other day when Mavis was with her because she and Maude both wore wigs and costumes when they were playing their roles. Mavis needed to find out what in the world he was planning.

"Hmm, I don't know who that could be," Mavis squeaked.

"She about dis tall," Earl said. He showed Mavis with his hand how far the women measured from the ground up. "Wearin' a big old robe and makin' money hand ova fist at her magic table! Just a little ol' thang. Shouldn't be no problem!"

"No problem?" Mavis asked. She had started to sweat, and her hands were starting to shake a little from her nerves.

"Oh yea," Earl nodded. "Madame Opalina or somethin like dat. I visited with her a few days ago and didn't see no money, but I knowed what happened. She and dis otha old lady been stashin it outta da way. She don't look like she put up a fight. I have all dat money in no time."

"A fight? You can't fight an old lady!" Mavis gasped.

"I ain't gotta hurt her," Earl shrugged. "Not if she tell me where da money is. Rumor have it dat she got it all buried out back behind her house. Dats what I heard. Just gotta get her outta da way first and I'll find it. Dis ain't my first time, suga. I know how to make people talk." His nonchalant manner made Mavis more nervous than she had ever been around him. She knew that he was devious, but he had never seemed altogether dangerous. Maybe prison had changed him.

"This is not like you, Earl," she whispered back. "I've never known you to be violent."

Earl laughed heartily. "Oh suga, Earl T. don't gotta get rough all da time. I'm a lover, not a fighter. If I get what I want, dat is. And you know just what I like. We can talk about dat later because now we gots to get on da road. You bring your car? I want to see da Manor and den go finds dis lady's house so we can scope it out. She probably got a mansion of her own and we can make it a nice little motel for our guests!"

"You sure have changed, Earl," Mavis said. She saw his eyes flash and she quickly scrambled to cover her tracks. "I mean, you're so much more confident and stronger." She was relieved to see that he bought it. He nodded and licked the sugary glaze off of another donut.

"What happened after you left Rhinestone last year?" Mavis asked. She had not kept up with his trials or anything regarding him once he was carted back to Louisiana. Life was easier that way.

"Since you had me locked up?" Earl mused. He looked angry, but Mavis needed to know.

"I'm so sorry, Earl," Mavis winced. She rubbed her eyes and tried her best to fake some tears for added effect. "I've just missed you so much! I missed you every day. I just couldn't find you." She was lying through her teeth, but Earl was lapping it up. He eyed her cautiously but smiled.

"I did some time in Baton Rouge," he spit.

"Oh my," Mavis hiccupped. "Tell me all about it."

"Well, I don't know," Earl said. "Dere's ears all around."

There was no way that he could know about the undercover police officers who had been trailing him. Mavis assumed he was just trying to be even more mysterious than usual. She batted her eyes and looked around before leaning in closer. "You can trust me. I'm so sorry for ever making you think you couldn't. I'm just all to pieces." She poked out her bottom lip and pouted like an award-winning actress.

"Well, it's just dat I ain't supposed to be here," Earl whispered.

"Whatever do you mean?" Mavis asked in a hushed tone.

"Well, you see, da judge in Baton Rouge said that I was a fight risk," Earl began.

"A fight risk?" Mavis interrupted. "Don't you mean a flight risk?"

"Earl T. don't know how to fly!" Earl cackled. "I'm like da strong bold eagle on da American flag. We can't fly but we still powerful." He boasted the last bit proudly and puffed out his weak chest. Bald eagles could definitely fly, but Mavis didn't want to burst his bubble just yet. She needed him to keep talking.

"Right," Mavis nodded. "My apologies."

"It's alright," Earl said. "Not everyone can be as smart as me. Anyway, he said I was a fight risk. You know he saw my muscles and knowed I was a fighter. So, he didn't give me no bail. I had to sit in dat cold dark cell for months before dey let me have a trial. I didn't need no attorney, ya know. I knows da law and I know I ain't guilty of nothin. But da judge and jury mans said I was. Couillons!"

Mavis could see that his dander was up. She bit her tongue and watched as he took another sip of his soda before continuing. "Dey lock me up and throwed away da key. But den dey needed some strong men to pick up trash on da roadside. I seen my way out a few weeks later. Dey called in da bloodhounds and everything, but I ain't scared of no water or gaytuhs, ya know. Swam all da way down da river and saw da light at da end of da tunnel."

"What was it?" Mavis asked with widened eyes.

269

"What?" Earl asked.

"What was the light?" Mavis repeated.

"Ain't no light," Earl shook his head. "It's a matador, ya know. It uh, means dere was something dere waitin for me."

Mavis scrunched up her nose and tried to discern what he was talking about. "Oh! A metaphor!" she nodded.

"Dat's what I said. I seen dis here travelin carnival and walked right on in. Found me dis here uniform and followed it where it go. I had seen on da schedule it was comin to Junction and I knowed it was right. It was all part of da plan," he grinned wickedly. "Didn't even need to borrow no car to come find you. You found me all on your own!"

"Of course," Mavis nodded.

"I made a few stops and deals along da way. I'm an enterprisin man, ya know. But now all I gotta do is pack up da money and we can ride ova to da Manor. Ya know, I'd like me a big steak dinner and a nice long soak in da tub while you cook it," Earl continued.

"Right," Mavis muttered. "Um, how do we, I mean, how do you get the money you have hidden?"

"I just need to get it in my special hidin spot," Earl shrugged.

"Let's go now!" Mavis said with sudden gusto. She saw a look of concern flash across Earl's face. "I just mean that I know that you're hungry and have been working so hard. Let's get on back to the Manor and I'll fix us up some supper." She hoped she had sounded convincing. She wasn't sure where the officers were, or where Mona had

270

scampered off to. She hoped that they were writing all of this down. She didn't know what she would do if she actually had to pull the car around. There was no way she was taking him home to Magnolia Manor.

Earl polished off another donut and wiped his hands on his ripped-up pants. He picked up the box and noticed that it was empty, so he put it back on the table and took one last sip of his drink. When it too was empty, he tossed it on the ground and beckoned for Mavis to follow him. She quickly picked up and discarded the trash before hurrying after him.

It didn't take him long to lead them to the disgusting smell of the portable toilets. Mavis held her nose as he opened the furthest portable toilet that had a sign on it saying it was unusable. He found a shovel in there and asked Mavis to help him push the structure over a little. "I'm a good hider," he nodded passionately. As soon as they had it moved over to his liking, he began to dig.

Mavis bit her lip in anticipation. She heard his shovel hit what sounded like a metal box. Earl hurriedly pulled the metal box out of the ground and looked around to make sure that no one was watching. "Is that it?" Mavis whispered.

Earl nodded and wiped off the dirt with his sleeve. Mavis silently willed him to open it, but she knew that he wouldn't take that chance. "Give me yo' jacket," Earl requested.

Mavis handed over her sweater and watched as he wrapped the box in it. She really wanted to see what was inside of it, but she did not want to be the one to open it. She did not want her fingerprints on any of the evidence, nor did she think that Earl would hand it over.

Once Earl was satisfied that the box was well hidden in her sweater, he tucked it under his arm and said it was time to go. He said he would come back for the box of other treasures hidden under his rack in one of the trailers later. Mavis froze. She had hoped that it would be like a scene out of the movies where officers jumped out of their hiding spots and wrestled him to the ground, but that was not the case. There was no one around them. No one was coming to save the day, so she would have to be the one to do it.

Since no officers showed up, she scanned the area looking for Mona. Or better yet, maybe Wilbur would stumble on the scene, but there was no one she knew. Wilbur was probably still trying the deal with Opal and Maude, and given the fact that Earl had his sights on Opal's money, she was relieved that Big Mama's two best friends were nowhere to be seen.

"What's the matter with you Suga Bear?" Earl watched her closely. "Aint you ready to go?"

"I guess I'm not used to so much excitement," Mavis fanned herself wildly. She continued to scan the area around her.

"Dis is only da beginnin,' Suga," Earl said. He looped his boney arm in hers and started walking toward the exit, half dragging Mavis along in the process.

Mavis wasn't exactly sure what happened next. As Earl began to drag her away from the fair, Wilbur yelled her name from the far end of the port-o-potties. He wasn't the only one who yelled.

Mavis could hear Mona closing in from the other side. Earl turned and saw Wilbur running straight for them. He dropped the box and bolted for the tree line.

"There he is!" Opal yelled.

Mavis turned to see Maude and Opal giving chase after Earl. Where in the world had they come from?

"Maude! Opal!" Wilbur yelled as he got closer to Mavis.

"Are you alright?" Mona wheezed as she reached Mavis.

"Yeah, but he wants to steal Opal's money," Mavis told both Wilbur and Mona. There was so much to tell them, but that was the most pressing.

"That'd be the ticket. They'd both kill him," Wilbur said. "Come on, let's go stop them from hurting him too bad."

Earl had climbed the nearest tree like a bear, but he had, unfortunately for him, not seen the hornet nest a few feet above his head.

Mavis stomped her foot and demanded that he come down, but he refused. She couldn't understand a word that he was saying. She saw a rock on the ground and picked it up. She would have to knock him out the tree after all. She reared back and hurled the rock at Earl's head, but she missed him by two feet.

"Ooh!" Opal gasped. "You done done it now."

Mavis had inadvertently stirred up the hornets above Earl's head. Earl fell out of the tree and landed on his behind. He jumped up and ran as fast as he could to escape the stingers from the angry nest.

"He's getting away!" Mavis cried. "What are we going to do?"

"I'm calling the police!" Mona yelled. She pulled out her phone and began shouting into it. "They're on their way!"

"They should already be here," Wilbur grumbled.

"Hold your horses! I ain't got all day!" Maude hollered. She was going to have to do this all on her own. No more waiting for the so-called professionals to step in. At the rate the cops were going, they were going to lose him again. She tossed her bag on the ground and opened it quickly. She reached inside and pulled out a lariat.

"Get him, Maude!" Opal yelled in encouragement. She held onto her baseball bat for added effect.

Maude twirled the lasso around her lead and let it fly. She caught Earl by his left leg and tugged. The birdlike man fell flat on his face, but quickly scrambled to stand up. Maude tugged again on the rope and held her ground with Opal's help. With a burst of sudden ferocity, Earl lunged forward and ended up sending Maude and Opal toppling to the ground. Maude dropped the rope as she fell.

"Maude! Opal!" Mavis cried. She and Wilbur ran towards them and helped them to their feet. "Are you ok?" Mavis gasped.

"We're fine," Maude said curtly. She was madder than a hill of ants that had just been kicked over. She looked at Opal who had some dirt on her elbows, but otherwise was no worse for wear. "I'm going to whoop him!" She hurried off after Earl leaving Wilbur, Mavis, and Opal in the dust.

"She really can move fast for an, well," her voice dropped off as Opal eyed her warily. She didn't need to finish her sentence and call Maude an old lady in front of Opal who was holding a wooden baseball bat.

"You get him, Maude!" Opal yelled. "I'm coming with my bat!" She took off like a racing horse at the starting gate.

"Good grief! How are both of them outrunning us?" Mona held a stitch at her side as she scampered off after Mavis and Wilbur who were trying to catch up to Maude, Opal, and Earl. Earl and the two women were already in the field full of parked cars by the time they caught up to them.

"Freeze!" Harlan's voice echoed off the nearby cars in the field. Earl paid him no mind and continued to run. The rope was still tied around his left foot and thrashed wildly after him. Opal did her best to grab it, but Earl was all over the place ducking behind random cars and trucks.

As Earl ducked behind a large Chrysler minivan, Maude closed in and lunged toward him. She threw a clean tackle just above the knees that would have made a defensive lineman proud. Opal saw that as the perfect opportunity. She landed on him with her knees square in his back and took aim. Fortunately for Earl, Wilbur showed up in the nick of time to grab the bat before Opal could make contact.

Harlan helped Maude and Opal off Earl while three other officers lifted Earl off the ground and handcuffed him. Maude dusted herself off and sneered at him. "You broke my best sunglasses," she hissed. She held up the snapped pair of glasses and shook her head. "Don't come back now, you hear me!"

"She should have played on the football team!" Mona said to Mavis in awe.

"They didn't let girls do that back then," Mavis said. She was so winded, but she also felt intense relief at the sight of Earl once again being handcuffed. "Girls had to be cheerleaders and stuff back then."

Opal began to cackle loudly behind them. "Maude wasn't a cheerleader," she howled. "She was too busy smoking behind the bleachers. Ruby was the cheerleader. She sure did keep us in line."

[Chapter Twenty-Five]

After Harlan carted Earl away in his car, Mavis breathed a sigh of relief. She dropped down to her knees and breathed heavily. Mona knelt down next to her and patted her on the back. "You did great!" she said. "He's gone for good."

"That's what we thought last time," Mavis wheezed. She tried to catch her breath as best she could.

"Come on, get up," Wilbur said gently. "This time we're going to make sure." He had handed off the metal box wrapped in Mavis' sweater to Harlan, along with his witness statement. Mavis, Mona, Maude, and Opal had each given their own account of the evening to the other officers.

Once Mavis calmed down, she invited everyone back to the Manor for pizza. She and Mona followed Wilbur, Maude, and Opal back to Rhinestone. Wilbur offered to pick up the pizza while Mavis went to the Piggly Wiggly. Mona called Harry on the way and invited him as well. They had lots to catch him up on.

Harry was waiting for them when they pulled into the Manor an hour later. He followed the caravan of people inside and listened as they caught him up on the events of the day. Mavis, Maude, Opal, and Mona all began talking at once which made it difficult to keep up with. He looked to Wilbur for help, but he merely shrugged. After they all gushed about what happened, Wilbur filled in the missing details and helped answer Harry's many questions. After Harry sat back in the chair and laughed, "Lord, you have all been busy!" Mavis declared that it was time to eat. She poured everyone a big glass of sweet tea and Wilbur handed out paper plates and everyone ate their fill of pizza and garlic bread. Once the empty pizza boxes were thrown away, Maude said she needed something sweet to counteract the savory pizza.

Mavis ushered them all to the living room and said she would bring them all a cup of coffee and some dessert. Mona stayed behind to help her.

"I still for the life of me don't know how Opal and Maude can run circles around half this town,' Mona said.

"We've had years of practice," Opal said as she exited the kitchen. She looked around for her bat and Maude's rope, but she couldn't find it. Wilbur had made sure that Opal's bat and Maude's lasso were safely stored away before they could get into any more mischief.

"Ms. Maude, I found something special for you at the Pig," Mavis smiled. "I found you a peach praline upside down cake." She lifted the plastic container to show her the decadent dessert.

"Ooh, that looks good," Maude smiled. "Cut me off a big piece." She followed Opal out of the kitchen towards the living room where Wilbur and

Harry were already sitting on the larger couch in front of the television. She and Opal each sank down in the pair of recliners that had been Jameson and Ruby's favorite spots to relax many years ago.

Mavis got the dessert plates from the cabinet and began to cut a piece of cake for everyone there, cutting an especially large piece for Maude. She and Mona carried the plates into the living room and began passing them around.

"That's for making sure Earl didn't get away," Mavis smiled as she set Maude's plate in front of her. Maude nodded and sighed happily. "This sure looks good!"

Mona and Mavis returned a few minutes later with cups of coffee for everyone. They sat down on the couch and ate in relative silence. Wilbur's cell phone buzzed on the coffee table, and he walked out of the room to answer it. He walked back in from the hallway a few minutes later putting his cellphone in his pocket. "That was Harlan. He's going to stop by in a few minutes and give us an update on Earl," Wilbur said.

"Good, I need to tell him what I learned today as well," Mavis said.

They still had no idea why Harlan and his men weren't nearby to capture Earl like Wilbur said they would be. Thankfully, Mona had the sense to call for help. Not that they necessarily needed them, but after Maude rugby tackled Earl, they weren't sure what they would have done with him aside from hogtying him with the lariat.

"Mavis, I'm sure that he has a pretty good idea of everything that happened," Wilbur told her, taking the plate of cake that she offered him. "We all gave our statements."

"Well, I keep remembering more. And I'm guessing that Earl told me some things that he hasn't shared with the general law enforcement community," Mavis snapped. She was exhausted and was definitely glad that Wilbur had shown up when he did, but she wasn't ready to listen to the smug way he talked about her investigative skills or his idea that she probably shouldn't have gotten involved.

"He'll probably have you make a more formal statement or something in a few days," Mona said. Her eyes lit up at the thought of it. "Ooh, this is exciting. We're going to be on Court TV!"

"Hold on Judge Judy," Wilbur said, trying to stem the rising excitement between Mavis and Mona. "Before you get too busy planning your closeups, maybe we should hear what Harlan has to say first."

"Wilbur takes the fun out of everything," Mavis told Mona.

When the knock at the back door came a few minutes later, Harry went to let Harlan in. He had a piece of cake in front of him as soon as he sat down thanks to Mona.

"You don't know how lucky you were," Harlan looked at Mavis in between bites of cake.

"What do you mean?" Mavis asked.

"This guy is a real piece of work. You should have never tried to go after him by yourself," Harlan said.

"She wasn't by herself. She had me," Mona said proudly.

"That's not exactly the tactical backup I would have chosen for a sting operation," Harry said.

"It worked, didn't it!" Mavis countered.

Harry opened his mouth to say something else, but Wilbur shook his head. They both knew that once Mavis or Mona get an idea in their heads, it was pointless to try and reason with them.

"I told you we should have handled this," Maude said to Opal. "These young kids today don't know how to catch the perps like we do. It's all in the wrist!"

"Perps?" Opal asked.

"Saw it on Blue Bloods," Maude nodded.

"I always liked Tom Selleck," Opal said absentmindedly from the recliner next to Maude. "But he just isn't as good since he left Magnum."

"Well kudos to him aside, this Earl fellow is something else," Harlan repeated. "He's dangerous."

"But Harlan, I know Earl," Mavis said. "He talks a big game, but he's not really violent."

"Mavis, you told me he wanted to beat up Opal," Mona said.

"I know, but," Mavis trailed off.

"He what?" Maude roared. She leapt out of the recliner and landed on her feet. "Where's that bat, Opal? I'm going to wallop him good for you!"

"No need to, Ms. Maude. We have him on a whole list of charges," Harlan said. "He's wanted for burglary, battery, criminal trespass, criminal damage to property, unauthorized entry, extortion, credit card fraud, forgery, harassment, theft, theft of a motor vehicle, purse snatching, robbery, illegal possession of stolen things, stalking, and a fake explosive device, just to name a few."

"Stalking?" Mavis couldn't believe it.

"Yeah," Harlan replied. "He was stalking a couple of the residents who lived close to the fairgrounds in Jackson. The fair was there a few weeks ago."

"Did you say he had some explosives?" Wilbur asked.

"Fake ones, but yeah," Harlan nodded. "Apparently he was trying to go fishing from the dock and he hoped the fish would simply come up to the surface."

"It's a wonder he didn't blow himself up," Wilbur said, shaking his head.

"Harlan just said they were fake," Mona reminded him.

"Earl is just dumb enough to figure out how to mix it with something like fireworks that really would make them explode," Wilbur said.

"He always did like the fireworks," Mavis agreed. She shook her head thinking about Earl blowing up half the county.

"Read that list again," Mona said. "I must have misheard a few of those. Did you say something about a stolen car?"

Harlan flipped back through his notes and nodded. "Stolen car, stolen livestock, theft of timber, and identity theft. Multiple counts of identity theft."

Wilbur shook his head and turned to look at Mavis. "This is insane," he breathed.

"Did you say arson?" Harry added.

"It's believed that he made a fire in a trashcan in Mobile that got out of control and burned down one of their livestock barns. Thankfully, no one was injured. They were able to get all of the horses out in time," Harlan explained.

"He's always been afraid of horses," Mavis nodded. Wilbur looked at her like she was crazy. "But all that doesn't explain why you weren't there today. Wilbur said you were going to snatch him up!" she exclaimed.

"I don't think I said those exact words," Wilbur countered.

"We'd been following him for a few days. Since today was the last day of the fair, we had to hurry and tie up some loose ends. We were waiting on a fax from a guy I know over in Jackson. That's why we weren't there when you, um, conducted your own, well, anyway. Earlier this morning, some of my guys searched his bunk and found a box full of wallets and purses and loads of credit cards. They're still sorting through them down at the station. When we ran his name and fingerprints in the database, he came up under lots of different names. People from Monroe, Jackson, Gulfport, Mobile, and now Junction have reported a man who sounds and looks an awful lot like Earl for a multitude of crimes. He had a different name in every town. Teddy Bear, Ben Dover, Chuck Wagon, Seymour Wieners, and a few others," Harlan blushed.

"Good Lord," Wilbur sighed.

"Theft of timber? What's he need with timber" Mona asked. "This is all crazy."

"Not to mention the more dangerous ones," Wilbur added.

"I can't believe he would do all that," Mavis said. "I knew he was trouble, but I had no idea he was doing all that."

"And when did you find out about his interest in Ms. Opal's estate?" Harlan asked.

"Today," Mavis said. "That was the first I had heard about it. I've never seen him threaten violence against anyone. Not really," she explained. "He's got an awful temper, but he never physically hurt anyone, I don't think." She frowned and tried to remember during her time in Louisiana if he had ever mentioned getting physical with anyone. He had thrown quite a few tantrums which entailed him trashing the trailer and breaking a few things every and then, but he had never hit her.

"Tell me more about Opal," Maude demanded.

"Well, he just mentioned that there was a lady at the fair that he had met, and he learned more about her. He said her name and everything. He said he saw all the money she was making," Mavis paused. She saw Maude's eyes widen in anger. "And, well, he learned somehow that she had a lot of money to her name. He said he knew how to get the money from her because he heard where it was hidden."

"Where my money was hidden?" Opal asked.

"Yes ma'am," Mavis nodded. "He said he'd fix you up and then he said he would grab all the money because it was in, well, I don't want to tell anyone where it is."

Opal smiled and leaned back in the recliner. "I can tell you that it won't ever be found. Not until I want it to be."

"But he said it was," Mavis closed her mouth and tried to communicate with Opal with her eyes, but it didn't work. Mavis stood up and whispered into Opal's ear. The old woman cackled loudly.

"My back garden?" she howled in laughter. "That's the best!"

"Oh Mavis, it ain't in her garden," Maude joined in laughing. "That man really is a fool! I'd like to see him try to dig in Opal's yard. Her damn chickens would have attacked him."

"And there's one or two plants he probably doesn't want to mess with," Opal smiled.

"One or two?" Maude chackled. "Every damn one of them is poisonous. He'd come out of that place looking like God knows what, not that he's a far cry from that already."

"I almost wish Opal would have gotten a few good whacks in before she was pulled off," Harry said.

"The last time she decided to whack somebody, I was the one who got hit," Wilbur said. He rubbed his eye with the mostly faded bruise.

"Don't worry, Wilbur. My aim has gotten a lot better since then," Opal assured him.

"But that was only a couple of days ago," Wilbur told her.

Opal nodded. "Like Maude said, it's all in the wrist."

"I'll take y'all's word for it," Wilbur said.

"So, what happens now?" Harry asked. He was almost disappointed that he hadn't been at the fair today to witness it all for himself.

"Well, we take a look at what crimes he's committed here," Harlan began. "I'm not exactly sure how many charges are pending here, but I suspect he's got a notebook full waiting on him for all the stuff he pulled while he was working at the fair. Then the judge will probably extradite him back over to Louisiana since he escaped from their custody. Once he's served his jail time for all that stuff, then he can serve time in Mississippi, then Mobile, then come back over here and spend some time in our jail. If I had to guess, I'd say he's looking at forty or fifty years, give or take a month or two, just in Louisiana. Of course, you never know once a jury gets involved, but I can tell you, the state of Louisiana doesn't take too kindly to escaped convicts running away from their work details."

"I don't want him back here!" Mavis cried.

"Mavis, forty or fifty years," Wilbur said softly. "I think it's going to be ok."

Harlan nodded affirmatively. "Let's just say that he won't be back in Rhinestone anytime soon. I know we've said that before, but there won't be a next time. I give you my word."

"So, you think we're finally rid of him then?" Mavis asked.

"I'd say so," Harlan said.

"That's worth another slice of cake," Maude said.

Opal leaned over to Mavis. "See, I told you it would work itself out."

"You sure did," Mavis said. "You sure did."

[Chapter Twenty-Six]

The excitement from the day before had driven all the tasks of tearing down Madame Opalina's booth from everyone's mind. When Opal had decided to close down her booth earlier in the week, they had packed her costume trunk and filled the wagon with all of her personal items, but they still had to tear down the booth and counter area that they had left behind for Morris, the sweet man with the birdhouses, to use. Wilbur called Mavis early Sunday morning and told her that he was heading over to get started early so he could watch the football game with Harlan and Harry later that afternoon.

"That's fine," Mavis told him. "I'm going over to pick up Maude and Opal and we'll head on over there."

By the time Mavis pulled into the driveway of Opal's house an hour later, Maude and Opal were ready and waiting. Maude pulled the wagon behind her on the way to the car. Thankfully, Opal had decided she no longer needed to know what happened to her bat. The large bundle she had carried with her the day before was nowhere to be seen and Maude no longer had the rather cumbersome looking bag that held her lasso. Mavis didn't know where Wilbur had stashed those items, but she didn't care as long as they didn't need to use them anytime soon.

"Do you think we'll need the wagon?" Mavis asked.

"Better to be safe than sorry," Maude said.

"Ready to face the enemy?" Opal asked as she climbed into Mavis' car.

"What enemy?" Maude asked.

"It's a figure of speech," Opal explained. She climbed into the passenger seat leaving Maude to sit alone in the middle row.

"Doesn't make much sense," Maude said. "Especially since we were doing all the fighting yesterday. You're getting battier as you get older."

"Me? If that's the case, we're just going to have to put you down," Opal to Maude who swatted at Opal with her purse.

"My brain hurts listening to y'all sometimes," Mavis said. She backed out of the driveway and turned on the radio to try and change the subject.

"Sometimes I feel like my brain won't turn off," Opal mused.

"Sometimes I feel like your brain hasn't even turned on," Maude muttered.

Opal ignored Maude and launched into a new subject about the animal auction later this afternoon at the fairgrounds. "I don't want to hear about that," Mavis shuddered. "Those poor little cows and pigs getting sold to eat."

"They do have that auction," Opal lamented. "But there's another one after that where they sell the petting zoo animals, like the llamas. There's even a camel for sale today! The one that people could pay to ride. I've always wanted a pet camel."

"You do not need a camel," Maude told her.

"Doesn't mean I can't want one," Opal reasoned.

"Why are they selling the petting zoo? Besides, a camel belongs in a big zoo," Maude said. "Or in the desert. We don't have a desert around here."

"Llamas?" Mavis asked, ignoring Maude's soliloquy.

"Yep," Opal nodded. "I saw a few of them the other day at the petting zoo. The man who owns it is retiring and doesn't want them anymore. He's got a camel, some goats, a tortoise, some sheep, a parrot, and three llamas. I'm sure there was more than that, but I can't remember."

Mavis made a mental note to go over to the livestock area and see if there were any animals that needed a good home after they tore down Opal's booth. She knew she had plenty of room for a few rescues since Clive had been released back into the wild. She also hoped to see some of the other vendors packing up, especially the food vendors. They would be sure to have some good deals on any leftover cakes and treats. She was completely lost in thought as they drove through the countryside to the fairgrounds for the last time in a good while.

"Stop the car!" Maude suddenly yelled from behind Mavis' seat.

Mavis slammed on the brakes which squealed wildly. "What in the world?" Mavis gasped. She looked in front of her and didn't see a deer or stray dog on the road. Why else would Maude suddenly yell?

"There's nothing like a good roadside market," Maude said. She pointed through the window at the little old man on the side of the road with a wooden stand and sign that boasted the freshest vegetables and boiled peanuts.

"You've got to be kidding me!" Mavis hissed.

"You can't be too careful where you get your produce from," Opal said. "Homegrown is best. Too many pesticides and junk from the store."

"Yep, whatever she said," Maude nodded. "Let's go look and see what he's got." She and Opal hurried out of the car leaving Mavis breathless behind the wheel. Once she had steadied herself, she pulled over to the side of the road and put the car in park and joined them.

"Oh look, he's got some tomatoes and cucumbers," Maude said. "And boiled peanuts!"

"Yep, won't have the tomatoes too much longer, maybe another month or so," he told them. "Same with the cucumbers."

"But you grow your own produce," Mavis said to Opal.

Opal nodded and looked through his baskets. "But I don't grow sweet corn," she explained. She bought a few ears while Maude haggled over the price of boiled peanuts with the man's wife. Things started to get heated, so as an act of mercy, Mavis bought a watermelon and some peanuts from the man while Opal dragged Maude away from the stand.

"I can boil my own peanuts for that price," Maude huffed.

Opal shook her head and sighed. "You tried that once. You're lucky you still have your eyebrows." They climbed back in the car while Mavis loaded the watermelon in the trunk. She handed Maude a Styrofoam cup of hot boiled peanuts before pulling back onto the highway. Maude carefully ate one and remarked how good they were.

"Then why didn't you buy any?" Mavis asked.

"Because they were overpriced," Maude said plainly with her mouth stuffed.

Mavis rolled her eyes and continued the drive to the fair. She had traveled this road so many times during the past week and a half that she could probably get there with her eyes closed. When they neared the fairgrounds, she saw that the field had considerably fewer vehicles since it was no longer open to the public, but she still had to park a ways back from the giant tent that housed most of the indoor vendors.

They found Wilbur inside the tent with most of the booth already broken down. He had been able to back his truck near the entrance of the tent which made loading up the boards much easier. Maude had taken the wagon with her to walk around and see what the other vendors were doing while Opal wanted to use the drill to remove the hand painted sign from the front of the booth. "I want to hang this up in the carport," she smiled.

Wilbur handed her the drill and kept a close eye on her while she used it. Thankfully, she didn't need any help. The sign was down in no time completely intact. Once everything was loaded and cleaned up, Wilbur hopped in his truck and said he would drop the wood off at Opal's and catch up with them later. The two football teams were set to kick off right after lunch, and he needed to hurry if he was going to make it on time. "Don't get into any more trouble," he called out of his window as he drove off.

"Who? Us?" Opal asked. She waved him off and skipped off to find Maude laying in one of the show floor hammocks a few aisles over. "I'm surprised you got back into one of those," Opal mused. She saw the confused look on Mavis' face and laughed. "She got trapped in one when she was a kid. I swear a bear had gotten her, but it was just her old self."

Maude stuck her tongue at Opal and pulled the hammock sides over her. "I'm like a butterfly in a cocoon," she said.

"Nah, you're just an old caterpillar. Now come on," Opal directed. She lifted Maude from underneath the fabric and turned her swiftly over. Maude held onto the fabric for as long as she could, but gravity won out and she tumbled to the ground.

"That was rude!" Maude snapped.

"Oh, hush," Opal said cheerfully. "The food vendors are clearing out. I bet we can get you some stuff half off."

Maude perked up instantly and rushed off towards the line of food trucks that were breaking down picnic tables and piling them and chairs and tables into their trailers. They asked around until they finally found the couple who ran the cake booth. They had a few cakes and platters of dessert left that they hadn't sold. Maude bought them all at a generous discount and loaded the boxes into the wagon. "See," she told Mavis and gestured to the wagon. "It's better to be safe than sorry."

Maude was considerably happier now that she had bought two chocolate layered cakes, a coconut cream cake, a plate of brownies, and two plates of assorted cookies. None of the other food trucks or vendor booths had anything left for sale, but Maude was content with her find. She peeled off the plastic wrap from one of the cookie platters and tasted a few different samples. She must not have found a bad one because Mavis noted that ate half the platter while they watched the various horses being loaded up into their respective trailers near the horse arena.

"Let's go check out the auction for the petting zoo," Mavis suggested. She had no desire to watch the bidding of the animals doomed for slaughter, but she really wanted to see what other animals would be at the sale.

They made it just in time to see the camel and tortoise go to another local petting zoo. The goats and sheep went to a local farmer who bought them for his grandkids. The parrot came down to a bidding war between a college-aged girl and an older woman who narrowly won.

"That thing will outlive her," Maude whispered not so loudly. The woman glared at her but walked on by without another word. "They live for like fifty years," Maude continued.

"Some up to eighty," Opal nodded.

"No thank you!" Maude hissed.

"Wow!" Mavis said. She was glad she hadn't bid on the parrot. She didn't need any animal that could potentially outlive her, nor did she particularly enjoy how loud the brightly colored bird was acting. She swore she heard him mutter a few curse words when the auctioneer yelled into the microphone.

Opal had been right about the llamas. There were three females that the owner was hoping to sell all together. Two were white and fluffy while the other one could best be described as resembling a calico cat. They needed a good bath and brushing, but otherwise looked healthy. The man stated that they were all about five years old and were up to date on all of their vaccinations. It wouldn't hurt for Mavis to offer the starting bid. She raised her hand to open up the bidding of one hundred dollars and frowned when the man behind her raised the bid. The llamas were certainly popular. Before long, there were five different people bidding for them back and forth. The price quickly soared to a solid four figures. A few of the bidders dropped out, but the man behind her held firm. He countered each offer she made. She looked over at the calico llama. It smiled broadly at her as only a llama could. She wasn't sure what came over her, but she stood up and called out an enormously high offer.

"Good lord! I didn't pay that much for my first house!" Maude yelled.

"That's a bit of an exaggeration," Opal said.

"Not by much," Maude replied.

The auctioneer looked around, but no one else spoke. "Going once, twice, three times! Sold to the lady in the third row!"

Mavis applauded herself and sat back down in between Maude and Opal.

"I didn't know you were looking to get llamas," Opal said.

"Wilbur's going to have a conniption," Maude added. She stuffed another cookie in her mouth and stared at the llamas in the round pen.

Mavis hadn't thought about Wilbur. He was definitely not going to be happy, but it was her money and her house. The barn was more than big enough to house them. He would just have to build her a little grazing pen, or better yet, a sturdy fence in part of the pasture for them to frolic. Surely llamas liked to frolic in the grass. She didn't know a thing about llamas, but they were so cute, and she had felt so drawn to them. Her heart needed some cheering up, and those three llamas were the answer.

The auction ended after the last animal, a massive bunny rabbit, was bought by one of the elementary school teachers from Rhinestone. She was excited to show her students their new class pet.

Maude and Opal followed Mavis over to the round pen where the llamas were munching on a bale of hay. Maude reached through the bars of the pen to touch the wool of the closest llama but snatched her hand back when it reared its ears. "Oh, Mavis! That one looks feral. I bet it bites!"

"No ma'am, none have ever bit me," the man from the petting zoo interjected. "This one does spit though. Gotta be careful."

While Maude and Opal ogled the animals, Mavis settled up with the man who owned the small zoo. He told her that he would be more than happy to deliver the animals to her house later on in the evening since she had paid so much. Mavis was delighted because she had been unsure how she would get them to Rhinestone in her new vehicle, and she didn't want to call and bother Wilbur just yet.

"Do they have names?" Mavis asked.

"They don't really answer to anything except food," the man shrugged. "They'll let you pet them for hours as long as you keep the food coming."

Mavis thanked the man and wrote down her address. She had a few hours to come up with their names. These precious llamas were leaving the life of show business for a grand retirement at Magnolia Manor where they wouldn't get tugged on constantly from toddlers and children from all over the country.

"What are you going to name them?" Opal asked.

"I'm still thinking," Mavis said. "We'd better get on back to the Manor so I can make sure I'm ready for them. I need to stop on the way and get some supplies. I don't even know where to go!"

"We've got this," Maude interrupted her meltdown. "There's a livestock store down the road from here on the way to the highway. They'll load you up with what you need."

Mavis nodded and clutched the bill of sale in her hand. She hoped the store had a book or two about llama ownership, because otherwise she was going to be perusing the internet all afternoon. She wanted to become an expert before she called Wilbur to tell him the good news.

[Chapter Twenty-Seven]

Mavis pulled into the livestock store's parking lot on two wheels. She was so excited to buy all the nice things for her new pets.

"This is going to be fun!" Opal exclaimed as she jumped out of the vehicle. "Come on Maude!"

Maude was already at the store's automatic door. They burst through the front door like two kids in a candy store with Mavis following close behind.

"I wonder where the llama section is," Mavis said aloud. She looked around for Maude and Opal to direct her, but they were nowhere to be seen.

Two teenage girls looked up from the counter and watched the three women run off in different directions. Most of their customers weren't quite so lively. They went straight to the back to get their manager to see if he could offer them some assistance.

"Found it!" Opal said from a row toward the back. "Follow my voice!"

Maude and Mavis rounded the opposite corners of the aisle.

"Oooh!" Mavis exclaimed. She began tossing a little bit of everything into her buggy.

The store manager came out of his office and took one look at Mavis' spree. "Looks like we'll be needing a larger cart," he smiled.

"Oh yeah, she's Ruby's granddaughter. We should have brought a bigger truck," Maude laughed as she watched Mavis fill the buggy with every contraption she could find.

After Mavis checked out at the register, Maude and Opal helped her pack all of the goodies in the trunk. There wasn't much room left in the car between the wagon and Mavis' shopping bags, but they managed to find more space at Maude's feet and in the empty seat next to her. It was now time to call Wilbur and let him know what they had done. Mavis climbed back into the driver's seat and sat in the parking lot and gritted her teeth waiting for Wilbur to answer his phone.

"You did what?" Wilbur bellowed on the other end of the phone. Mavis could hear Harry and Harlan cheering in the background. The football game must still be raging on.

"Oh Wilbur, if you would have seen them, you'd understand!" Mavis protested. "They're three of the cutest little llamas ever!"

"Three of them?" Wilbur clarified.

"They're rescues," she explained.

"Why did you need three?" Wilbur asked.

"I couldn't just leave one behind. They'd get lonely," Mavis said.

"Mavis!" Wilbur interrupted. "They don't get lonely, and they aren't rescues. You just told me you bought them off a petting zoo!"

"They're rescues to me!" Mavis countered. "If you think about it, this is all thanks to you."

"How in the world is this my fault?" Wilbur asked. There were once again loud cheers in the background.

"You made me get rid of Clive," Mavis began.

"Not this again," Wilbur sighed. "I have explained to you that you can't keep a dolphin sized catfish in an aquarium."

"But I miss him," Mavis said.

"Mavis, the game is tied with four minutes to go. I'll be at the Manor later." He hung up the phone and returned to his living room to watch the last few minutes of the game. There was never a dull moment when Mavis Montgomery was around.

"How did he take it?" Opal asked in the passenger side of the car when Mavis put her cell phone back in her purse.

"He's elated," Mavis lied.

"Sure," Opal laughed. She turned to Maude who was busy ripping into one of the cake boxes crammed at her feet. "Are you eating again?"

"All that shopping made me hungry," Maude shrugged. She fished around her purse and found the plastic fork that she was looking for. She dug into the chocolate cake and sighed happily.

Mavis buckled her seatbelt and pulled out of the parking lot of the livestock store. She was thankful that she had purchased a large vehicle because it was now filled to the gills with supplies. Who knew that llamas needed so much! She had bought three bedazzled bridals, lead ropes, blankets, brushes, insect repellant, vitamins and minerals, various medicines to keep on hand, llama treats, and a book that the manager at the store said would tell her all she needed to know. Unfortunately, that didn't leave any room for the feed and hay that she needed, but she could send Wilbur out for that later.

"Want me to take yall home or?" Mavis started to say.

"Oh no!" Maude interjected. "We're invested in this." She leaned in closer to Opal and whispered loudly, "Plus, I want to see Wilbur blow a gasket when he sees them."

"Wilbur's going to love them," Mavis said confidently. How could he not? The llamas were well trained and would be the perfect addition to Magnolia Manor. The old barn wasn't getting much use out in the yard. It was like they were already bringing new life onto the property.

They pulled up at the Manor and unloaded their haul. Mavis wasn't sure when Irwin, the llama's previous owner, would be dropping them off, but she was ready for them! After thirty minutes of sitting in the swing, she retired back inside the Manor with Maude and Opal who were looking through one of Ruby's old photo albums. "Which one is that?" Mavis asked.

"This is from our time in New York," Maude said proudly. "That was before your time, of course. There we are in front of the World Trade Center. Who would have thought they'd ever be able to bring them down. I remember it like it was yesterday." She turned the page and pointed out the pictures of slices of pizza and random pictures of pigeons. "Ruby sure liked to document everything," she laughed.

"Is that Ms. Waters?" Mavis asked. She pointed to a picture on the opposite page of a woman standing in front of a giant Ferris wheel.

Opal nodded and smirked at Maude. "She was in New York the same time we were. She won a radio contest," she started to explain.

"She cheated," Maude interrupted.

"Anyway, we ended up in the same hotel and just kept running into each other! We even went to Coney Island on the same day. She gave Ruby this picture of her once we got back and Ruby added it to the album," Opal explained.

"Did y'all hang out on the trip?" Mavis asked.

"Indirectly," Opal chuckled.

Before Mavis could ask for an explanation, Maude jumped in to tell the story. "There were these nuns, you see," she started.

"And Maude's afraid of nuns," Opal reminded Mavis.

"What? Afraid of nuns?" Mavis laughed.

"And they were on our airplane and wouldn't stop singing and talking and I swear, there they were again on the blasted rollercoaster I was forced onto," Maude continued.

"What rollercoaster?" Mavis asked, but Maude and Opal were talking circles around her as they reminisced.

"She rode it with the nun!" Opal cackled. "It was hilarious."

"It was an experience," Maude grumbled.

"A religious experience?" Mavis gasped.

"You could call it that!" Opal howled in laughter again.

"If cursing out everyone on the damned ride is considered a religious experience, then yes," Maude scowled.

"Ms. Maude! You didn't!" Mavis gasped.

"Mavis, you've known Maude for forty years. You know durn well she did," Opal said plainly. "Ahh, those were the days."

"You act like I didn't just cuss out the man at the carwash the other day," Maude huffed.

"What in the world?" Mavis exclaimed.

"He got the inside of my car all wet!" Maude declared.

Opal turned to Mavis and explained, "Maude's jumbo thumb hit the power window button and it started to go down as he was scrubbing her windshield."

There was a sudden knock at the door that made Mavis jump. "Ooh! I bet they're here!" she exclaimed. She rushed to the door and smiled at Irwin who was ready to knock again. She could see his truck and trailer parked on the other side of the magnolia tree. She bounded down the steps and squealed in excitement at the sight of them in the trailer munching on hay.

"Where do you want them?" Irwin asked. He unlocked the trailer and grabbed the three lead ropes and held them out to Mavis who took them gingerly. "You sure you're ready for this?" he asked.

Mavis was speechless but nodded exuberantly.

"Alrighty," Irwin shrugged. "Have a good one." He peeled out of the driveway faster than his old truck and trailer looked like they could handle.

"Now what?" Maude asked as she walked down the porch steps. "What do you do with them?"

"We could take their wool and weave matching sweaters," Opal suggested.

Maude rolled her eyes and sat down on the last step. She intended to give the llamas a wide berth for a while. She didn't trust their beady little eyes that followed her. "Did you ever decide on names?" she asked. "What about Betty? That's a good solid name."

"For an eighty-year-old," Opal laughed. "What about Cloud?"

"They're llamas, Opal! Not some hippie you met at the moonlight festival," Maude snickered.

"She was a nice lady!" Opal stuck her tongue out. "What about Moonbeam then?"

Mavis shook her head while Maude launched into baby name trends from over the years. "Names used to be strong. Take my name for example!"

"Maude Winfred," Opal laughed. "Real strong."

"Hush up Clementine!" Maude snapped.

"I think I've got it," Mavis announced.

"Got what?" Opal asked.

"I heard it was going around," Maude nodded. "Back away, Opal. We don't wanna get sick, too."

"What?" Mavis asked. "No, I think I've got their names!"

"Well spit it out," Maude said. "We ain't got all day."

"Winifred, Clementine, and Morgan. Winnie, Clem, and Morgan for short," Mavis beamed. Naming them after Maude, Opal, and Ruby seemed like the perfect thing to do.

"Ruby got the way better end of the stick with her middle name," Maude said.

Opal smiled widely and reached out to pet the nearest llama. "Hello little Clementine," she gushed. The llama's ears reared back. "Oh, this must be Winnie instead. My apologies."

"Why do I have to be the mean one?" Maude frowned.

"None of them are mean!" Mavis corrected. "Don't talk like that in front of them. They've had such a hard life, haven't you little Winnie?" She scratched underneath the llama's chin and then squeezed it around the neck. "Oh, they're going to love it here! I can already tell!" She handed Maude and Opal each a rope attached to a different llama and beckoned them to follow her to the barn to show them their new home.

Maude picked up the rope with two fingers and handed it to Opal. "I'll follow behind to make sure they don't run away or anything." Opal rolled her eyes and took the rope in her other hand and followed Mavis and Winnie across the yard to the barn.

"Here comes trouble," Opal called out as Wilbur's truck came into view. Wilbur pulled up next to Mavis' car and stared out the window at the two women holding the ropes before turning to Maude. "Are you not part of this little adventure?"

She shook her head and threw her hands up in the air in an act of surrender. "I told them it was a bad idea, but have you ever told Ruby, I mean Mavis, no?" she asked.

"Good point," he nodded. Mavis was Ruby Montgomery's stubbornness through and through. When she put her mind to something, she saw it through no matter what. If she wanted something, she moved hell and high water to get it.

"Oh Wilbur, aren't they adorable!" Mavis gushed when Wilbur stepped out of his truck and walked over to where Mavis and Opal were walking with the llamas. Maude followed behind at a distance.

"They're something," Wilbur said.

"Oh, don't be mean," Mavis said. "They're the cutest little darlings in the world." Mavis made kissy faces at the one closest to her.

Wilbur shook his head. "What in the world are you going to do with them?"

"I'm going to love them forever!" Mavis gushed.

Wilbur looked at Opal who handed him one of the ropes. "This is Morgan," she smiled. "Say hello!"

"Say hello to the llama?" Wilbur asked.

"Her name is Morgan," Opal repeated in case he hadn't heard her the first time.

"Why is Maude all the way over there?" he asked looking back over his shoulder.

"She's afraid of them," Opal shrugged. "Say hello to Morgan. And this one," she held up the rope in her hand, "is Clem. Mavis has Winnie right there."

"Morgan, Clem, and Winnie. Those are um, unusual names," he murmured. "For unusual pets. Makes perfect sense."

"Morgan, Clementine, and Winifred," Mavis explained. "For Big Mama, Opal, and Maude. You have to admit they're the perfect names!"

Wilbur's heart softened at the thought of the Stone Sisters being honored, even if it was by llama namesakes. Though he wasn't sure how Maude felt about the honor. She stayed at least ten feet behind them as they walked into the barn. Wilbur held the first stall door open and ushered the three llamas inside. "Do you want them all to have a separate stall?" he asked.

"No!" Mavis gulped. "They've never been apart. But we do need to build a fence for them to graze. The book says they need a lot of room to roam. They're very energetic." She walked inside the stall and closed the gate behind her so they couldn't run out. She unhooked their lead ropes and removed their dirty bridles. Opal handed her the new sparkly ones from the shelf that they had organized earlier. Mavis thought about which color bridle to put on each animal.

Wilbur looked at the three llamas on the other side of the gate staring back at them. "I talked to Harry before I came over here. He said they're going to be a lot to look after. I take your comment to mean that I need to build them a grazing pasture out yonder. And in the meantime, what are they going to eat?" He looked around the barn and didn't see any bales of hay.

"Oh, I got them a few snacks and the book says we can give them some fruits and vegetables,"

Mavis explained as she struggled to put the purple bridle on Morgan. "But I figured you could run into town this evening or tomorrow and pick up the rest of it in your truck."

"And how much do they eat?" Wilbur asked. He sighed and opened the gate to help her get the bridle on.

"I'm sure they don't eat much," Mavis said. "I mean, the sooner you get the fence built, the sooner they can graze on all those grasses and weeds out there." She handed him the pink bridle next for Clem, which left the bright red one for Winnie.

Somehow Wilbur sincerely doubted Mavis' calculations. She had never been accused of putting any of her pets on a diet, and Wilbur was certain these llamas would be no exception. He didn't know how much llamas usually ate, but he felt certain that these creatures were going to get double rations on a regular basis, especially since they were named after Big Mama, Opal, and Maude. These three creatures had just landed in the lap of luxury, although they probably didn't know it yet. He made a mental note to double check the loft in the barn to make sure it was ready to hold a winter's worth of hay and whatever other supplies llamas needed.

"On second thought, they do look a little underweight," Mavis frowned.

Wilbur laughed.

"What's so funny?" Mavis asked indignantly.

"I was just thinking the same thing," Wilbur smiled.

[Chapter Twenty-Eight]

"Wilbur definitely took it better than I thought he would," Maude said. She was sitting in the backseat of Mavis' car as Mavis drove them back home later that evening. She yawned loudly and stretched her arms high over her head.

"How could he not? They're so adorable," Mavis said. "All rescues are."

"They certainly are," Opal agreed. "I think they'll give you lots of adventures."

"If they're anything like their namesakes," Mavis nodded. "Wilbur's going to love them. I just know it! Maybe I should look around and see if there are any more that need a good home. We could have a little llama farm and everything!"

"Mavis, Wilbur is a saint," Maude interjected from the backseat. "But one of these days he's going to snap."

Opal laughed and added, "She's got a point."

They continued chatting about the new additions at Magnolia Manor during the ride back to Opal and Maude's houses. After the excitement from the previous few days, it was wonderful to sit back and enjoy something as relaxing as adopting new pets, even if those pets were a bit unconventional and spit when they were tired or annoyed. Mavis was already dreaming of ordering them matching blankets and embossed name plates for their stall when she got home. Thanks to the internet, the world of all llama related things was at her fingertips. As soon as Wilbur got the new fence up for them, they'd be free to have all kinds of adventures across the acres of Magnolia Manor. She planned on making sure Wilbur worked hard and fast on the fence. She could even take a little break from all her overseeing and visit Clive tomorrow, maybe with the llamas in tow.

As she turned down Maude and Opal's road, she marveled at the stillness of the old country road and homes. Things were quiet down where Opal and Maude lived. Most of the town was in for the evening getting ready for the week ahead. There were a few porch lights left on, but Mavis noticed that the lights were off at Nadine's and there were no cars in the driveway. She didn't want to make anyone uncomfortable, but neither Maude nor Opal had mentioned Nadine since she was taken to the hospice center Friday morning.

"Have either of you heard how Ms. Waters is?" Mavis asked. She looked in the rearview mirror and saw Maude shake her head. Opal sighed and said, "no. They took her to Junction Friday morning. With all the craziness going on, I haven't stopped by to see her." She turned around in the seat to face Maude. "Let's ride over there in the morning and check in on her."

"Ok," Maude shrugged sadly.

When Mavis pulled up in Opal's driveway, she helped them get the wagon out of the trunk and wheeled it to Opal's porch. Maude silently carried her cake and treat boxes into her house next door.

"She's really taking it hard," Mavis noticed.

"It's hard getting old," Opal nodded. Mavis smiled glumly and helped Opal pull the wagon inside her house. "I'll unpack it tomorrow," Opal said.

Mavis hugged her goodbye and said, "Send my love to Ms. Waters. If you can think of anything she needs, please don't hesitate to let me know. Call me when y'all get back home tomorrow and let me know how things are."

"Of course," Opal nodded. She watched Mavis as she walked down the porch steps back to her car. She waved as she backed out of the driveway and disappeared down the road back towards the Manor.

Mavis called Wilbur on the way home. He answered on the third ring out of breath. "I'm hurrying," he breathed.

"Oh, well, that's not why I'm calling," Mavis said.

"What's wrong?" Wilbur asked.

"Nothing like that," she replied. "I was just going to tell you that I dropped Maude and Opal back at their houses. I made the mistake of asking about Nadine and I think Maude's really torn up about this. I didn't know if you had heard anything new."

"Not since they moved her to hospice Friday," Wilbur said. "I honestly have been so contained with this Earl drama that she slipped my mind. Have you heard any updates?"

"No," Mavis lamented. "We haven't been the best at keeping up with her or any of Big Mama's other friends, besides Maude and Opal. I'm going to call Michael and see what he can tell me. You don't think it's too late, do you?"

"I don't know," Wilbur said. "It's after dark. Maybe send him a text, and I'll ask Harlan on my way back with this last load of hay if he knows anything." Harlan's mother was Patsy Collins, a former member of the Ladies Auxiliary with Ruby. She and Nadine had always been close. Even though she was ailing herself, her mind was as sharp as a tact. She lived with Harlan's sister, Elizabeth, in Junction.

"Ok," Mavis agreed. "I'll see you back at the Manor. I've got some lasagna I heated up earlier with Maude and Opal. I'll make you a plate."

Wilbur thanked her and they hung up the phone. When Mavis pulled up next to her beloved magnolia tree a few minutes later, she sent Michael a quick text checking in on Nadine. By the time she got out of the car and into her kitchen, he had already texted back telling her that it would be any day now. He said she had gone downhill over the weekend more rapidly than anyone had expected. She didn't seem to be in any pain, but if anyone wanted to see her, it could be hours or a few more days, and they had better hurry.

She let him know that Maude and Opal were planning on coming by in the morning. He said that he would let Maureen know and she would see them then. He promised to keep her posted. Mavis knew that Michael's word was good. Michael and Maureen, Nadine's niece, had been together for nearly twenty years, and though Nadine had never had any children of her own, Maureen and Michael were the closest family she had left. They were both in their late fifties and had worked at the bank together for longer than Mavis could remember. Michael had always taken care of Ruby and Jameson's accounts, which were transferred to Wilbur and Mavis when they both passed. Mavis knew that Nadine's passing would be hard on both him and Maureen. She understood exactly what they were feeling.

Wilbur pulled up a few minutes later and unloaded the last of the hay into the barn. When he was done, he walked inside the Manor and took off his boots at the door and washed his hands in the bathroom sink. He thanked Mavis for the plate of food she had waiting for him at the table and sat down hungrily. He downed an entire glass of ice water and then began to eat the lasagna and garlic bread ravenously.

"Michael said it's a matter of days, maybe even less," Mavis sighed. "I sure hate to hear that."

Wilbur nodded. "That's what Harlan said, too. He said his mama is all to pieces, but there's nothing more to be done. I can't imagine living so long and watching all of your friends pass away. Maude and Opal have seen so much."

"I thought Opal would take it hard, but I swear it's going to be rougher on Maude," Mavis said. "Opal has always been the feeling one out of the two of them, but Maude is not doing well with it."

"Did she say anything?" Wilbur took a large bite of the lasagna.

"She's hardly said a word about it," Mavis said. "Anytime Nadine is mentioned, she gets really quiet and distant. I've never seen her like this."

Wilbur gave a weak smile. "I guess she never really hated Nadine as much as she always said she did."

"Oh, we both knew she didn't really hate Nadine," Mavis said. "They just loved to aggravate each other, but if one of them was really in a pinch, the other was there every time."

"That's true," Wilbur smiled. "You remember that time Nadine sent Maude a singing telegram on Valentine's Day? She said she didn't want Maude to be lonely."

"That was the ugliest cupid I ever saw," Mavis laughed. "He came right up to the Comb Over in just his red long johns and knelt down right in front of her while she was in the hair dryer. Shirtless, bald, and had flimsy little wings on his back. Sang the entire song twice in case she didn't hear it the first time."

"I would have loved to have seen Maude's face," Wilbur chuckled.

"She was mortified," Mavis said. "I was just a teenager, but I'll never forget it. I was so glad I was there that afternoon. I wish I could have recorded it! Maude's secret admirer was the talk of the town for weeks."

"I forgot what Maude did in return," Wilbur said.

"There's no telling. That's been so long ago," Mavis said. "They were always one upping each other. I don't know if they even remember it all."

"Someone could write a book about those two one day," Wilbur laughed. "About all of them really."

"No one would believe it," Mavis chuckled.

Wilbur laughed and finished his meal. Once he was done, he stood up from the table and rinsed the plate in the sink. "I'll get started on the fence in the morning. Harry's going to come out and help me. He said it'll be nice to be out in the open air for a change. It'll go much faster with his help." He put his boots back on and walked down the steps to his truck.

Mavis locked the door behind him and watched him back out of the driveway. He was such a good big brother. She knew she didn't deserve him, but she was sure thankful for him being a constant in her life. Wilbur had come into all of their lives like a rescued puppy, but if truth be told, he was the one who constantly rescued them all. It was fate all those decades ago. She couldn't imagine her life without him.

She walked back to the kitchen and found Ruby's old cookbook and found the recipe for homemade tea cakes. She checked the fridge and cupboard to make sure she had all the necessary ingredients. She planned to get up early and make some for Wilbur as a small gesture of thanks. Then she would go visit Clive at his new home and take him some tasty treats to make sure he knew she had not forgotten him. She checked the clock above the stove and was surprised to see how late it was. She needed to take a shower to wash off the smell of the fair and barnyard animals and get into bed. She was hoping for a night of restful sleep now that her yard was full and Earl had been officially sent back to Louisiana in handcuffs. After a hot shower, she climbed into bed and drifted off into the most peaceful sleep.

Early the next morning, Opal woke up with the rising sun shining into her bedroom. She got dressed and grabbed her favorite blanket from the couch and draped it over her shoulder as she brewed her morning tea. She enjoyed having a cup of hot herbal tea out in the garden before the day really got going. She grew her own butterfly pea flower that she used in her lotions, skin care products, and tea. It was her favorite tea to steep in her kiln fired mug.

The cool autumn breeze blew gently through her hair as she walked through her garden to her swing. It had been a few weeks since she had been able to start her day off the right way. Even though she was technically retired, she still ran herself ragged most days. That mainly meant seeing what adventures she could get into with Maude, but she knew that Maude wasn't looking forward to today. If she had to guess, she would have bet Maude hadn't slept much last night. She would offer her a mug of tea, but she knew Maude would rather eat the dirt that the flowers grew in.

As she expected, Maude came over a few minutes later. "I saw you through the kitchen window," Maude said.

"It's a nice way to start the day," Opal said. "Would you like some tea?"

"No thanks," Maude said.

They sat for a few minutes while Opal sipped her tea. "You about ready to head over there?" Opal asked after a few minutes of silence.

Maude nodded.

"I'll drive," Opal said.

"Not a chance," Maude countered.

Opal took her empty mug back inside and set it in the sink. Maude was waiting for her in the driveway in her car. "I don't mind driving," Opal said again as she slid in the passenger side.

"Opal, the day I let you drive my car is the day I lose my license. And even then the answer is still no," Maude replied.

"Dare I remind you that between the two of us, only you have more tickets than you do fingers and toes," Opal said.

"That's because these young folks don't know the laws," Maude retorted.

Opal knew that wasn't the truth, but she could see that Maude was not in a joking mood this morning. She even turned down Opal's idea of swinging through her favorite donut shop's drive thru for some sausage kolaches. They rode the entire way to Junction in near silence. When Maude turned into the parking lot, she let out a huge sigh. "Let's go on in," she said quietly.

Opal gave her a smile, but Maude wasn't paying attention. They walked inside the hospice center to the front desk and asked to see Nadine Waters. The man behind the desk looked up her room number and showed them which hallway to take. The sterile hall was eerily quiet. Maude grew paler the longer they walked. When they came to her room, Opal knocked gently. The door opened

321

slowly and Nadine's niece, Maureen, ushered them both inside.

"How is she?" Opal asked. She glanced at the bed where Nadine looked fast asleep.

Maureen shook her head and replied, "It's a waiting game. She's been asleep since yesterday before supper. She's so peaceful." She glanced back at Nadine and then at Opal. "I know she's glad you two are here."

Opal patted Maureen on the back and walked over to Nadine's bedside. Maureen walked back to the window and sank down in the uncomfortable chair. After a few encouraging nods from Opal, Maude walked over to the bedside and leaned against the wall. There was nothing left to do or say at this point.

[Chapter Twenty-Nine]

Mavis had spent the past two hours watching Wilbur and Harry put up the pasture fence. They weren't going quite as fast as she had hoped they would, but they were doing the best they could on such short notice. They had ignored her help from the get-go, but she persisted.

"Maybe if you add a little water, the dirt will be softer and easier to move out of the way," Mavis offered helpfully.

Wilbur and Harry looked at each other. "Why didn't we think of that?" Harry grinned sarcastically. "Thanks, Mavis! We'll get right on it."

Before she could offer another suggestion, Wilbur turned on his chainsaw to cut through some limbs. There was so much vegetation in the overgrown pasture for the llamas to chow down on. She was giddy with excitement. Maybe she could get a few goats to go with her new babies.

Mavis had been up since daybreak making a few batches of tea cakes for them all to enjoy. They ate them for a mid-morning snack and got back to work quickly. After another water break, Mavis grew tired of supervising the boys and sauntered back into the house and called Mona to see if she wanted to meet Magnolia Manor's newest residents.

"Of course!" Mona exclaimed. "I'll be right over. How is the fence coming?"

"They're doing their best, but they're not as young as they used to be. They seem to be slowing down a bit," Mavis sighed.

Mona laughed. "None of us are as young as we used to be."

"I'm in my prime," Mavis declared with a chuckle. She talked to Mona for a few minutes more before hanging up and heading to the kitchen to chop some fruit for the new additions.

As soon as Mona arrived at the Manor, Mavis took her over to the barn to meet Clementine, Winifred, and Morgan. She told Mona how she had bid for them and how she had arrived at their new names. She even showed her how sweet they were as they ate bananas from her hand. Mona was a little skittish around them, but she had to admit that they were cute.

"What do you think?" Mavis beamed.

"They sure are something!" Mona admired. They were bigger than she thought they would be, and their teeth freaked her out. They reminded her of her first ex-husband in a way, and that wasn't doing him or them any favors. "I'm glad to see you've healed from Clive being gone," she surmised.

Mavis nodded and hugged the nearest llama tightly. "How about we go visit him? We can take Wilbur's truck through the woods and check on him."

Mona shrugged and said she had nothing better to do. Mavis walked over to Wilbur and retrieved his keys from him and told him she would be back soon after visiting Clive for a bit. He tossed her the keys and she hurried into the house to pack a basket of treats for the giant catfish. Once she was ready, they piled into Wilbur's truck to head through the woods towards Wilbur's cabin. Mona waved at Harry and Wilbur who were hard at work. Even though the sun was out, there was a cool breeze floating through the trees. She mentioned to Mavis that they should probably head into town after visiting Clive and pick up a nice lunch for them all. Mavis readily agreed.

When they neared the large pond in front of Wilbur's cabin, Mavis put the truck in park and grabbed the basket in the backseat. Mona followed her to the edge of the pond and watched Mavis kneel down in the mud and call out loudly, "Clivey! It's mama! Clivey boy!"

Mona held back a smile and hung back away from the mud. She had never heard of a fish coming when called. Mavis called out again a little louder this time and dipped her fingers in the water to cause ripples. Mona gasped when a few seconds later, the giant catfish surfaced in front of them.

"Oh, Clivey! You've gotten so big!" Mavis cooed.

It had only been a few days, and Mona wasn't sure if he had grown or not since he was already massive in size. She watched as Mavis fed the catfish strips of bacon and pieces of sausages as she told him all about the new llamas. "But they haven't replaced you!" Mavis assured him.

After Mavis ran out of food, Mavis patted the fish's head and stood up to shake the dirt and mud from her pants. They drove back to the Manor for Mavis to change clothes and wash the fish and dirt off her hands. As soon as she was ready, she took Wilbur his keys and told him that she and Mona were going into town to pick up lunch.

"Where to?" Mavis asked as she backed her car out of the driveway. Mona thought for a second and shrugged. "I honestly don't have a hankering for anything in particular. What about you?"

"I'm honestly craving some of your specialties from the diner," Mavis smiled.

"I can cook anything you want for you anytime. Just say the word," Mona laughed. "You know, they're supposed to open back up in a few days. Would it be weird if I went by there on their first day?"

"I don't think that's weird," Mavis said. "I'll come with you!"

"Great!" Mona smiled. "That would make me feel less awkward. I'm so happy with how it all turned out, but I know it'll be strange walking in there seeing how different it is being on the other side of the counter for the first time ever."

Mavis nodded and listened as her friend reminisced. The Starlight Cafe had been a staple in Rhinestone for so long. Mavis couldn't imagine passing the torch of her family's legacy to someone else. "Let's celebrate," Mavis said once Mona was finished talking. "Anywhere you want to go, my treat! We'll bring Wilbur and Harry something back."

"In that case, let's go to Pepperonis! I haven't been back since the whole fiasco with Earl last year," Mona laughed. "I did bring Giovanni a bunch of pies the next day to hopefully make up for all the drama, but I haven't dined in properly."

"Giovanni is such a good sport," Mavis agreed. "I love the chicken parmesan there. Let's go!" She took the next right and drove downtown towards the Italian eatery near Mona's old cafe. As they passed by the cafe, Mona stared out the window at the new paint job and new sign that had been installed. "They kept the name after all," Mavis pointed out.

"That was part of the agreement. I just couldn't bear to see Mama and Daddy's cafe name be changed," Mona explained.

The parking lot at Pepperonis only had four cars in the lot. Mavis didn't reckon that there would be many people there on a Monday afternoon, especially the first Monday after the fair had left. She and Mona were seated at a table near the center of the restaurant and were waited on by the owner, Giovanni.

They both gave their orders of chicken parmesan for Mavis and spaghetti for Mona. Giovanni wrote their entrees down and sped off to the kitchen. He returned a minute later with their drinks and a basket of bread for them to share as they planned their next adventure. Mona jokingly tossed out the idea of traveling to New Orleans for Mardi Gras next year, but Mavis almost choked on her garlic bread. "Never will be too soon," Mavis gagged.

When the food arrived, Mona inhaled the steam coming off the sauce. "It's been too long since I've had this good of a meal!"

"What about Vegas?" Mavis exclaimed. "We can gamble and see all the shows. And Mona, can you even begin to imagine the food we could eat!"

Mona's eyes grew wide with excitement. "I've always wanted to go to Las Vegas! Harry's been, but I didn't get to go!"

"Then it's settled!" Mavis nodded.

"Who's going to look after the llamas?" Mona asked. "Maude and Opal?"

"I'm sure I can ask someone else," Mavis said. "I'd come back from Vegas and the llamas would be on the roof or something. Speaking of Maude and Opal though, I need to check in with them today."

"Everything ok?" Mona asked.

Mavis nodded and pulled out her cell phone. "They went to Junction to visit with Nadine Waters this morning." She shook her head and sighed. "I'm afraid she isn't doing well at all and could pass any time now."

"That sure is a shame," Mona said. "She was always very kind to us."

There were no unread messages or missed calls from anyone, but Mavis decided to call them just in case. She knew that neither one of them were good about answering their phones, and she wasn't sure either of them knew how to text, but it was worth a shot. She dialed Opal first, but when she didn't answer, she tried Maude to no avail. In a panic she called Michael.

"Hey Mavis," Michael said. "I guess you heard. I was just about to call you."

"What?" Mavis gasped. "Oh no, Michael. Is it Ms. Nadine?"

"She passed about an hour ago," Michael said. "Isn't that why you're calling?"

"I'm so sorry," Mavis said. "I didn't know. I was trying to reach Maude or Opal to make sure they made it safely to see her. I can't get them on the phone, and I was hoping you'd seen them. Do they know?"

"They're right here next to me. They've been here since this morning. Want me to hand one of them the phone?" he asked.

"No, that's ok," Mavis quickly said. "Is there anything I can do?"

"Not right now," Michael sighed. "The funeral home's on the way and we'll finalize the arrangements. She had most everything worked out already. I'm thinking Wednesday night for the visitation and Thursday morning for the service."

"We'll send food over to your house this evening," Mavis said. "You or Maureen call me if you can think of anything. I know it's overwhelming right now."

She hung up with Michael and met Mona's gaze. "Sure is a shame," Mona said. "What can we do? Maude and Opal ok?"

Mavis nodded and told her what Michael had said. "I better let Wilbur know. I'll step outside and be right back." Mavis hurried outside to the covered porch and sat down on a bench to call

Wilbur. He didn't answer on the first few rings, but when he did, she could tell that he already knew.

"I just got off the phone with Harlan," he explained. "Sure is a shame. He said that Michael wants me to be a pallbearer, so I've got to make sure my suit still fits. Harry and I have the main grazing pen done, but I think we're going to call it a day."

"Absolutely," Mavis agreed. "Thank you and Harry so much. We're getting food now and will be back at the Manor shortly." She hung up the phone and hurried back inside where she ordered two more chicken parmesan dinners and extra bread. Giovanni said he would put a rush on their order and had it bagged up not long after. Mavis paid the bill and drove rather quickly back to the Manor where Wilbur and Harry were sitting on the porch drinking water and polishing off the last of the tea cakes.

Wilbur and Harry followed Mavis and Mona into the house and sat down to eat their late lunch. Mavis thanked them both profusely and cleaned up the mess she had left from baking earlier that morning. Wilbur's phone dinged and he read off the text from Harlan. "Visitation will be at Beaver Crossing Wednesday evening and the funeral will be Thursday morning." Mavis nodded and added the information to her calendar on the fridge.

"He also said Maude and Opal just left the funeral home and should be heading back to Rhinestone," Wilbur continued. "Why don't you head over there, and I'll meet you once I've showered. I'm sure they'll want to talk."

Mavis agreed and said she would stop by the Piggly Wiggly for something to make Maude and Opal feel better. She knew the way to their hearts was a good treat from the bakery.

Mona and Harry left and asked for them to keep them posted about things. They promised to see them Wednesday night at the visitation as well. Mavis thanked Harry again and told Mona she'd call her tomorrow. Once they were gone, Wilbur jumped in his truck to go shower and Mavis headed to the store.

News had spread fast of Nadine's passing. Mavis ran into so many people that she knew in the marketplace, and they were all full of sorrow. After she picked up some rotisserie chicken and sides to drop off at Michael's house on the way to Maude's, she browsed the shelves in the bakery and found a pineapple upside-down cake, a caramel cheesecake, and an apple pie. She picked up a jug of lemonade and sweet tea and checked out. She dropped off the dinner at Michael's house with Michael's parents who had flown in from Orlando. Michael and Maureen were still at the funeral home.

Mavis and Wilbur pulled up in Maude's driveway at the same time. Maude's car was under her carport, so they knew they had to be there. Wilbur unloaded Mavis' car while Mavis knocked on the front door. Opal answered the door and smiled warmly. Mavis hugged her tightly and held the door for Wilbur as he came up the steps. "Maude's in the shower," Opal explained. "She's been in there for a good while. Wasting water and whatnot."

"Should we check on her?" Mavis gasped.

"I've seen enough of her behind over the years," Opal shook her head. "No thank you."

Mavis looked at Wilbur for help. "Don't look at me," he said. "No way."

"Fine!" Mavis sighed. She walked down the hallway towards Maude's bedroom and knocked on the door. There was no answer, so she gently pushed the door open and saw Maude in all her glory picking out clothes from her dresser. "Oh my God! I'm so sorry!" Mavis yelled. She slammed the door and hurried back down the hallway to the kitchen.

"What in the world?" Wilbur asked.

Mavis' hands were over her eyes, and she shook her head. "She's out of the shower," Mavis explained.

Opal sat down in the recliner and laughed heartily. "Good luck getting that sight out of your brain!"

Maude emerged from her room a few minutes later more cranky than usual. "I'm so sorry!" Mavis squealed.

Maude frowned and walked past them to the kitchen. She opened up the top cabinet and found a bottle of wine. She popped the cork and poured herself a large glass. "Anyone else want any?" she asked.

Wilbur shook his head and instead poured himself a glass of lemonade.

"I'll take some wine," Mavis said sheepishly.

Maude handed her a glass of wine and looked at Opal who said she preferred lemonade, too.

"Mavis, I used to change your diapers. I've seen you naked, too," Maude said.

"And one day you can change her diapers," Opal said knowingly.

"Oh, dear Lord," Wilbur said. "Mavis, please tell me there's something besides lemonade and tea in those bags." He gestured towards the remaining grocery bags and Mavis nodded. She pulled out the desserts and arranged them on the counter. "Thank God," he continued. He found a serving knife and cut himself a generous slice of the cheesecake and sat down at the table to eat it. He was finished with the talk of naked relatives and hoped they were too.

Maude took the serving knife and served the rest of them cheesecake. They all sat down around the table to eat and relax. There wasn't much to say. They could all feel the sadness in the air.

[Chapter Thirty]

The visitation Wednesday night had been full of people from all over the county coming by to pay their respect to Nadine. After the visitation was over, Mavis and Wilbur took Maude and Opal out to eat at the local Mexican restaurant. Even though Maude was a bit quieter than usual, her appetite had returned. She didn't complain about the wait time either, which was a nice change of pace. After dinner they all retired back to Maude's house to her screened-in back patio for a glass of fancy wine that Opal had bottled years ago. Opal's line of wine was sold all around the world, but she winked and said she always saved the best for them. Besides the bottle of wine, Opal lugged over a heavy photo album and spread it open on the coffee table. The cracked leather held firm so many pages of black-and-white photographs.

"What are all these?" Wilbur asked. He touched the worn leather and inhaled its aged smell.

"If I'm not mistaken, I think this is the early seventies," Opal smiled. "I don't think either of you have seen this book," she said to Mavis and Wilbur.

Mavis looked at her and asked, "Is my mother in there?"

Opal smiled and nodded. "I haven't looked at this old book in years, but I know there's many a good picture in here." She opened the aged cover to read the inscription on the inside cover. "Yes, 1970 to 1975. Your mother would have been around ten years old at the time."

"She was born in 1961," Maude added. "January of that year. I'll never forget it." She leaned over the table and turned to the first page of photographs. "Oh, dear God, Opal! Why in the world do you have this one?"

Mavis and Wilbur laughed heartily at a photograph of Maude in a fluffy robe with a towel wrapped around her head. Opal shrugged. "I don't even remember taking that one," she smiled.

Maude, Opal, and Ruby called themselves the Stone Sisters ever since they were young girls. The album was full of their adventures. They were in their early thirties in these pictures, and they looked so happy and full of life. Maude pulled a set of pictures from the page and laughed as she read the writing on the back. "This was the time we went to the Kentucky Derby. Look at Ruby's ridiculous hat. She insisted that we all wear matching ones. Those were the ugliest, most uncomfortable things!"

"I still have mine," Opal chuckled.

"So do I," Maude nodded. She flipped the page and pointed out Jameson's Halloween costume. He was dressed like a vampire with a long black cape and stood next to Ruby who was dressed like a witch. Melanie stood in front of them dressed like a scarecrow. She looked to be around twelve years old in that photograph.

"I've seen this one," Mavis smiled. "It's still framed in the living room."

Wilbur nodded and leaned in closer to the book as Maude turned the page again to reveal a large photograph of what looked like the front of Beaver Crossing Holy Church. There was a group of ladies standing on the front steps. He pointed to the picture and asked Opal, "is that? Wait a minute," he smiled. "That is you! And there's Big Mama! Is that Ms. Nadine and Mrs. Patsy behind y'all?"

"Sure is," Opal nodded.

"That's the first Ladies Auxiliary meeting," Maude explained. "I don't reckon Beaver Crossing would be what it is today without them."

"We had so much fun," Opal nodded. "Finally got Maude to join eventually."

Maude rolled her eyes and turned the page quickly.

"Oh wow," Mavis gasped. She held her hand over her heart and breathed in deeply. Wilbur glanced at the picture that had captured her attention. It was a formal photograph of Ruby, Jameson, and Melanie on Melanie's fourteenth birthday. Mavis resembled her mother so much. Their long dark hair and cheek bones were carbon copies of each other.

"You've never seen this one?" Maude asked.

"I have seen it, it's just been a long time," Mavis whispered. Mavis had lived with her grandparents, Ruby and Jameson Montgomery since the day she was born. She had no recollection of her mother who had passed away a few months after her second birthday. Melanie, her mother, had been an aspiring actress in Hollywood, but instead of fame she found drugs. She visited her daughter across the country sporadically, but she died from an accidental overdose less than three weeks before her twenty-second birthday. Ruby and Jameson had made sure that Mavis knew how wonderful her mother had been, even through the years of addiction, and how proud she would be of the woman Mavis had grown to be.

Mavis had never met her father. She had no indication of who he could be. Jameson and Ruby had said that Melanie had had an on and off again relationship with a man in Hollywood, but that he was not her father. He had submitted to a court ordered DNA test, per Melanie's request, around Mavis' first birthday. Melanie had admitted only one time that she was unsure who Mavis' father really was, but it didn't matter to Ruby or Jameson. They had cared for and raised Mavis the way that every child deserves.

Mavis had been curious about the identity of her father over the years, but she had never pursued it. She'd even read online where DNA collection sites could track down long lost relatives. DNA results had even solved cold cases buried in evidence lockers for decades. Looking at the faded photographs of her family brought up those old feelings. Maybe she'd bite the bullet and order one of those ancestry DNA kits and see what the universe had in store for her. She was perfectly content with her life now, but she couldn't help but wonder if there was something more out there.

They spent the rest of the evening combing through the pages of the album. When they came to the last page, Opal closed the book and said she was ready to turn in for the evening. Maude said she would be ready in the morning, and they'd ride back over to the church for the service. Mavis offered to pick them up, but they both said they would be fine on their own. Wilbur had to be at the church early to go over his pallbearer duties, so Mavis would only be responsible for herself.

She drove to Beaver Crossing the following morning wearing a new black dress with a matching black cardigan and a set of pearls. It was a chilly, wet morning which added to the somber atmosphere. She opened her umbrella and left her thermal coffee mug of lukewarm coffee in the car and walked into the church to meet everyone. She left her umbrella by the door with the rows of other wet umbrellas and looked around.

"Look at you!" Mavis smiled as Wilbur walked over to her. She helped Wilbur knot his tie in the foyer of the church and saw Harlan round the corner. "And you, too, Harlan. Looking sharp in that snazzy suit."

Harlan laughed and told her thank you. "It's definitely an upgrade from my daily look." He and Wilbur waved goodbye to Mavis as she joined the throng of people heading into the sanctuary of Beaver Crossing Holy Church. She joined Mona and Harry on the fifth row and spotted Maude and Opal two rows ahead of her next to Patsy.

Mona tapped Mavis on the arm and handed her a tissue box from the pew next to her. "It's starting," Mona whispered. They watched as

Wilbur, Harlan, Michael, and three other men carried the casket down to the front of the small stage. Mavis blew her nose and settled back into the pew next to Mona as Reverend Ezekiel Simmons walked up to the podium with his Bible and smiled at the packed church. "Thank you all for being here today as we celebrate the life of our dear sister Nadine S. Waters who joined our Lord and Savior on Monday October 25th. Nadine was born October 1st, 1938, to her parents Nigel and Diana Waters in Junction. The eldest of three children, she had two younger brothers. She was the daughter," he paused and cleared his throat. He needed to settle down and follow his notes before he lost control of the service. "She moved to Rhinestone before her second birthday where she attended Rhinestone Elementary, Middle, and High School, before attending the University of West Alabama for college. She earned her teaching degree and returned to Rhinestone where she worked with her father at his company. Though Nadine never married or had any children of her own, her many friends and family members cherish her memory and thank you all for being here today. Mary McDowell and the choir here will now sing two songs specifically chosen by Nadine, before she passed of course." The Reverend's ears turned a bright shade of red as he sat down in his chair behind the pulpit.

Maude turned around and rolled her eyes at Mavis. She had never been the biggest fan of Reverend Simmons, but he was leaps and bounds better than when he first became the preacher at

Beaver Crossing a few years ago. Hopefully, he would organize his notes and finish strong.

"I've always loved that song," Mona whispered. She dabbed her eyes with a tissue.

Mavis nodded along to the harmony of the robed choir. It was a beautiful song selection indeed. When the musical numbers were over, Reverend Simmons stood back up and opened his Bible. He read a few passages and paused for intended effect. Then it was time for the choir to sing another song, this time with a slideshow of photographs playing on the screen behind them. There were pictures of a young Nadine all the way to a few weeks ago. Scattered across the screen were pictures of friends and family, including a few of Maude, Opal, and even Ruby over the years. It did Mavis' heart good to see her grandmother smile in photographs from high school in her cheerleading uniform next to Nadine on the football field. There was even a photo of Opal, Maude, Ruby, and Nadine from their New York trip in front of a wooden roller coaster.

Harlan's mother Patsy stood up at the close of the service. Harlan helped her up the two steps to the stage where she then shared a few words about Nadine. Reverend Simmons spoke one final prayer and the pallbearers lifted the ornate casket and walked it back down the aisle to the waiting hearse. There was no graveside service as Maureen and Michael knew that many of Nadine's friends were elderly themselves and had said their goodbyes already.

It had begun to rain hard, so Mavis turned to Maude and Opal in the foyer and asked if they would be alright driving home. She said she could always take them to their houses or back to the Manor until the storm let off. They agreed to ride to the Manor with her. It was just after lunchtime, so Mavis loaded them in her car and drove through the local pizza joint's drive-up window where she ordered two pizzas. Once the pizzas were ready, the young man handed the pizza boxes through the window to Mavis. She passed them over to Opal in the passenger seat and drove through the raging thunderstorm towards the Manor. When she pulled up next to a magnolia tree, the rain continued to come down in thick heavy sheets.

"Maybe we should wait it out for a bit," Mavis suggested.

"I'm starving," Maude huffed. She leaned forward and smelled the pizza boxes. "Pizza won't be good once it's cold."

"It's raining cats and dogs," Mavis countered.

"A little rain never hurt anyone," Maude said. She opened the door and trudged out into the deluge. Mavis watched as she scurried up the porch steps and beckoned for them to follow.

"She gets grumpier when she's hungry," Opal acknowledged. She handed Mavis the warm pizza boxes and opened the passenger door. She wasn't quite as fast as Maude had been, but she made it up the front steps in one piece.

Mavis sighed loudly and grabbed her damp umbrella from the backseat. There was no easy way to get out of the car with her purse, cup, and two pizza boxes, but she would have to manage. After struggling to open the umbrella, Mavis decided to leave her purse and cup in the car and make a mad dash for the porch. Grumbling the entire way, she finally made it to the porch with the pizza boxes. Maude took the drenched pizza boxes from her so that she could open the front door.

Once inside, Maude took the pizza to the kitchen while Mavis peeled off her cardigan by the front door and kicked off her shoes. She could hear Maude grumbling in the kitchen about how wet the pizza was. She told Opal that she was going to run upstairs really fast to change out of her soaking wet dress. When she got back downstairs, Maude and Opal were already sitting at the kitchen table eating.

"Saved you some," Opal said. She pointed to a plate piled high with pizza slices on the placemat next to her.

"Thanks," Mavis nodded. She poured herself a glass of tea and sat down next to Opal. "That was a lovely service."

"It was," Opal nodded.

Maude nodded and took another bite of cheese pizza. "Even if Mary did sound like a wailing calf," she mused.

"She's doing her best," Opal added.

"Then I'd hate to hear her at her worst," Maude shuddered. "And I swear, if that man doesn't start thinking before he talks!"

"He's come a long way," Mavis interjected.

"That's true," Maude nodded. "He's a weird one though. I remember one time he got to talking about some mighty inappropriate stuff at the pulpit. Opal remembers."

Opal nodded. "Something about horses and Uranus, right?"

"My what?" Maude snapped. "Geez, Opal! That's between me and my doctor." She stuffed another piece of pizza in her mouth and chewed loudly.

Opal shrugged and drank the rest of the tea in her glass. "Everyone's got one," she said matter-of-factly. "Some more than others. Anyway, how's Clive?"

"He's good," Mavis smiled. She was happy that the conversation had taken another turn. "I visited with him a few days ago. And Clementine, Winifred, and Morgan are packing on their missing weight. Before you know it, they'll be little butterballs!"

Opal looked at her like she had two heads. "You can't make butter from that," she said. She turned to Maude and whispered loudly, "I don't reckon anyone ever gave Mavis the talk. You should sit down with Mavis later and explain things."

"Ok," Maude nodded. "I knew this day would come soon enough."

Mavis shook her head and stood up from the table. Where in the world was Wilbur?

[Chapter Thirty-One]

Wilbur finally arrived back at the Manor two hours later. Mavis opened the front door and asked where in the world he had been. Before he could answer, she launched into, "I've got Maude trying to explain the birds and the bees to me one minute, and Opal wanting to ride one of the llamas the next!"

Wilbur laughed and followed Mavis back to the living room where Maude and Opal were sitting in the recliners with their feet propped up. "Where've you been?" Maude asked him.

"We just finished at the church," Wilbur explained. "We had to wait a good bit for the rain to slow down before we could load the casket in the hearse and take it over to Deerlane Cemetery. After the graveside, we all went back to the church and had to clean up a bit. There was mud and water everywhere in the foyer." Mavis noticed his cheeks had turned a little red.

"Who all was with you?" Mavis asked.

"Well, me and Harlan, and Mrs. Patsy, of course. Michael and Maureen and their families. And Mrs. Beulah, and Emily, and Reverend

Simmons, and you know," Wilbur's voice dropped off.

Who's Emily?" Mavis asked.

"No one," Wilbur said. His ears burned the same shade of red as his cheeks. He turned back to Maude and Opal and asked, "What have y'all been up to? I thought I saw your car, Ms. Maude, still at the church?"

"Mavis made us leave it there," Maude nodded. "She's scared of the rain."

"I'm not scared of the rain. I simply didn't want you to have to drive in the rain," Mavis explained once again.

"Never bothered me before," Maude began. "It's all the other idiots who don't know how to drive."

Mavis opened her mouth to respond, but Opal quickly interjected.

"She's trying to say you're too old to drive in the rain," Opal said gently.

"I'm not old," Maude said.

"It snuck up on you," Opal said.

"I'm not the one who's scared of the rain," Maude retorted.

"I, oh never mind," Mavis sighed. She was already exhausted from trying to entertain them for the last few hours.

Maude huffed loudly and opened her purse to see if she had any snacks hidden in the zipped pocket. Unfortunately, she couldn't find any, so she stood up and walked to the kitchen to see what she could find in the cupboards.

"I told you she gets grumpy when she's hungry. We got her some pizza to calm her down though," Opal explained. "Guess she didn't eat enough."

"Because it got all wet and soggy," Maude complained from the doorway. She hadn't found anything worthwhile in the kitchen either. "Have you eaten anything, Wilbur?"

Wilbur rubbed his stomach and said, "Not since breakfast. I thought about stopping for something on the way home, but I'll just wait until dinner."

"I want to try that new steakhouse in Junction," Maude said. "Let's go there for supper."

"It's a good one," Wilbur nodded.

"How do you know?" Maude asked cautiously.

"Because he and Harry went there the other day," Mavis tattled.

"You went to a steakhouse without me?" Maude gasped. That was an act of betrayal in her eyes. No one liked beef as much as she did. Wilbur should have known better.

Wilbur eyed Mavis and then smiled sweetly at Maude. "I would love to take you out there tonight," he offered. "My treat. We can all go."

"I guess I can be free tonight," Opal said with a shrug. "I need to change clothes first though."

"I can take you home. I guess we need to get Maude's car from the church on the way," Mavis said. She looked out the window and saw that the rain had finally slacked off.

"Then I'm going to run home and change out of this suit. Want me to meet you at Maude's, Mavis?" he asked.

"That'll be fine," Mavis nodded. "Then we can load up in my car and go have a nice dinner in Junction this evening." It would be good to get Maude and Opal out for a bit to get their minds off of Nadine.

Wilbur waved goodbye and walked outside to his truck. He was more than ready to get out of the suit. He much preferred a pair of jeans and an old t-shirt to the crisp black suit he had worn all day. He pulled up in his driveway and checked his watch. He knew that once Maude announced she was hungry, that she'd be raring to go, so he had better hurry up. He took a quick shower and put on a nice pair of jeans, his cowboy boots, and a new button-down shirt.

As soon as Wilbur left the Manor, Mavis redid her hair and checked her makeup to make sure she still looked ok. She changed into her third outfit of the day and ushered Maude and Opal back into her car. She dropped them off at the church and followed behind them as Maude drove towards her house.

Mavis decided to wait in her car as the two older women went into their respective houses to change. It only took Opal a few minutes to fix her hair and change clothes, but Maude was already pacing her front porch waiting for her when she came out. "Where is Wilbur?" she sighed. "We're always waiting on him!"

Opal cupped her hands over her eyes and said, "Here he comes!"

Wilbur pulled up next to Mavis' car and made sure he had everything he needed before getting out of his truck. Maude and Opal met him at his driver's side door.

"Don't you look nice tonight," Opal said as she saw Wilbur getting out of his truck. "I always did like the color blue on you. It brings out your eyes."

"Thank you," Wilbur said. He opened the door for Maude and Opal to get into Mavis' SUV. Maude ducked under his arm and jumped up in the front passenger seat, leaving Wilbur and Opal to ride in the middle row.

The drive to Junction was much more relaxed than many of the drives the previous week. Mavis told them all about the sweaters she had ordered online for her llamas, on account of the cold weather that would be setting in soon. Then they chatted about the service and who had attended and who had not. Wilbur also told them that Michael and Maureen had agreed to eventually put Nadine's house up for sale, which irritated Maude to no end. She asked why they wouldn't move into themselves.

"But they already have a house," Mavis pointed out.

"I don't want to have new neighbors," Maude pouted. "People are weird. You never know what kind of psycho could move in next door."

"Oh hush," Opal said from behind her.

"See what I mean!" Maude said. "Opal's lived next door to me for two centuries."

They were saved as Mavis pulled into the crowded parking lot a few minutes later. "Looks like it's almost a full house in there tonight," Wilbur said, as they looked for a place to park. "Let me jump out and get our name on the list."

"Y'all go with him," Mavis said to Opal and Maude. "No need for y'all to walk."

Wilbur shot Mavis a look and then helped Maude and Opal out of the vehicle. "We'll wait for you inside, I guess," he said. He closed the passenger door and looked around, but Maude and Opal had already walked off leaving him in the parking lot by himself.

By the time Mavis joined them inside, the hostess was ready to seat them. They made their way to the center of the room in front of a large fireplace with a fire quaintly burning in the grate. Wilbur waited until Opal and Maude had found their seats before sitting down. As he pulled his chair out, he glanced around the room and noticed Emily and her grandmother sitting at a booth in the corner.

"What are you looking at?" Mavis asked Wilbur.

"No one," Wilbur said. "I mean, nothing. Ready to order?"

"We just sat down," Mavis said. "Lordy, you must be hungry!"

"Famished," Wilbur agreed. He gave his drink order and entree order to the waiter as soon as the gentleman came by. Wilbur looked at the three women who stared at him and asked if they knew what they wanted yet.

"I'll take the stuffed mushrooms and a glass of water for now," Opal smiled at the waiter.

"I'll have what Wilbur's having," Maude said. She looked the waiter dead in the eye and said, "The biggest one you have." She pointed at Wilbur and added, "Bigger than his steak. He owes me one. Can you believe he came here without me?"

The waiter smiled and turned back to Wilbur and played along, "Oh no, that is terrible to hear! Sir, how could you not bring your grandmother with you?"

"My what?" Wilbur asked, right as Maude said, "His what?"

"I, um, my apologies, ma'am," the waiter stumbled over his words. "Is this your mother?"

"She's his wife!" Opal declared in a fit of laughter. The waiter gasped and didn't realize that Opal had been joking.

Mavis buried her face in her napkin and roared with laughter as Wilbur's eyes bulged out of his head. While Maude tried to kick Opal under the table, Wilbur explained to the poor waiter that Maude wasn't his grandmother, mother, or wife. He was mortified and hoped that no one had overheard any of the conversation. The waiter took Mavis' order and hurried back to the kitchen. Opal and Mavis were still cracking up as Maude balled up her cloth napkin and threw it at Opal's head. She missed, but it did land on a passing waiter's tray of dirty dishes.

"Nice one," Mavis said appreciatively.

Wilbur noticed Emily was staring at them out of the corner of his eye. It was not the impression he'd hoped to make.

"Can you believe anyone would think I was your grandmother?" Maude fumed.

"I'm surprised anyone would think you're his wife," Opal laughed.

"You hush up!" Maude hissed.

Mavis changed the subject to her upcoming vacation with Mona, which snagged Maude's attention. "Vegas?" she asked. "Be careful. They hand out SBD's there like it's candy."

"SBDs?" Mavis asked.

"STDs," Opal corrected. "Lord, Maude, I never could take you anywhere."

"Same difference," Maude said. "Just be careful Mavis. You don't want to catch something."

Wilbur groaned audibly and prayed that no one could hear their conversations. Finally, the waiter brought over the meals and refilled their drink glasses. Maude whispered a quick prayer for the saints and sinners that surrounded her and then sighed happily as she took the first bite of steak. "This is good," she said. "Not the best I've ever had, but pretty damn close."

Thankful for the distraction, Wilbur dug into his steak with gusto. He barely listened to the women discussing first one embarrassing topic and then another. Somehow, they had gotten on the subject of Maude's bathroom habits and dietary issues. Thankfully, that hadn't lasted long, but they had moved onto the bout of impacted crop in Opal's chickens. Wilbur had done his best to tune them out and not gag as Opal told them the way to cure it. Occasionally, he would glance over in Emily's direction. Twice he caught her looking toward their table and he scrambled to avoid eye contact.

"Wilbur, you're awfully quiet tonight. Are you feeling alright?" Maude asked.

"Just a bit tired, I guess," Wilbur replied. He took a sip of water while the ladies ventured onto another interesting topic.

Opal smiled to herself as Wilbur yet again looked over at Emily for what had to be the tenth time that evening. Beulah stood up and walked to the restroom, which gave Opal a bright idea. "Well, I'm going to run by the restroom before we head out. Anyone need anything?" Opal asked.

"From the restroom?" Maude asked. "No!"

Opal rolled her eyes and took the cloth napkin out of her lap and put it on the table. "Ok," she shrugged, and disappeared around the corner out of sight. "I'll be right back."

"She never ceases to amaze me," Mavis said as she watched Opal bound across the restaurant. "Diseased chickens one minute, and then who knows what the next."

"She's always been like that. Nobody could ever keep up with her," Maude said.

"Can you believe how well she did at the fair? I never would have imagined," Mavis said. "Of course, I knew she'd be a hit, but wow! That kind of donation is life changing."

Wilbur was quiet while they recounted the adventures of the previous week, including their adventures with Earl, who had planned all along to steal Opal's money. Opal's favorite charity would certainly be thrilled with the result of the fundraiser, which made Mavis even happier to have Earl out of the picture. As Mavis caught Maude up on the charges Earl had racked up, she noticed that Wilbur stole a glance across the room to the pretty brunette sitting with Beulah Johnson.

He had barely touched his dinner even though he had said he was hungry. The waiter offered to bring him a box for his meal, but Wilbur politely declined. "I'm going to finish it," he promised.

"Steak isn't good warmed back up," Maude said knowingly.

Wilbur nodded and quickly ate the rest of his ribeye and mashed potatoes while Maude prattled on about the importance of not overcooking steak and how she had yet to meet anyone who could cook it the way her father did when she was growing up.

Opal sat back down in her chair and smiled. "What did I miss?" she asked

"I think Wilbur's sweet on that girl over yonder," Maude said plainly.

"Beulah's granddaughter?" Opal asked. "I could tell from the moment I saw him first looking at her. The inner eye sees all, you know."

"You were right!" Mavis gasped. She pointed to Opal and covered her mouth with her napkin. "You predicted this very thing at the fair!"

Wilbur cleared his throat uncomfortably. "All I said was we chatted at the graveside. I didn't say anything about being sweet on anybody."

"You didn't have to. We've known you all your life," Maude said. "She looks like a really nice girl. You should ask her out. Is that what the kids are saying these days?"

"The kids," Mavis laughed. "Ms. Maude, Wilbur's an old man, according to the kids these days."

"Well, I mean, I'm not," Wilbur began.

"Wilbur! She's getting ready to leave. Go get her number. Or did you already get it?" Mavis inquired.

"I didn't get her number," Wilbur chuckled. "Besides, she doesn't live here anyway."

"That's ok," Opal said. "I got it right here! Besides, Beulah said Emily was staying in town for a little while. I'm sure we can work out something."

"Wait, you talked to Ms. Beulah about this?" Wilbur asked.

"Good for you!" Mavis cheered a little too loudly.

"Beulah has been coming to the Comb Over for years," Opal said. "Don't worry. We'll fix everything."

"You know that Opal knows everyone in this here state," Maude pointed out.

Wilbur wasn't sure if he liked the idea of Opal, Maude, and Mavis interfering in his love life, but he didn't know if he could stop that train once it had left the station.

Acknowledgments

We would never have been able to finish this book so quickly without the love and support of our families and friends. To our loved ones, once again we hope we haven't embarrassed you too much with this next installment of the Magnolia Manor series. If we have, let us know so we can write another book! We've got the ten in the series outlined thus far, but everyone knows these things practically write themselves!

To all of our family members who have inexplicably been mentioned in these pages, whether by name or not, we thank you for supplying us with laughter and stories for yet another book.

Finally, we'd like to thank the ladies at Southern Willow Publishing. Jaimie, Jennifer, and Victoria continue to believe in us and support our adventurous tales. It is due to their professionalism and experiences that we have been able to publish this series that keeps us young year after year. We look forward to many more adventures ahead.

About the Authors

Wanda Jennings and Louise Turner have known each other since they were young(er). They began their writing careers later in life after retiring from their professional careers in civil service and social work.

When not writing the Magnolia Manor series, Wanda and Louise find all sorts of new adventures. Louise finally got to go on her long-awaited cruise to Greece. She stuck out like a sore thumb, but did get to ride a camel in Egypt. Be careful, they spit!

Wanda has returned twice to her beloved New York City this year with plans to visit again soon. She isn't a fan of cruising like Louise is, but she is considering flying to Hawaii next spring.

Dear Reader,

We hope you enjoyed Hold Your Horses. We are truly blessed that you took the time (again) to spend a few hours with some of our favorite members of the Rhinestone gang. Rhinestone has a collection of true characters, that's for sure! It's hard to not fall in love with them over and over again.

We are currently working on the next book in the Magnolia Manor series that will be out in the spring of 2023. This next book takes place during the beginning of 2022. Mavis takes one of those new-fangled DNA tests and discovers more to her history than she ever bargained for. Maude and Opal encounter new adventures when Opal puts in to skydive, but Wilbur is the one who takes a giant leap of faith!

If you enjoyed Dirty Laundry, Saints & Sinners, Color Me Crazy, Double Trouble, Now & Forever, Round Trip, and Hold Your Horses, please make sure to join us on our next adventure in Over Yonder!

Thank you again for reading Hold Your Horses. We would really appreciate it if you could take a few minutes and leave us a positive review on Amazon.com and Goodreads.com. Your feedback is very important to us, and it helps spread the word about our series. Join us on Facebook (@LouiseandWanda) to keep up with all of our adventures. We love to interact with our fans!

Thank you again for humoring two old ladies. We always wanted to share the Rhinestone gang with the world, and we are so thankful that we found a way to do it. We look forward to sharing the last three books in the series with you all.

Love,

Louise & Wanda

Books in the Magnolia Manor Series

Dirty Laundry

Saints & Sinners

Color Me Crazy

Double Trouble

Now & Forever

Round Trip

Hold Your Horses

Over Yonder (Coming Spring 2023!)

The adventures will
continue next spring.
Join Mavis, Wilbur,
Opal, Maude, and the
whole Rhinestone gang
in

Over

Yonder

Available Spring
2023!